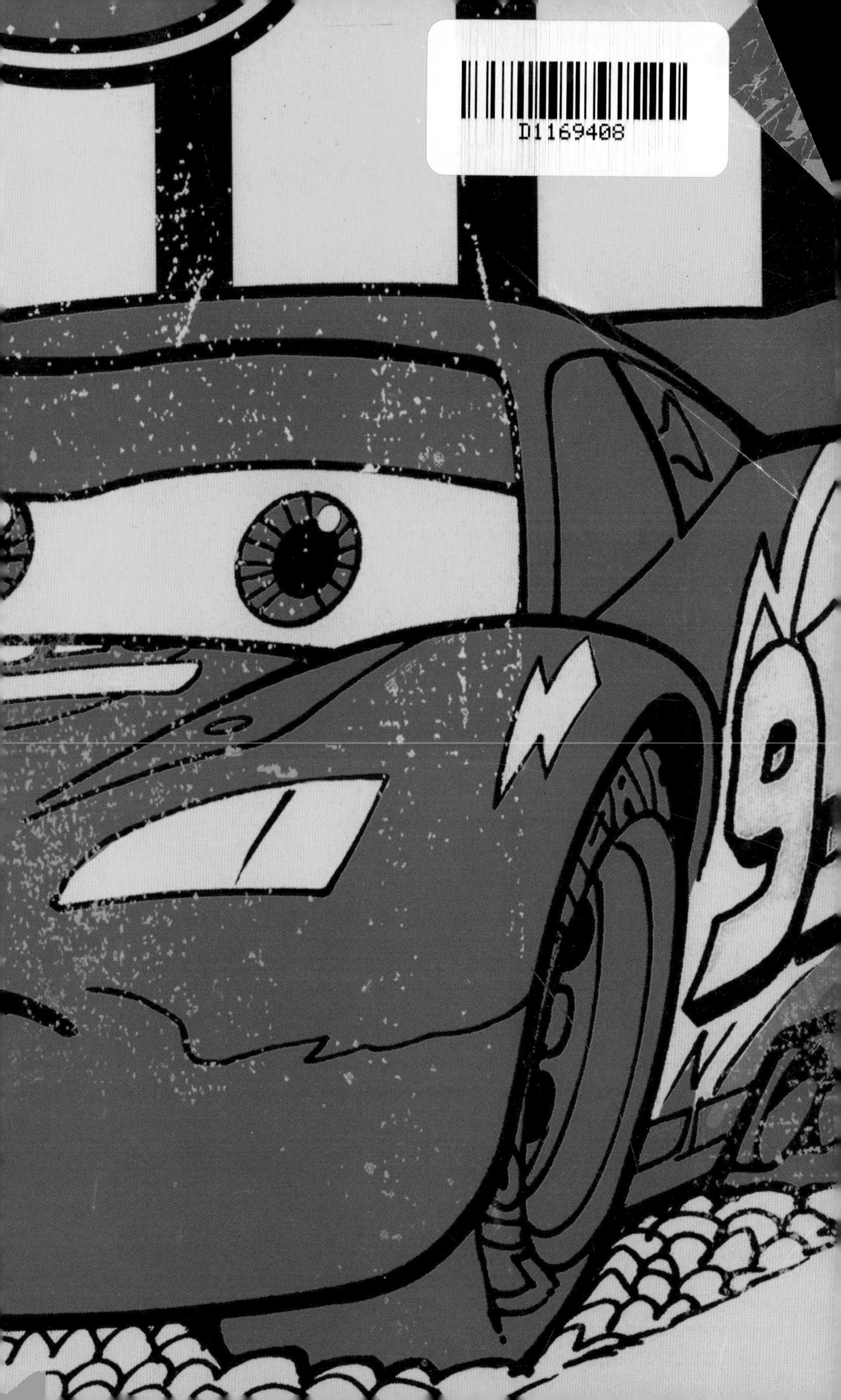

The Rookie

BOOM KIDS!

WRITTEN BY

ART BY

COLOR

ROSS RICHIE
chief executive officer

ANDREW COSBY
chief creative officer

MARK WAID
editor-in-chief

ADAM FORTIER
vice president,
publishing

CHIP MOSHER
marketing director

MATT GAGNON
managing editor

LETTER

COVER ARTIST

FIRST EDITION: JULY 2009

10 9 8 7 6 5 4 3 2 1
PRINTED IN CANADA

CARS: THE ROOKIE – July 2009 published by BOOM! KIDS, a division of Boom Entertainment, Inc. All contents © 2009 D
Pixar, not including underlying vehicles owned by third parties; Dodge is a trademark of DaimlerChrysler Corporation; Plyn
Superbird is a trademark of DaimlerChrysler Corporation; Petty marks used by permission of Petty Marketing LLC; Mac
registered trademark of Mack Trucks, Inc.; Mazda Miata is a registered trademark of Mazda Motor Corporation; Cadillac C
de Ville is a trademark of General Motors. BOOM! KIDS and the BOOM! KIDS logo are trademarks of Boom Entertainmen.
registered in various countries and categories. All rights reserved.

Office of publication: 6310 San Vicente Blvd Ste 404, Los Angeles, CA 90048.

Alan J. Porter
Albert Carreres

Emily Kanalz
ISSUES 1-3
Flavio B. Silva
ISSUE 4
Deron Bennett
Allen Gladfelter

Chapter One

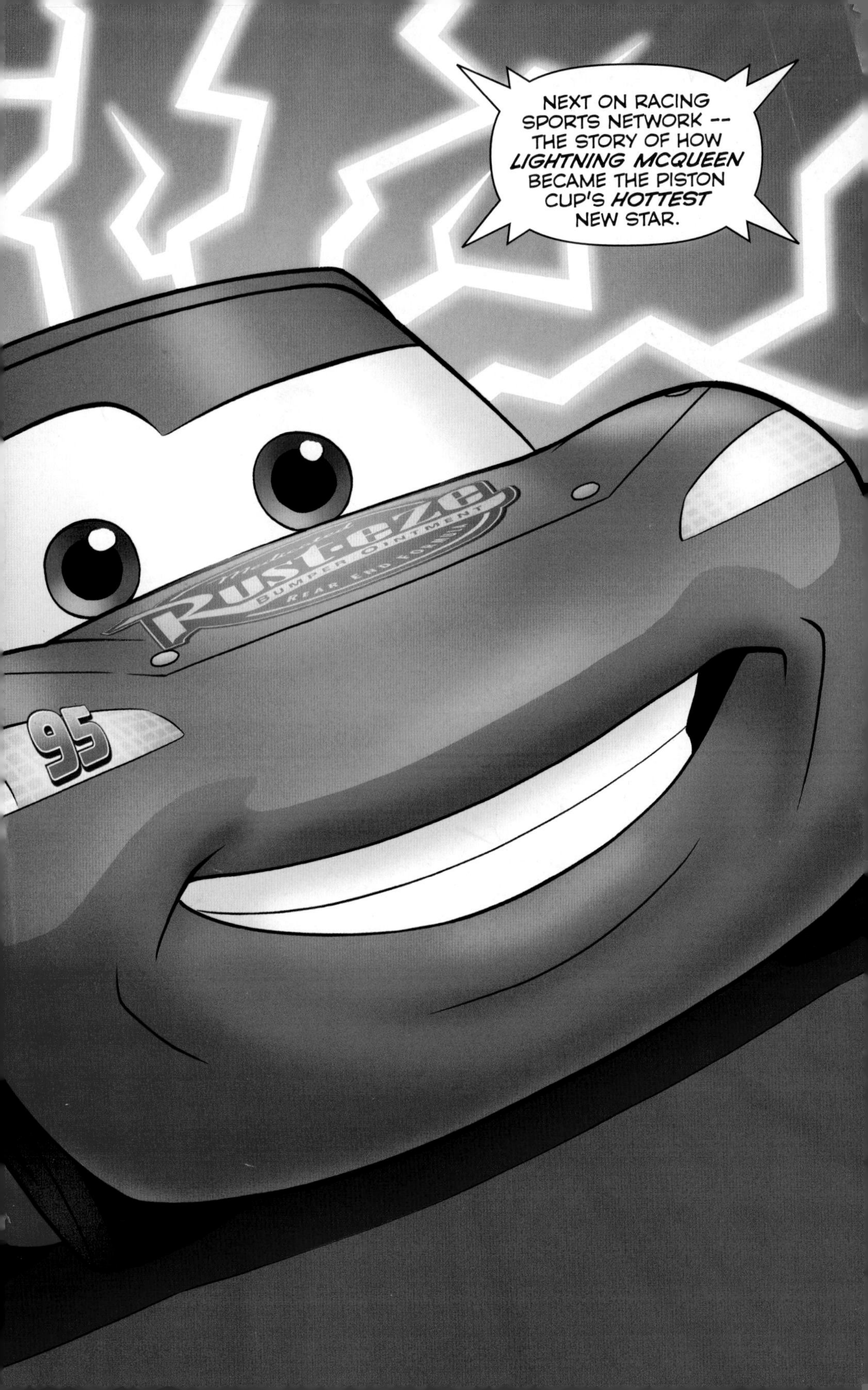
NEXT ON RACING SPORTS NETWORK -- THE STORY OF HOW *LIGHTNING MCQUEEN* BECAME THE PISTON CUP'S *HOTTEST* NEW STAR.

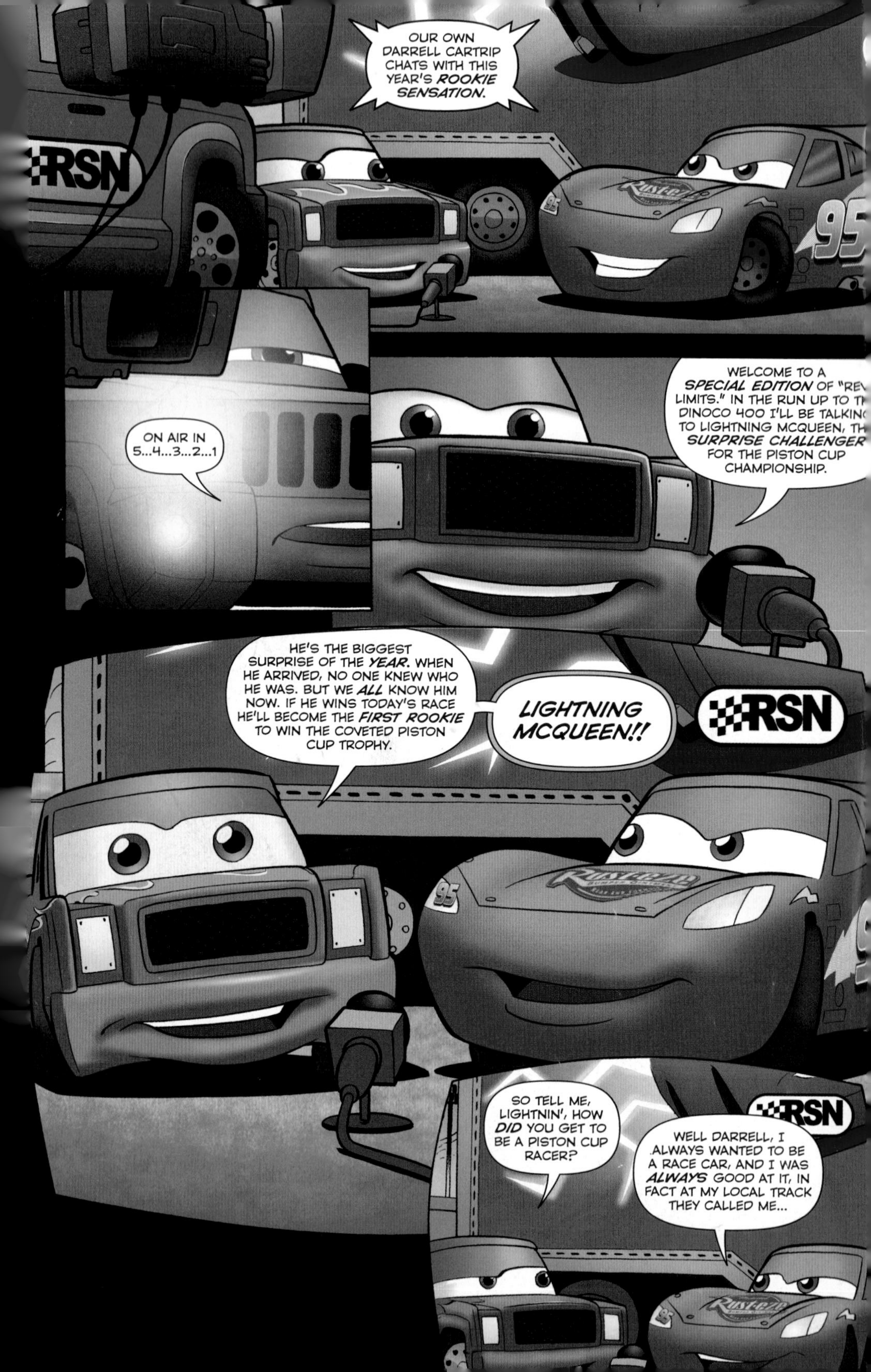
OUR OWN DARRELL CARTRIP CHATS WITH THIS YEAR'S ROOKIE SENSATION.
RSN
ON AIR IN 5...4...3...2...1
WELCOME TO A SPECIAL EDITION OF "REV LIMITS." IN THE RUN UP TO TH DINOCO 400 I'LL BE TALKING TO LIGHTNING MCQUEEN, TH SURPRISE CHALLENGER FOR THE PISTON CUP CHAMPIONSHIP.
HE'S THE BIGGEST SURPRISE OF THE YEAR. WHEN HE ARRIVED, NO ONE KNEW WHO HE WAS. BUT WE ALL KNOW HIM NOW. IF HE WINS TODAY'S RACE HE'LL BECOME THE FIRST ROOKIE TO WIN THE COVETED PISTON CUP TROPHY.
LIGHTNING MCQUEEN!!
RSN
SO TELL ME, LIGHTNIN', HOW DID YOU GET TO BE A PISTON CUP RACER?
RSN
WELL DARRELL, I ALWAYS WANTED TO BE A RACE CAR, AND I WAS ALWAYS GOOD AT IT, IN FACT AT MY LOCAL TRACK THEY CALLED ME...

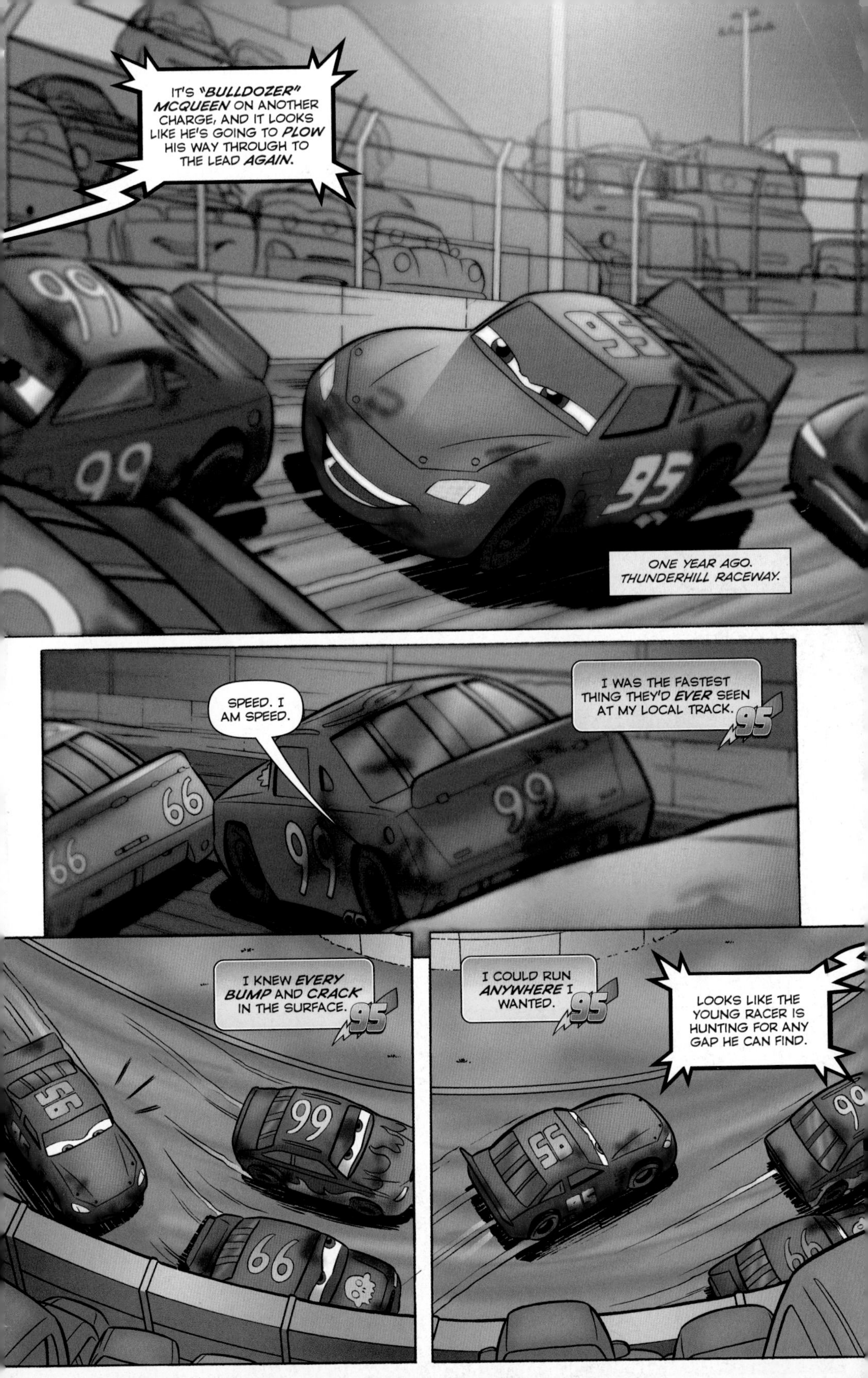
IT'S "BULLDOZER" MCQUEEN ON ANOTHER CHARGE, AND IT LOOKS LIKE HE'S GOING TO PLOW HIS WAY THROUGH TO THE LEAD AGAIN.
ONE YEAR AGO. THUNDERHILL RACEWAY.
SPEED. I AM SPEED.
I WAS THE FASTEST THING THEY'D EVER SEEN AT MY LOCAL TRACK.
I KNEW EVERY BUMP AND CRACK IN THE SURFACE.
I COULD RUN ANYWHERE I WANTED.
LOOKS LIKE THE YOUNG RACER IS HUNTING FOR ANY GAP HE CAN FIND.

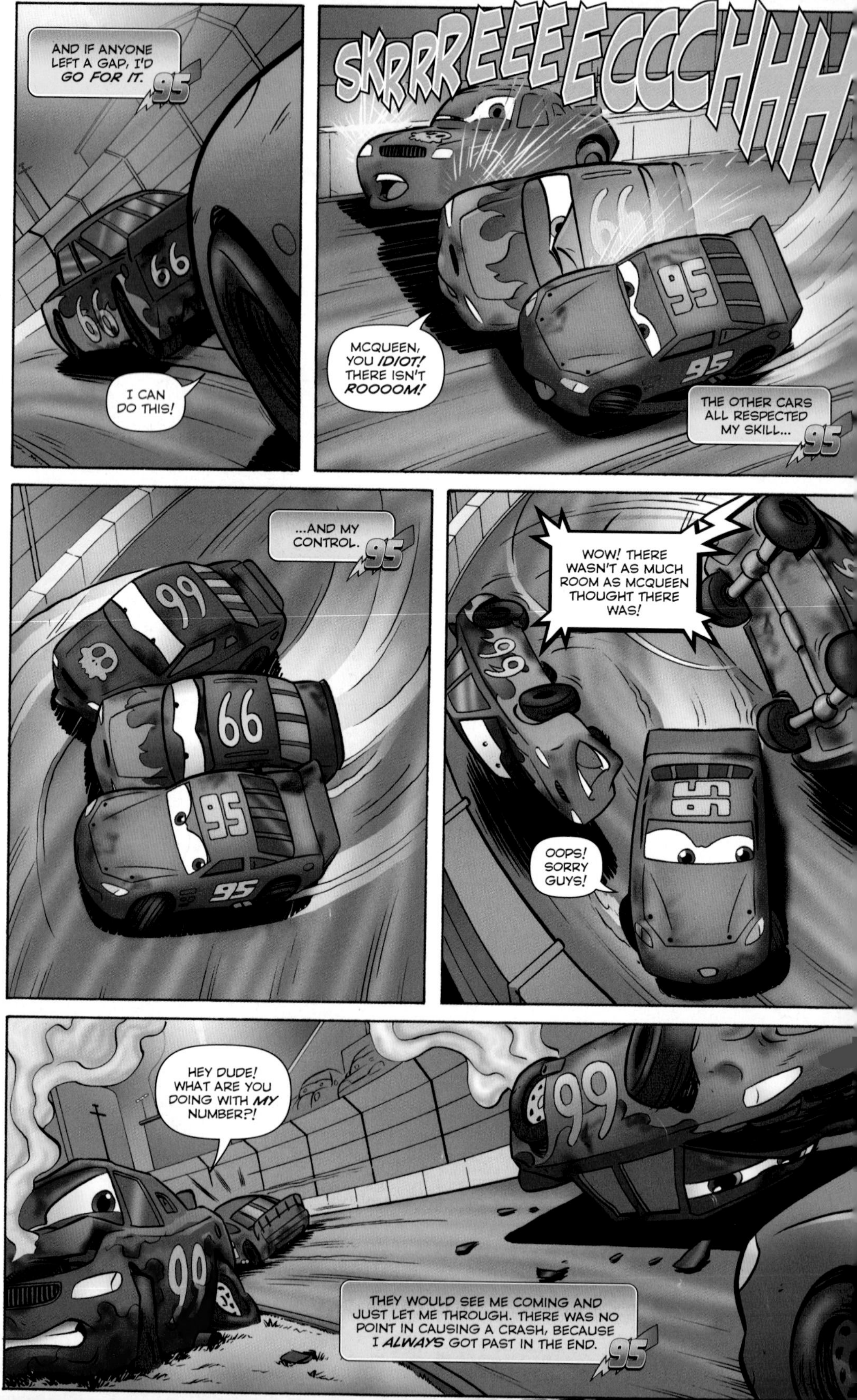

AND IF ANYONE LEFT A GAP, I'D GO FOR IT.
I CAN DO THIS!
SKRRREEEEECCCHHH
MCQUEEN, YOU IDIOT! THERE ISN'T ROOOOM!
THE OTHER CARS ALL RESPECTED MY SKILL...
...AND MY CONTROL.
WOW! THERE WASN'T AS MUCH ROOM AS MCQUEEN THOUGHT THERE WAS!
OOPS! SORRY GUYS!
HEY DUDE! WHAT ARE YOU DOING WITH MY NUMBER?!
THEY WOULD SEE ME COMING AND JUST LET ME THROUGH. THERE WAS NO POINT IN CAUSING A CRASH, BECAUSE I ALWAYS GOT PAST IN THE END.

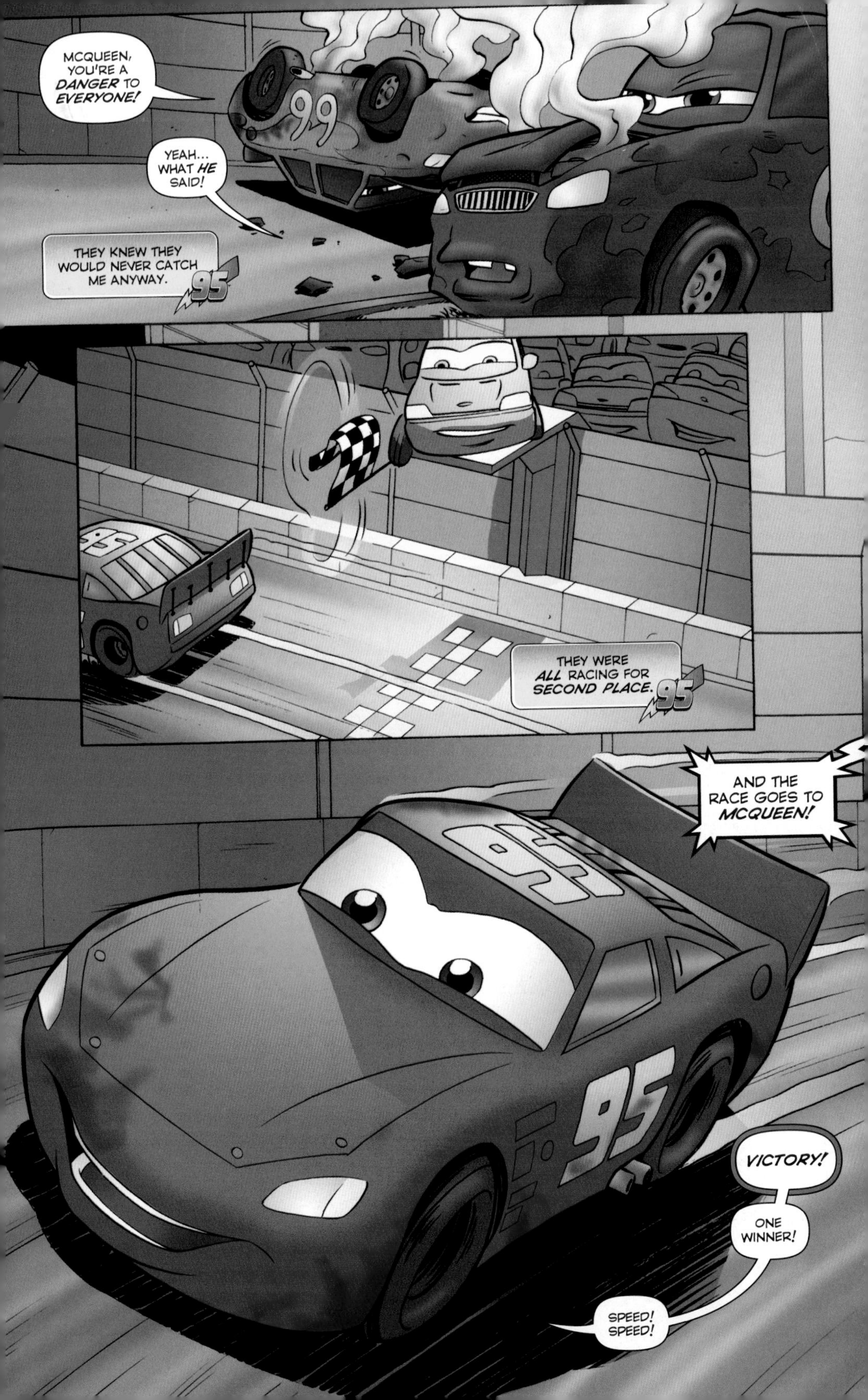
MCQUEEN, YOU'RE A DANGER TO EVERYONE!
YEAH... WHAT HE SAID!
THEY KNEW THEY WOULD NEVER CATCH ME ANYWAY.
THEY WERE ALL RACING FOR SECOND PLACE.
AND THE RACE GOES TO MCQUEEN!
VICTORY!
ONE WINNER!
SPEED! SPEED!

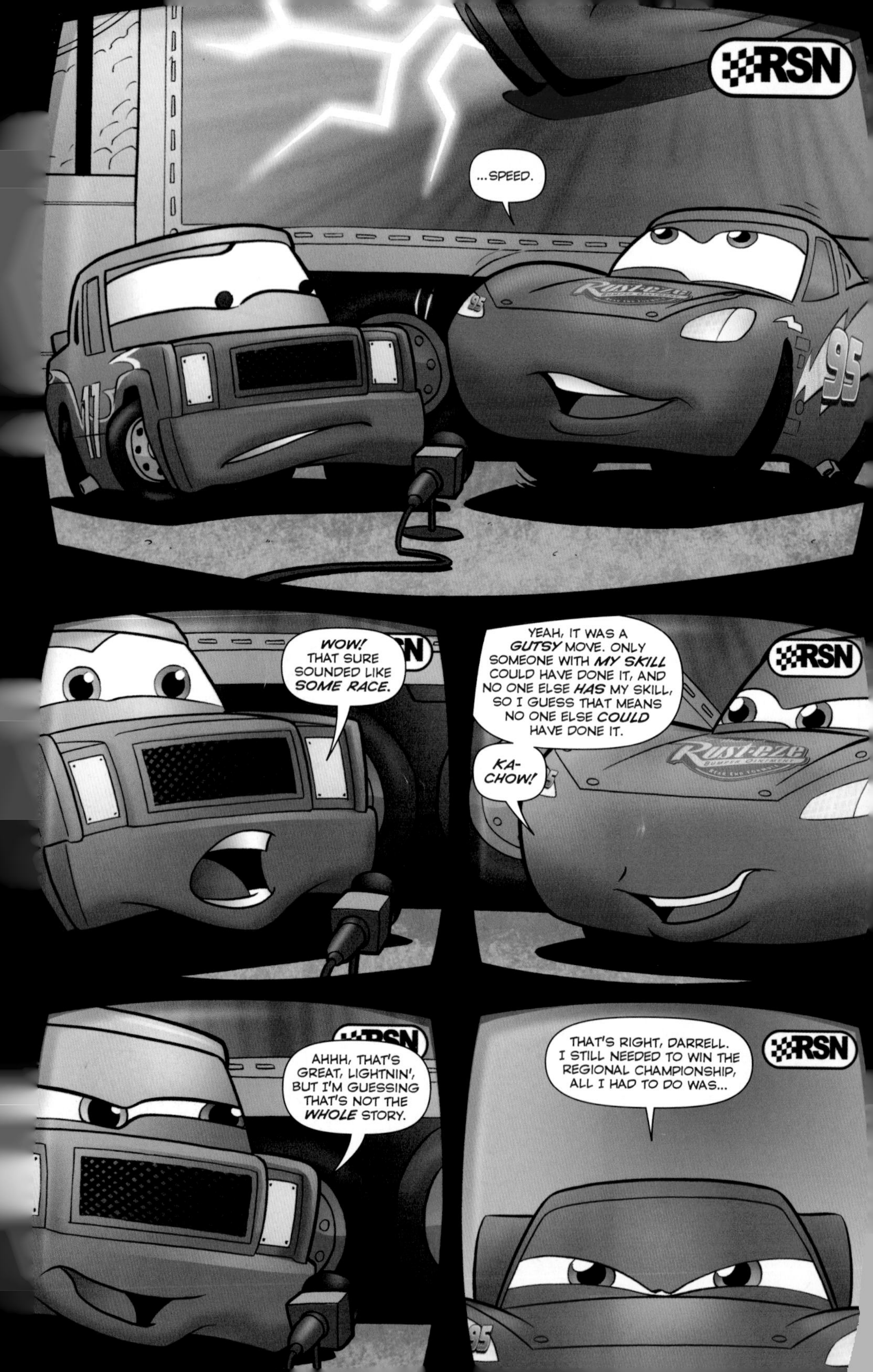
RSN
...SPEED.
WOW! THAT SURE SOUNDED LIKE SOME RACE.
YEAH, IT WAS A GUTSY MOVE. ONLY SOMEONE WITH MY SKILL COULD HAVE DONE IT, AND NO ONE ELSE HAS MY SKILL, SO I GUESS THAT MEANS NO ONE ELSE COULD HAVE DONE IT.
KA-CHOW!
AHHH, THAT'S GREAT, LIGHTNIN', BUT I'M GUESSING THAT'S NOT THE WHOLE STORY.
THAT'S RIGHT, DARRELL. I STILL NEEDED TO WIN THE REGIONAL CHAMPIONSHIP, ALL I HAD TO DO WAS...

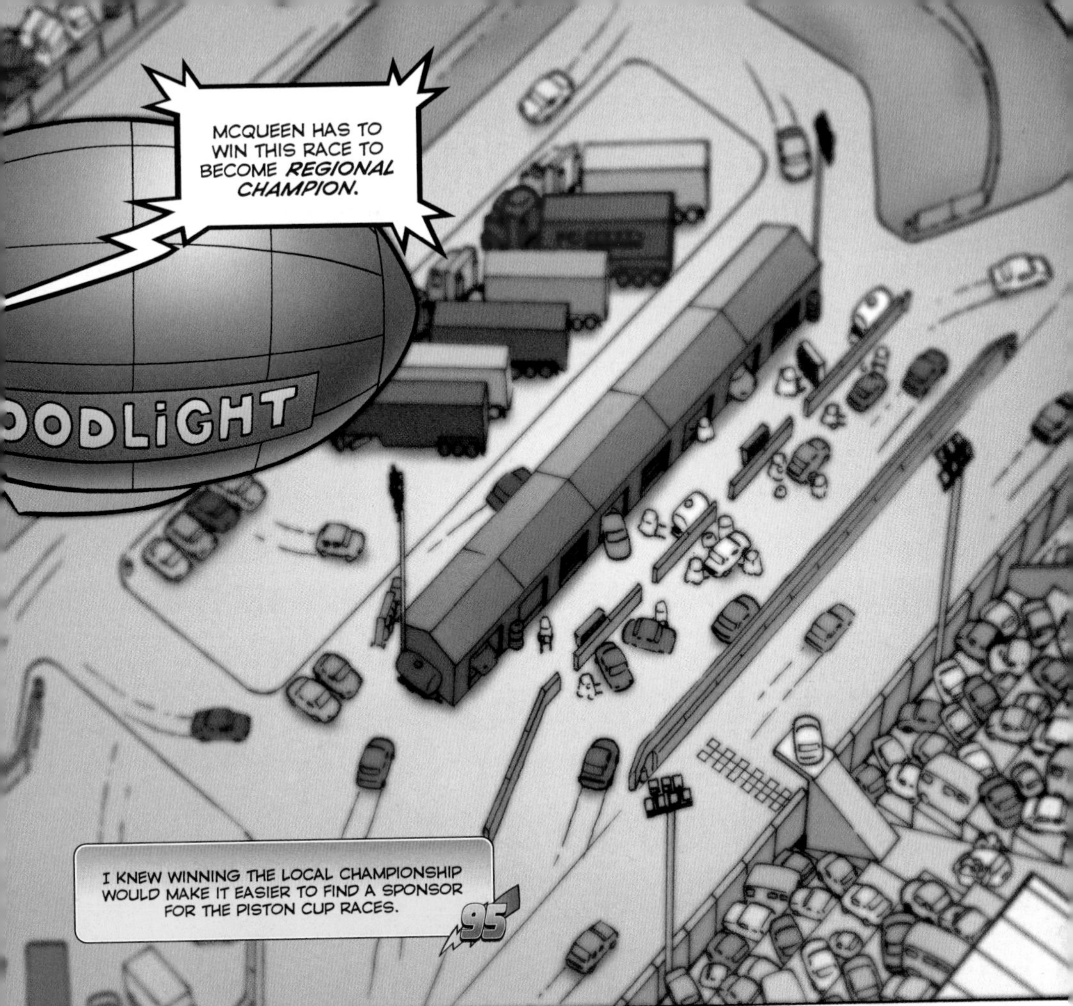
MCQUEEN HAS TO WIN THIS RACE TO BECOME *REGIONAL CHAMPION.*
ODLIGHT
I KNEW WINNING THE LOCAL CHAMPIONSHIP WOULD MAKE IT EASIER TO FIND A SPONSOR FOR THE PISTON CUP RACES.
95

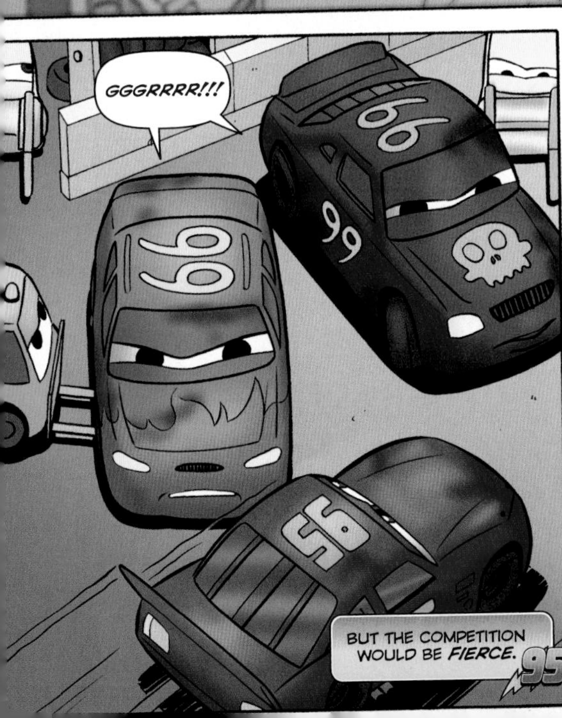
GGGRRRR!!!
BUT THE COMPETITION WOULD BE *FIERCE.*
95

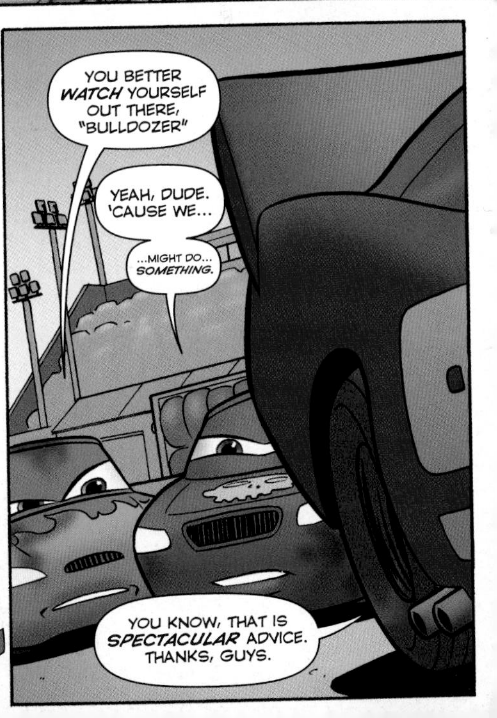
YOU BETTER *WATCH* YOURSELF OUT THERE, "BULLDOZER"
YEAH, DUDE. 'CAUSE WE...
...MIGHT DO... *SOMETHING.*
YOU KNOW, THAT IS *SPECTACULAR* ADVICE. THANKS, GUYS.

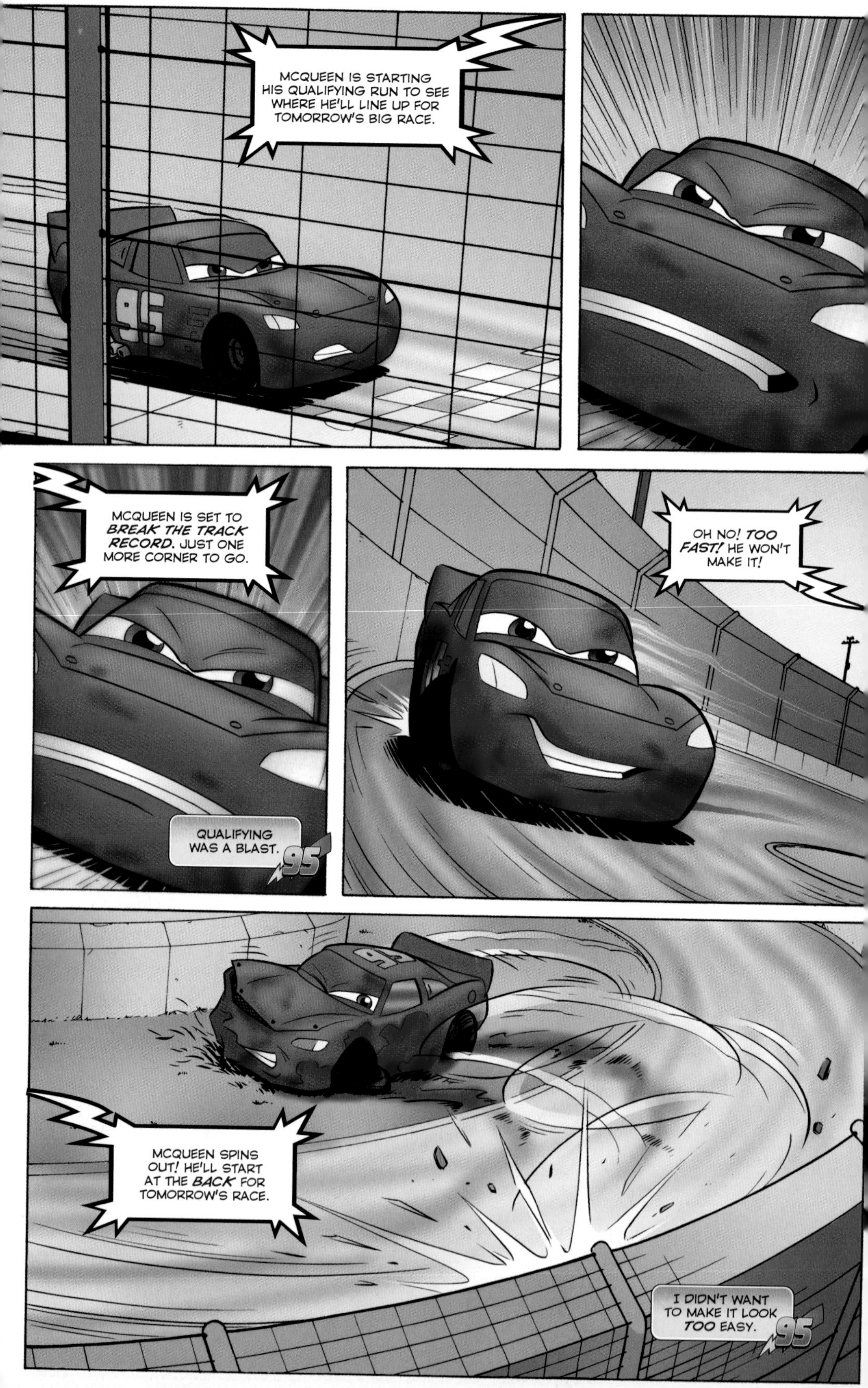
MCQUEEN IS STARTING HIS QUALIFYING RUN TO SEE WHERE HE'LL LINE UP FOR TOMORROW'S BIG RACE.
MCQUEEN IS SET TO *BREAK THE TRACK RECORD.* JUST ONE MORE CORNER TO GO.
QUALIFYING WAS A BLAST.
95
OH NO! *TOO FAST!* HE WON'T MAKE IT!
MCQUEEN SPINS OUT! HE'LL START AT THE *BACK* FOR TOMORROW'S RACE.
I DIDN'T WANT TO MAKE IT LOOK *TOO* EASY.
95

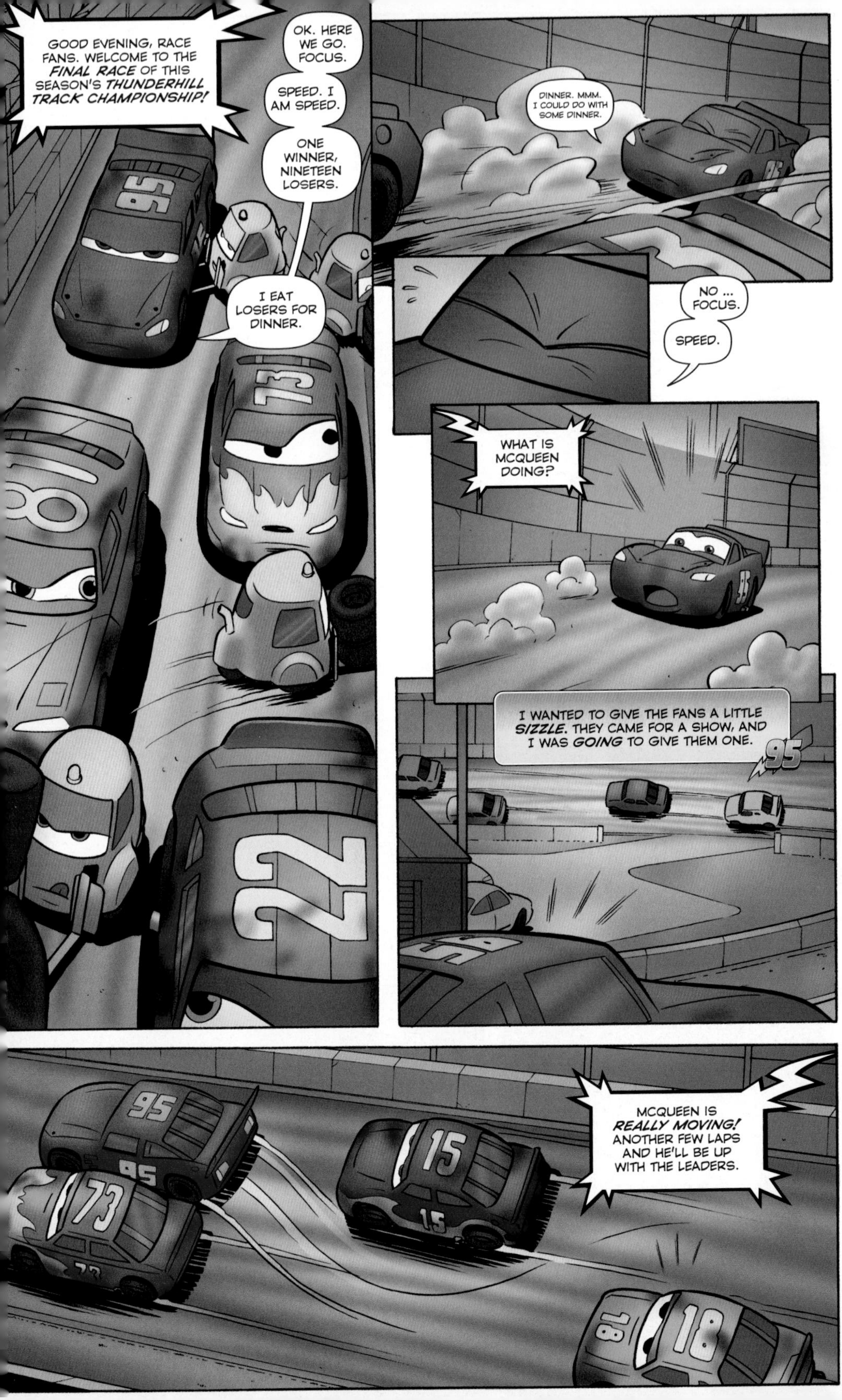
GOOD EVENING, RACE FANS. WELCOME TO THE FINAL RACE OF THIS SEASON'S THUNDERHILL TRACK CHAMPIONSHIP!
OK. HERE WE GO. FOCUS.
SPEED. I AM SPEED.
ONE WINNER, NINETEEN LOSERS.
I EAT LOSERS FOR DINNER.
DINNER. MMM. I COULD DO WITH SOME DINNER.
NO ... FOCUS.
SPEED.
WHAT IS MCQUEEN DOING?
I WANTED TO GIVE THE FANS A LITTLE SIZZLE. THEY CAME FOR A SHOW, AND I WAS GOING TO GIVE THEM ONE.
95
MCQUEEN IS REALLY MOVING! ANOTHER FEW LAPS AND HE'LL BE UP WITH THE LEADERS.

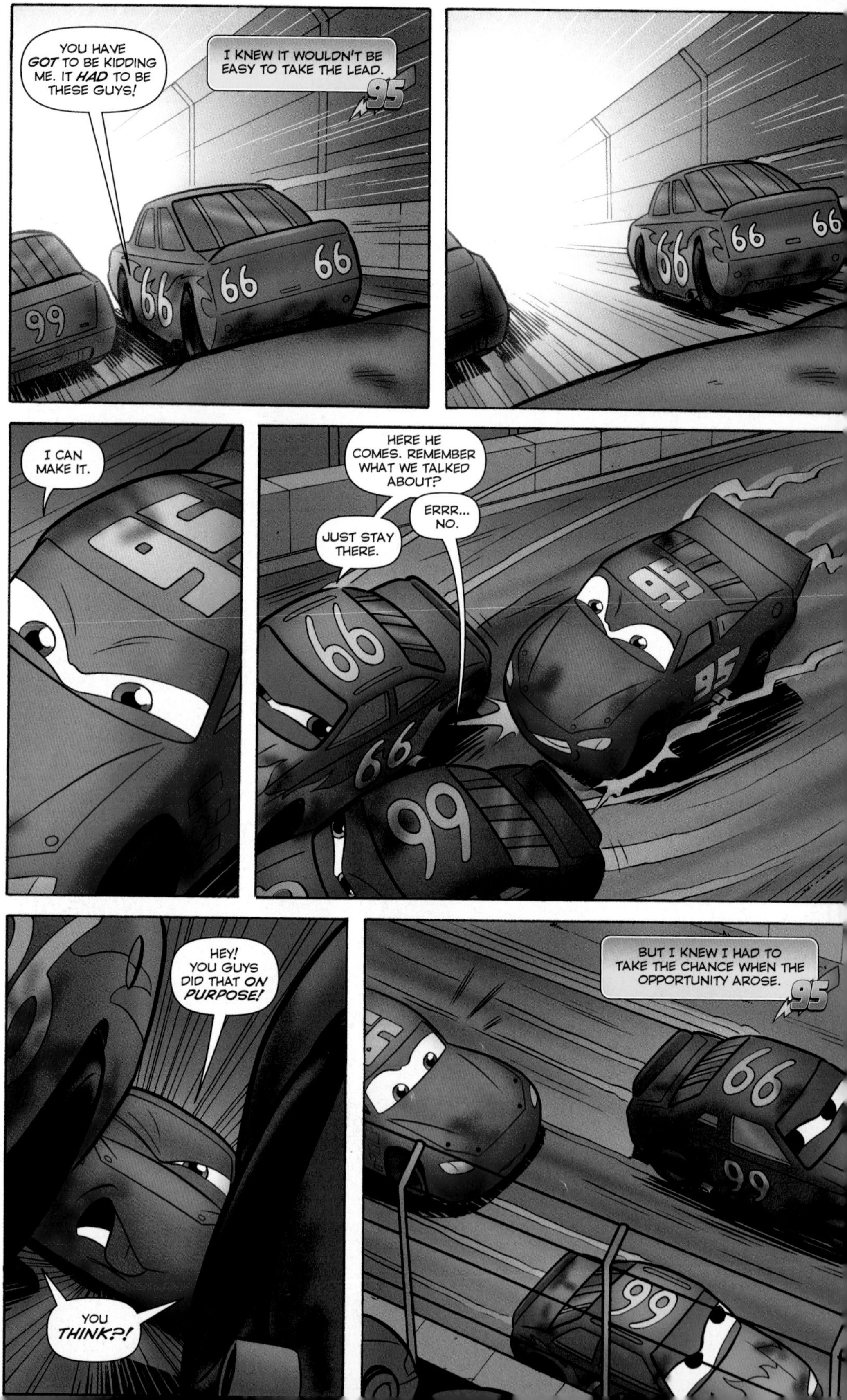
YOU HAVE GOT TO BE KIDDING ME. IT HAD TO BE THESE GUYS!
I KNEW IT WOULDN'T BE EASY TO TAKE THE LEAD.
95
I CAN MAKE IT.
HERE HE COMES. REMEMBER WHAT WE TALKED ABOUT?
ERRR... NO.
JUST STAY THERE.
HEY! YOU GUYS DID THAT ON PURPOSE!
YOU THINK?!
BUT I KNEW I HAD TO TAKE THE CHANCE WHEN THE OPPORTUNITY AROSE.
95

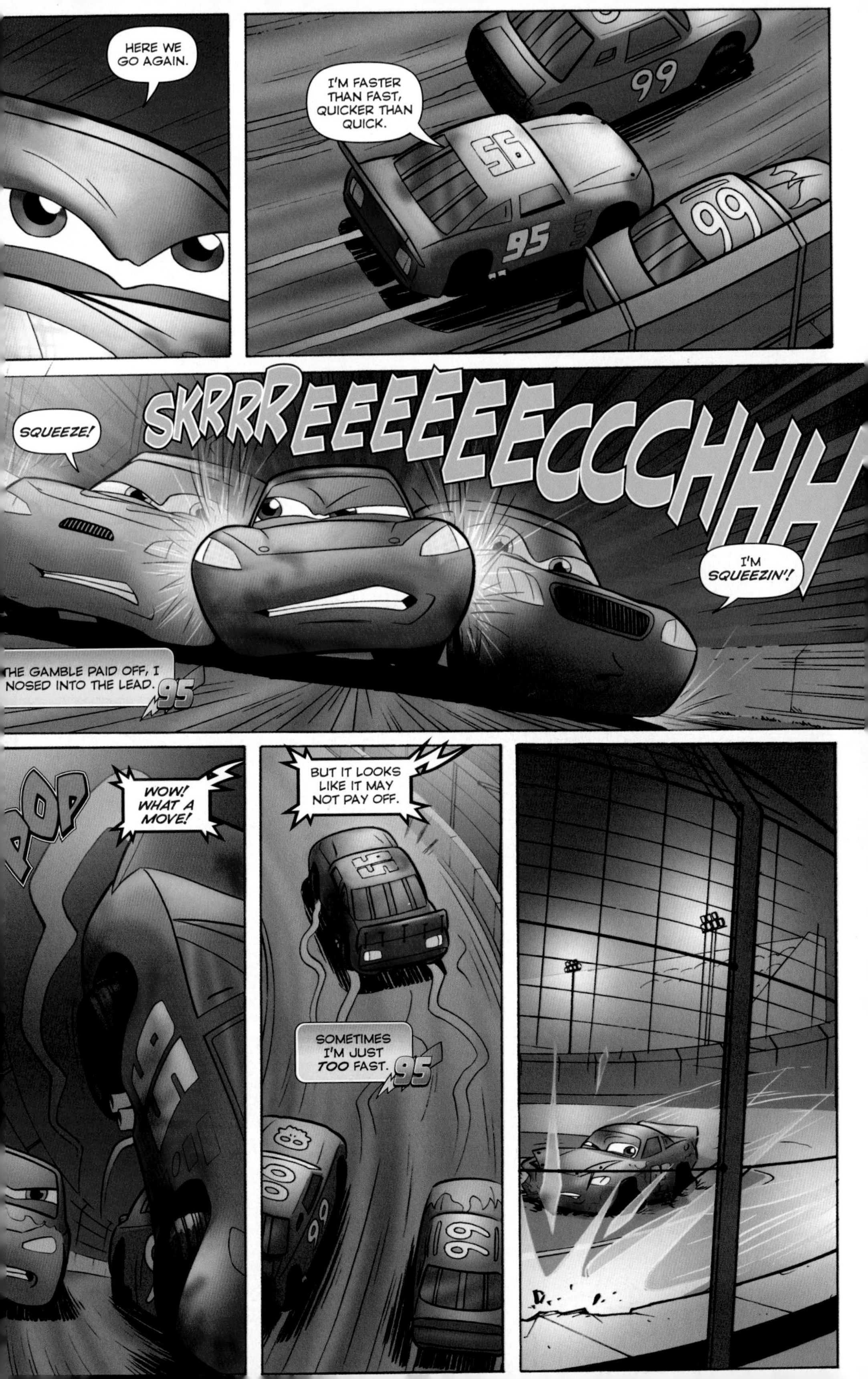
HERE WE GO AGAIN.
I'M FASTER THAN FAST, QUICKER THAN QUICK.
SKRRREEEEEEECCCCHHH
SQUEEZE!
I'M SQUEEZIN'!
THE GAMBLE PAID OFF, I NOSED INTO THE LEAD.
POP
WOW! WHAT A MOVE!
BUT IT LOOKS LIKE IT MAY NOT PAY OFF.
SOMETIMES I'M JUST TOO FAST.

HEY, BULLDOZER! WHAT GOES AROUND COMES AROUND!
YEAH! ROUND AND ROUND, DUDE!
YAAAAYYY
FWOOSSH
BANG
WOO-HOO
THE NEW TRACK CHAMPION IS...
...NOT ME.
BUT THERE'S A LOT MORE TO RACING THAN *WINNING*. I GAVE THEM *SIZZLE*.

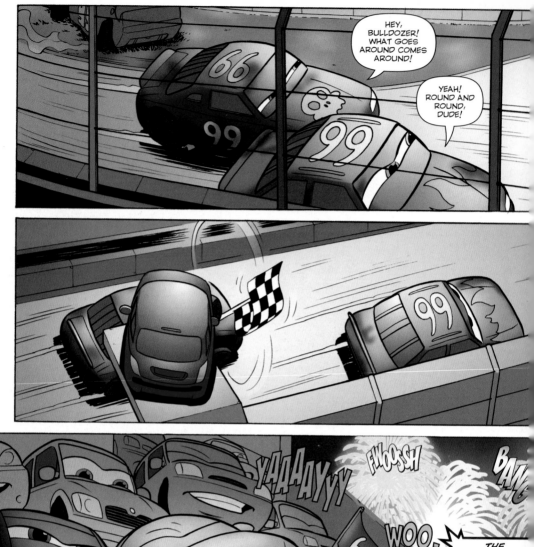

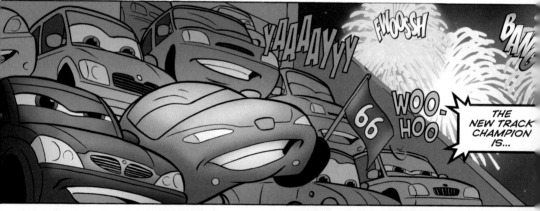

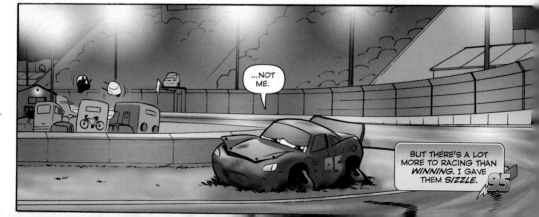

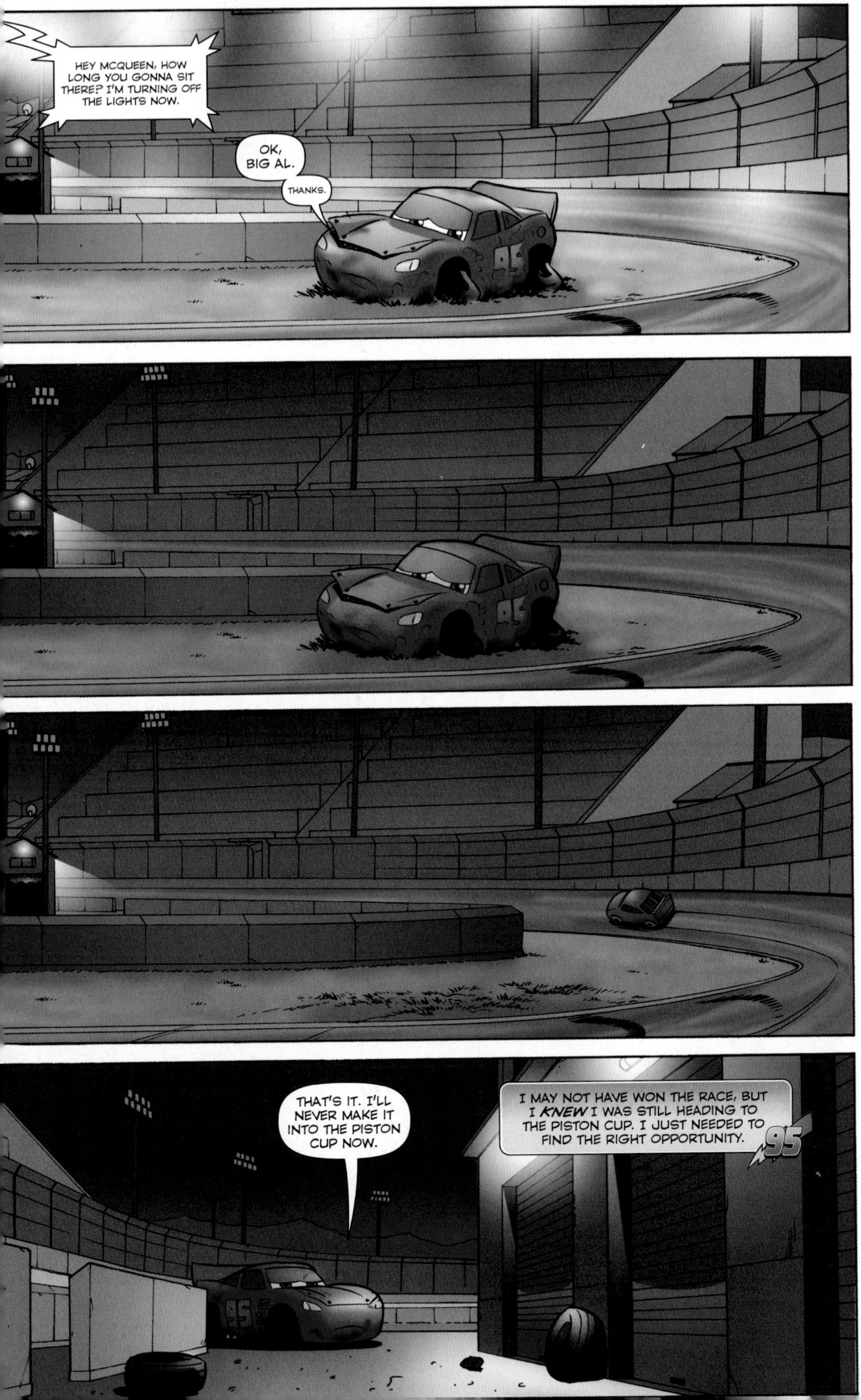
HEY MCQUEEN, HOW LONG YOU GONNA SIT THERE? I'M TURNING OFF THE LIGHTS NOW.
OK, BIG AL.
THANKS.
THAT'S IT. I'LL NEVER MAKE IT INTO THE PISTON CUP NOW.
I MAY NOT HAVE WON THE RACE, BUT I *KNEW* I WAS STILL HEADING TO THE PISTON CUP. I JUST NEEDED TO FIND THE RIGHT OPPORTUNITY.
95

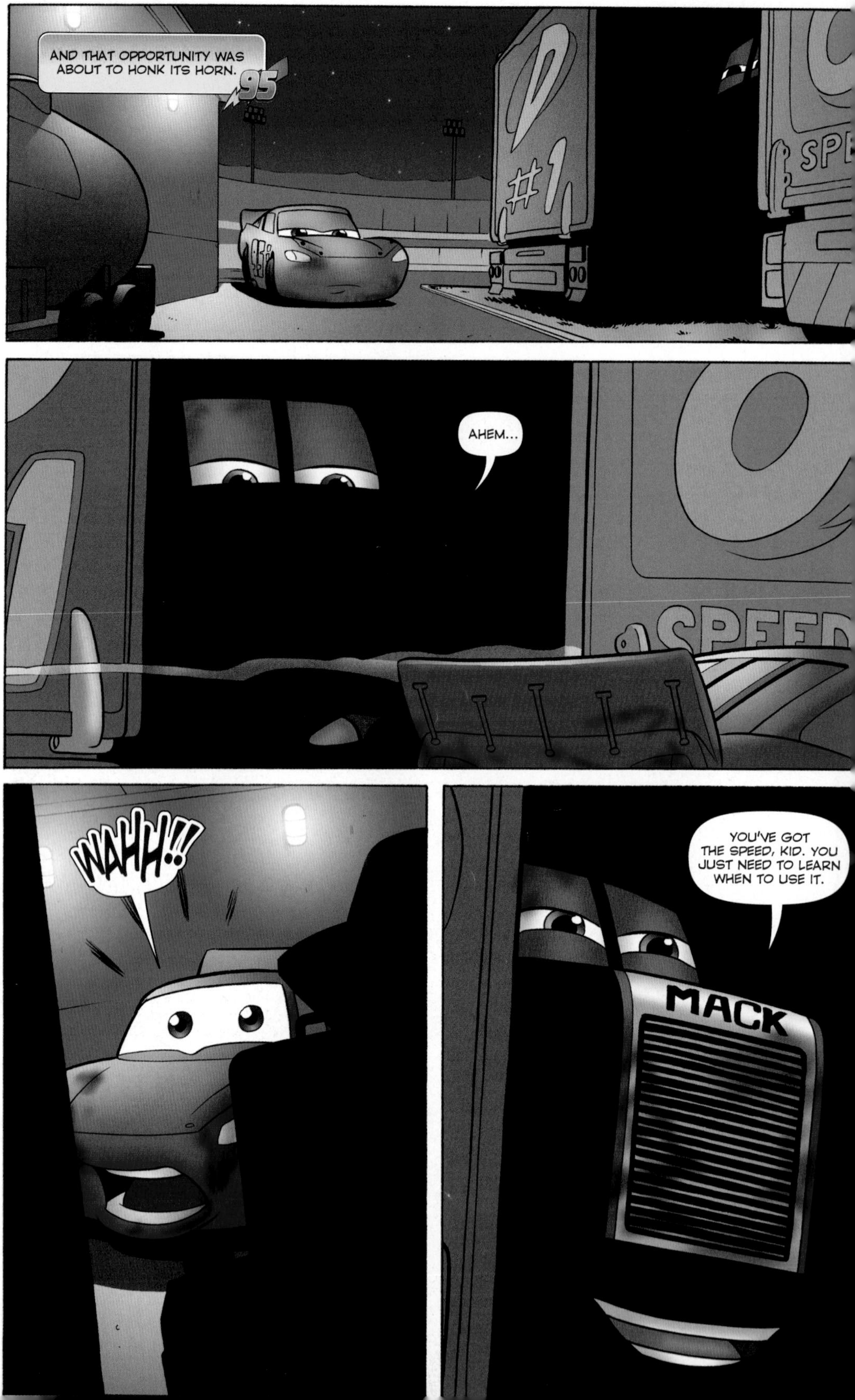
AND THAT OPPORTUNITY WAS ABOUT TO HONK ITS HORN.
95
#1
SPE
AHEM...
SPEED
WAHH!!!
YOU'VE GOT THE SPEED, KID. YOU JUST NEED TO LEARN WHEN TO USE IT.
MACK

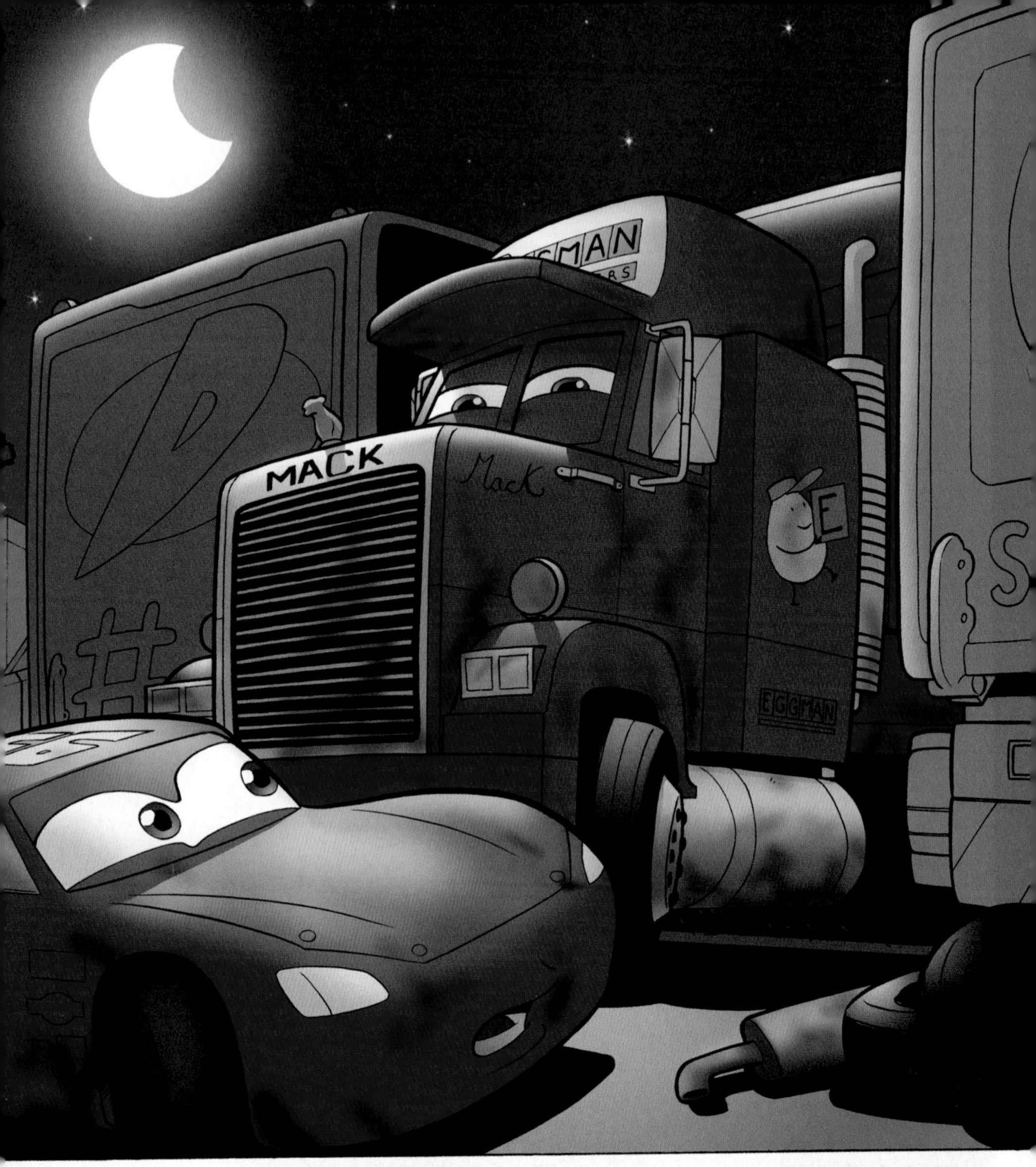
MACK
Mack
EGGMAN

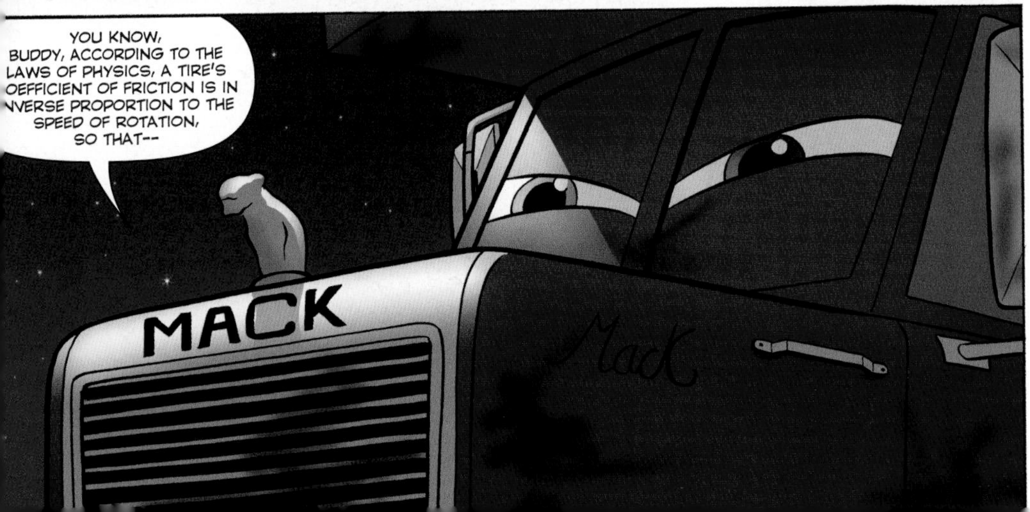
YOU KNOW, BUDDY, ACCORDING TO THE LAWS OF PHYSICS, A TIRE'S OEFFICIENT OF FRICTION IS IN NVERSE PROPORTION TO THE SPEED OF ROTATION, SO THAT--
MACK
Mack

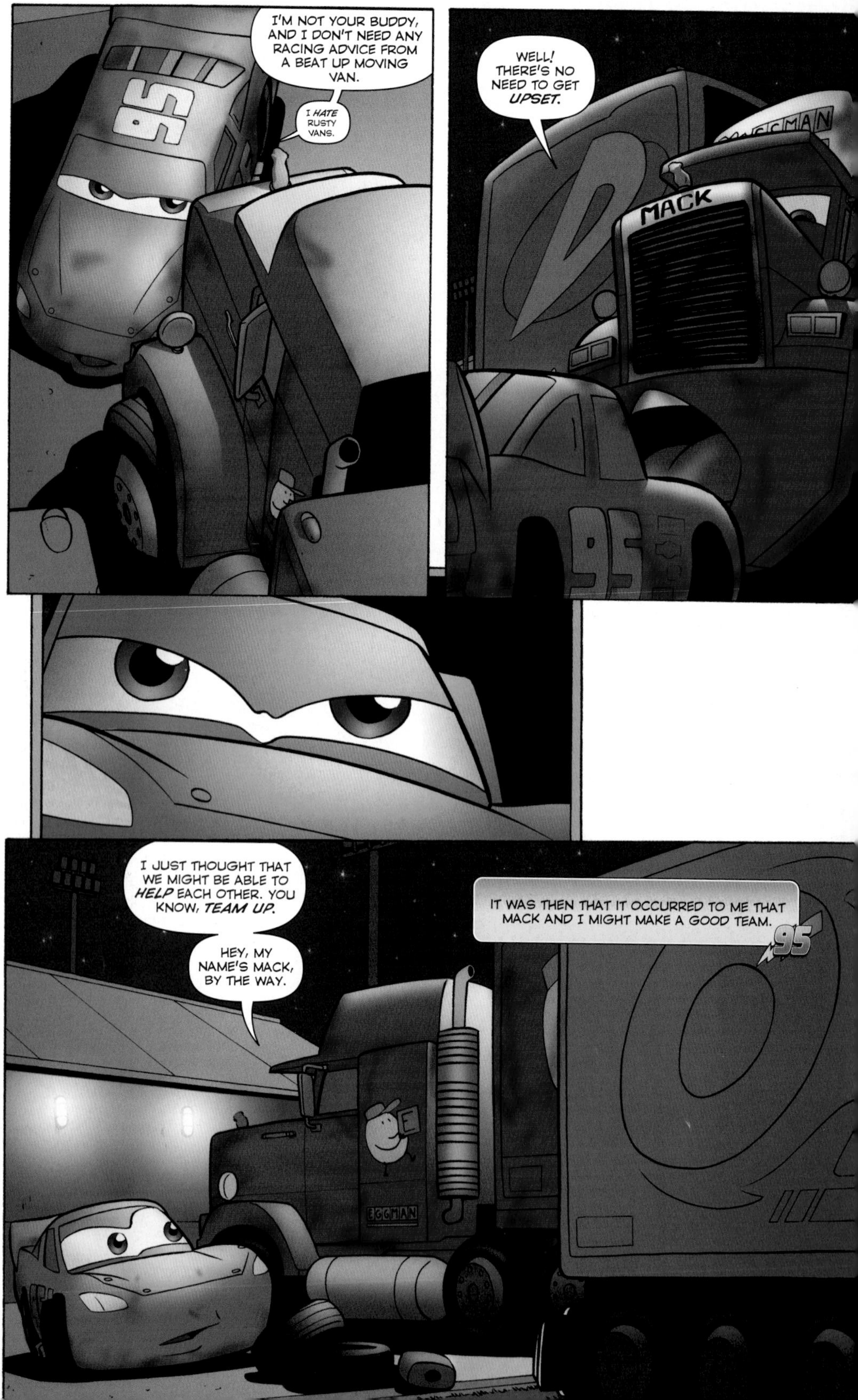
I'M NOT YOUR BUDDY, AND I DON'T NEED ANY RACING ADVICE FROM A BEAT UP MOVING VAN.
I *HATE* RUSTY VANS.
WELL! THERE'S NO NEED TO GET *UPSET*.
MACK
I JUST THOUGHT THAT WE MIGHT BE ABLE TO *HELP* EACH OTHER. YOU KNOW, *TEAM UP*.
HEY, MY NAME'S MACK, BY THE WAY.
IT WAS THEN THAT IT OCCURRED TO ME THAT MACK AND I MIGHT MAKE A GOOD TEAM.
EGGMAN

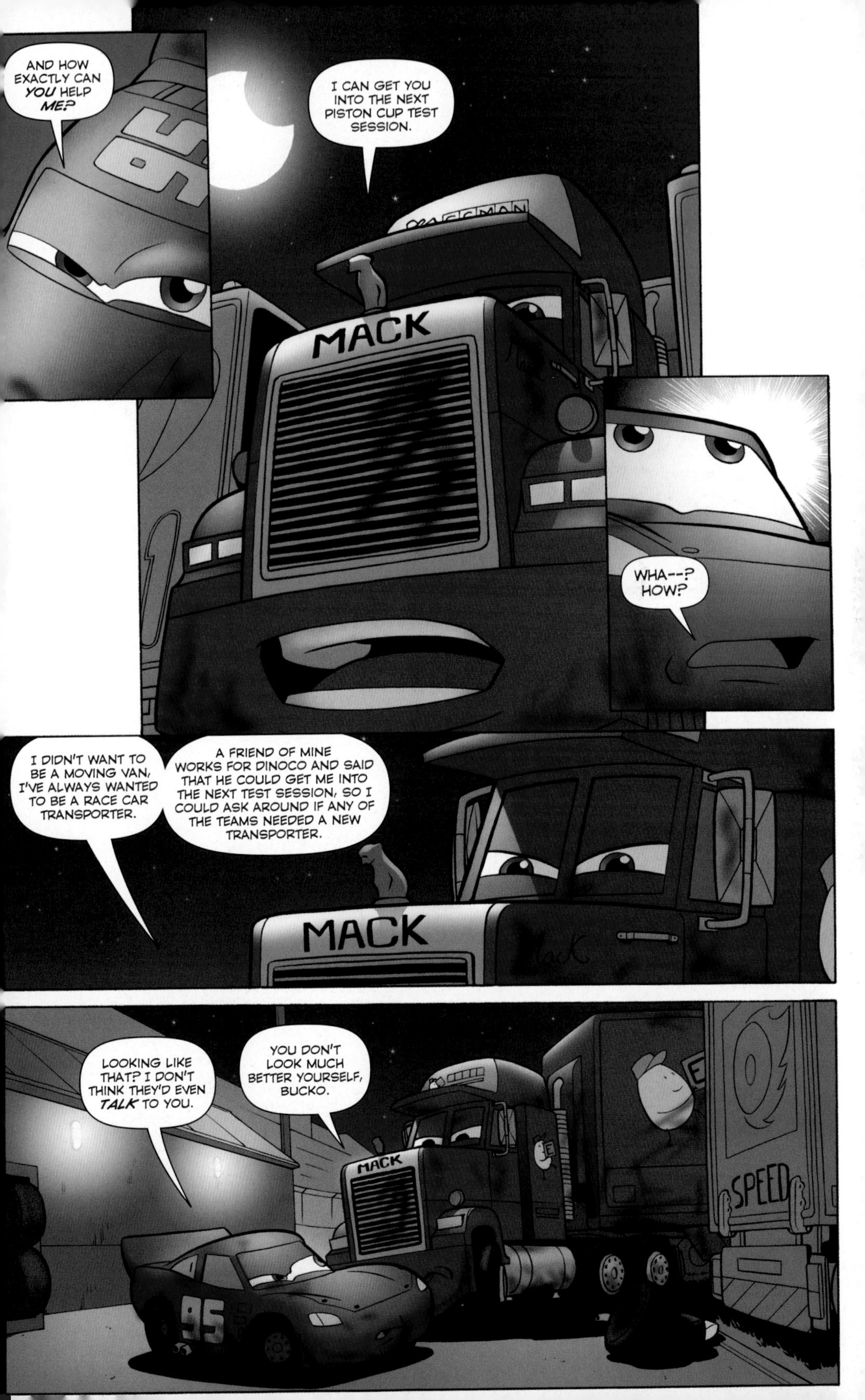
AND HOW EXACTLY CAN *YOU* HELP *ME?*
I CAN GET YOU INTO THE NEXT PISTON CUP TEST SESSION.
MACK
WHA--? HOW?
I DIDN'T WANT TO BE A MOVING VAN, I'VE ALWAYS WANTED TO BE A RACE CAR TRANSPORTER.
A FRIEND OF MINE WORKS FOR DINOCO AND SAID THAT HE COULD GET ME INTO THE NEXT TEST SESSION, SO I COULD ASK AROUND IF ANY OF THE TEAMS NEEDED A NEW TRANSPORTER.
MACK
LOOKING LIKE THAT? I DON'T THINK THEY'D EVEN *TALK* TO YOU.
YOU DON'T LOOK MUCH BETTER YOURSELF, BUCKO.
MACK
SPEED
95

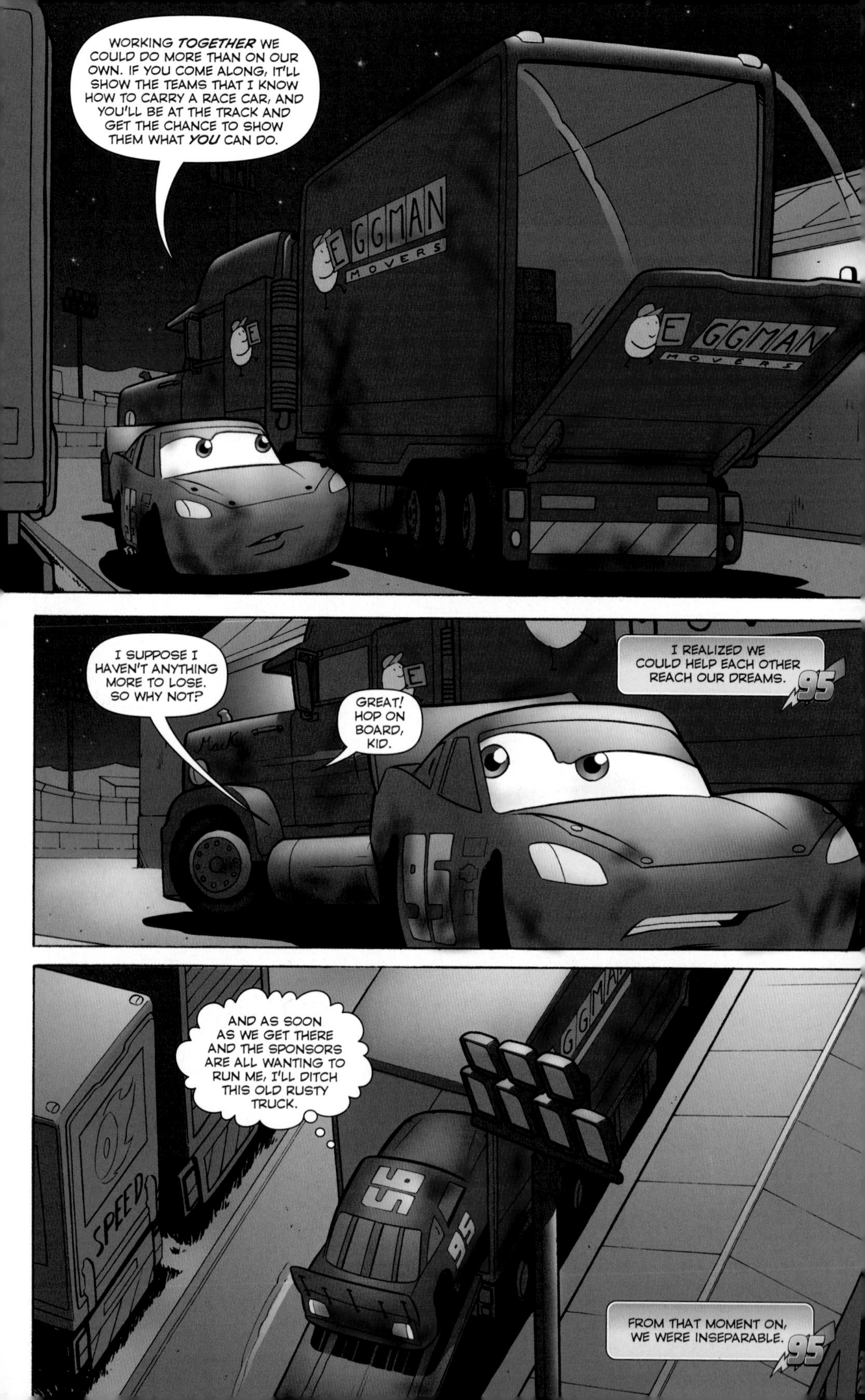
WORKING *TOGETHER* WE COULD DO MORE THAN ON OUR OWN. IF YOU COME ALONG, IT'LL SHOW THE TEAMS THAT I KNOW HOW TO CARRY A RACE CAR, AND YOU'LL BE AT THE TRACK AND GET THE CHANCE TO SHOW THEM WHAT *YOU* CAN DO.
EGGMAN MOVERS
I SUPPOSE I HAVEN'T ANYTHING MORE TO LOSE. SO WHY NOT?
GREAT! HOP ON BOARD, KID.
I REALIZED WE COULD HELP EACH OTHER REACH OUR DREAMS.
AND AS SOON AS WE GET THERE AND THE SPONSORS ARE ALL WANTING TO RUN ME, I'LL DITCH THIS OLD RUSTY TRUCK.
FROM THAT MOMENT ON, WE WERE INSEPARABLE.

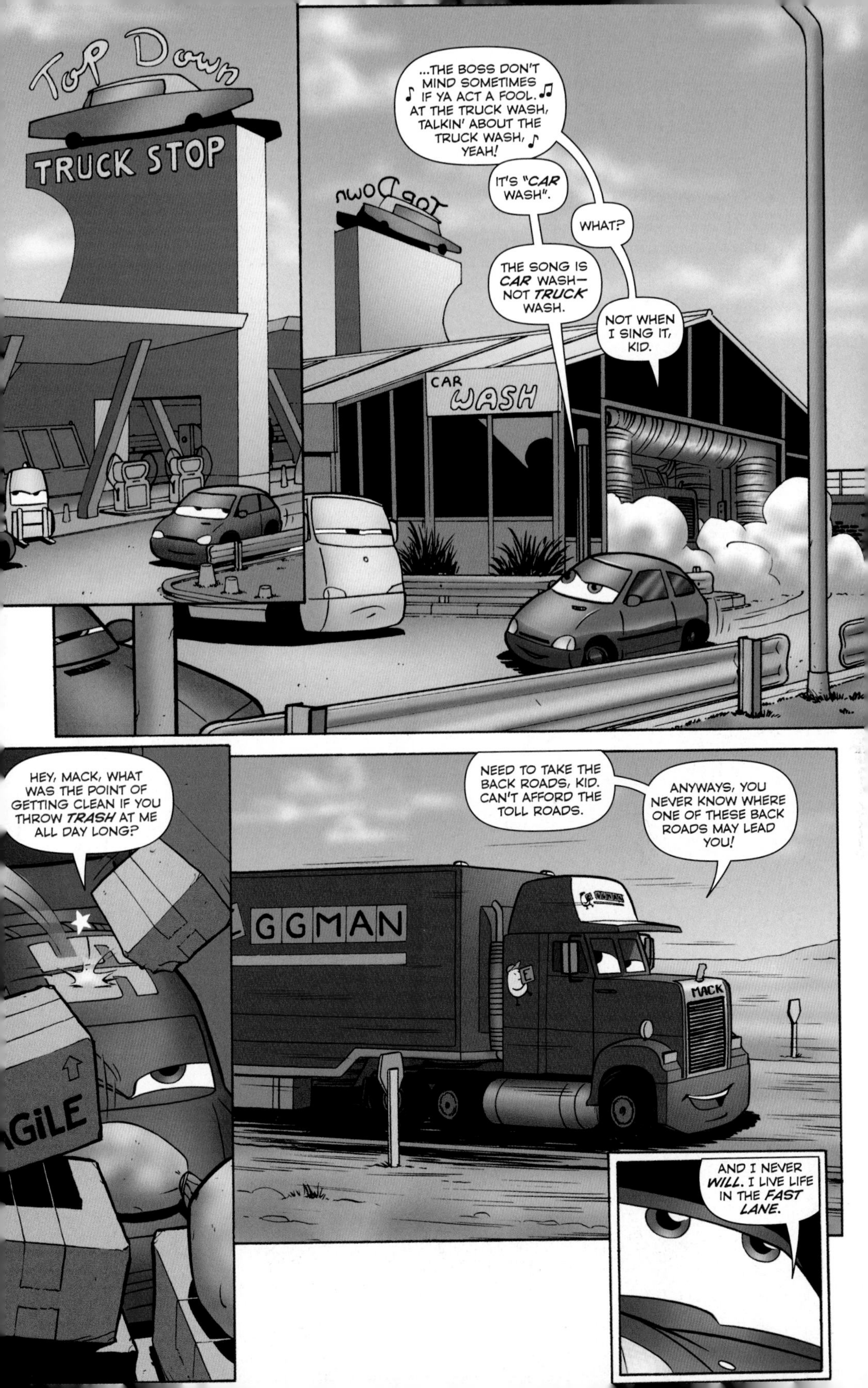

Top Down
TRUCK STOP
...THE BOSS DON'T MIND SOMETIMES ♪ IF YA ACT A FOOL. ♫ AT THE TRUCK WASH, TALKIN' ABOUT THE TRUCK WASH, ♪ YEAH!
IT'S "CAR WASH".
WHAT?
THE SONG IS CAR WASH— NOT TRUCK WASH.
NOT WHEN I SING IT, KID.
CAR WASH
HEY, MACK, WHAT WAS THE POINT OF GETTING CLEAN IF YOU THROW TRASH AT ME ALL DAY LONG?
NEED TO TAKE THE BACK ROADS, KID. CAN'T AFFORD THE TOLL ROADS.
ANYWAYS, YOU NEVER KNOW WHERE ONE OF THESE BACK ROADS MAY LEAD YOU!
GGMAN
MACK
AGILE
AND I NEVER WILL. I LIVE LIFE IN THE FAST LANE.

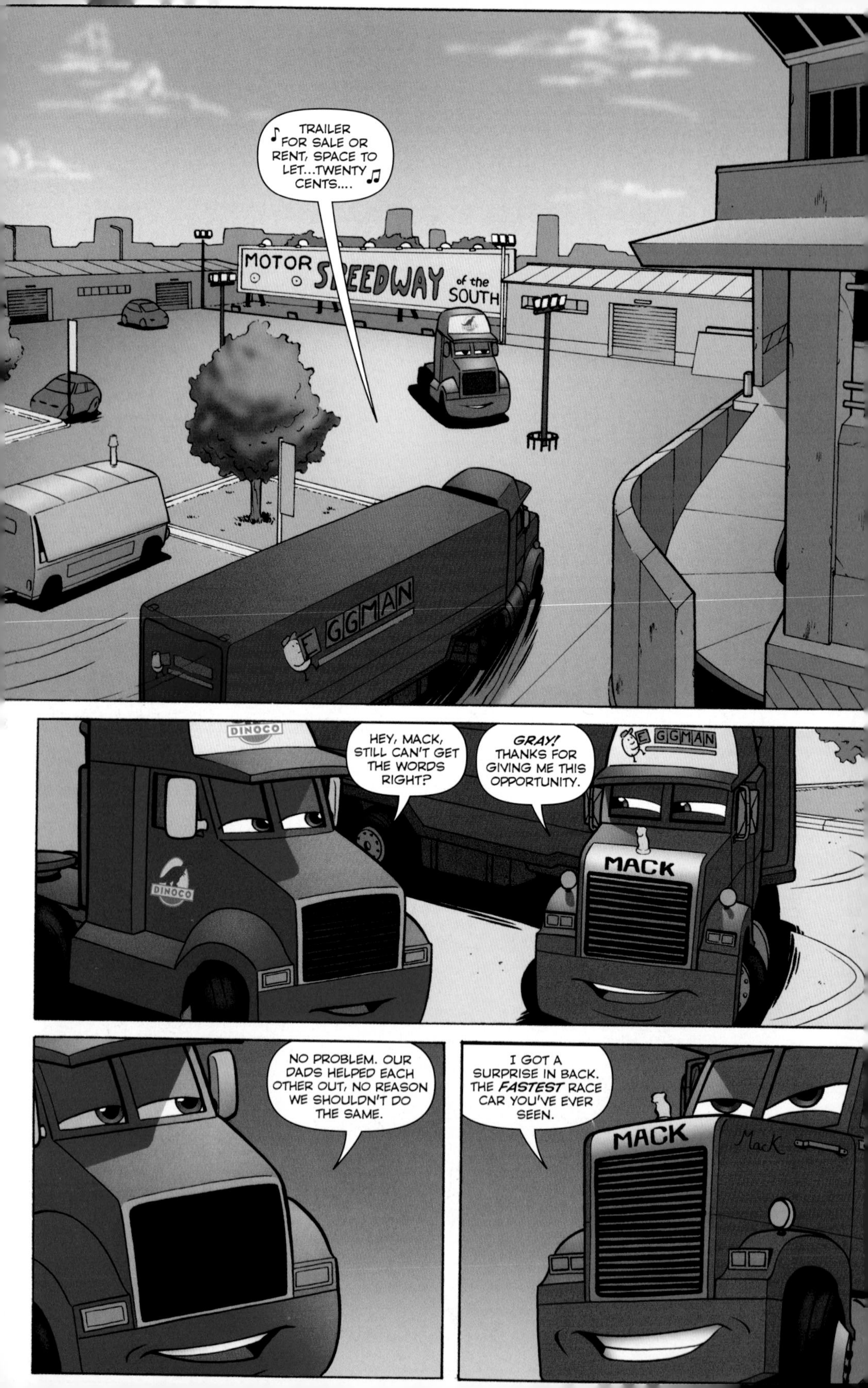

TRAILER FOR SALE OR RENT, SPACE TO LET...TWENTY CENTS....
MOTOR SPEEDWAY of the SOUTH
EGGMAN
DINOCO
HEY, MACK, STILL CAN'T GET THE WORDS RIGHT?
GRAY! THANKS FOR GIVING ME THIS OPPORTUNITY.
EGGMAN
MACK
NO PROBLEM. OUR DADS HELPED EACH OTHER OUT, NO REASON WE SHOULDN'T DO THE SAME.
I GOT A SURPRISE IN BACK. THE *FASTEST* RACE CAR YOU'VE EVER SEEN.
MACK
Mack

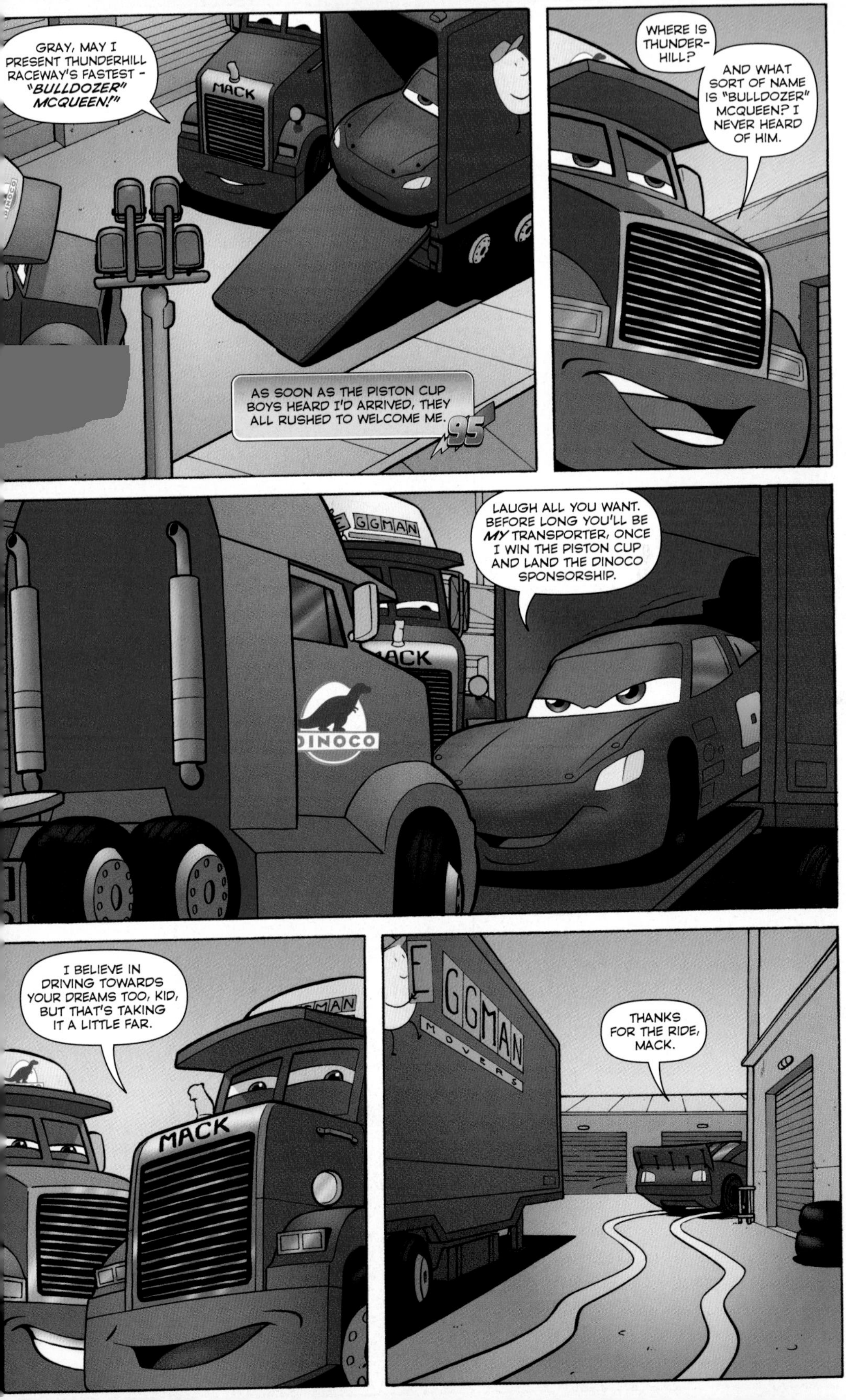
GRAY, MAY I PRESENT THUNDERHILL RACEWAY'S FASTEST - "BULLDOZER" MCQUEEN!"
MACK
AS SOON AS THE PISTON CUP BOYS HEARD I'D ARRIVED, THEY ALL RUSHED TO WELCOME ME.
95
WHERE IS THUNDER-HILL?
AND WHAT SORT OF NAME IS "BULLDOZER" MCQUEEN? I NEVER HEARD OF HIM.
LAUGH ALL YOU WANT. BEFORE LONG YOU'LL BE *MY* TRANSPORTER, ONCE I WIN THE PISTON CUP AND LAND THE DINOCO SPONSORSHIP.
EGGMAN
MACK
DINOCO
I BELIEVE IN DRIVING TOWARDS YOUR DREAMS TOO, KID, BUT THAT'S TAKING IT A LITTLE FAR.
MACK
EGGMAN
MOVERS
THANKS FOR THE RIDE, MACK.

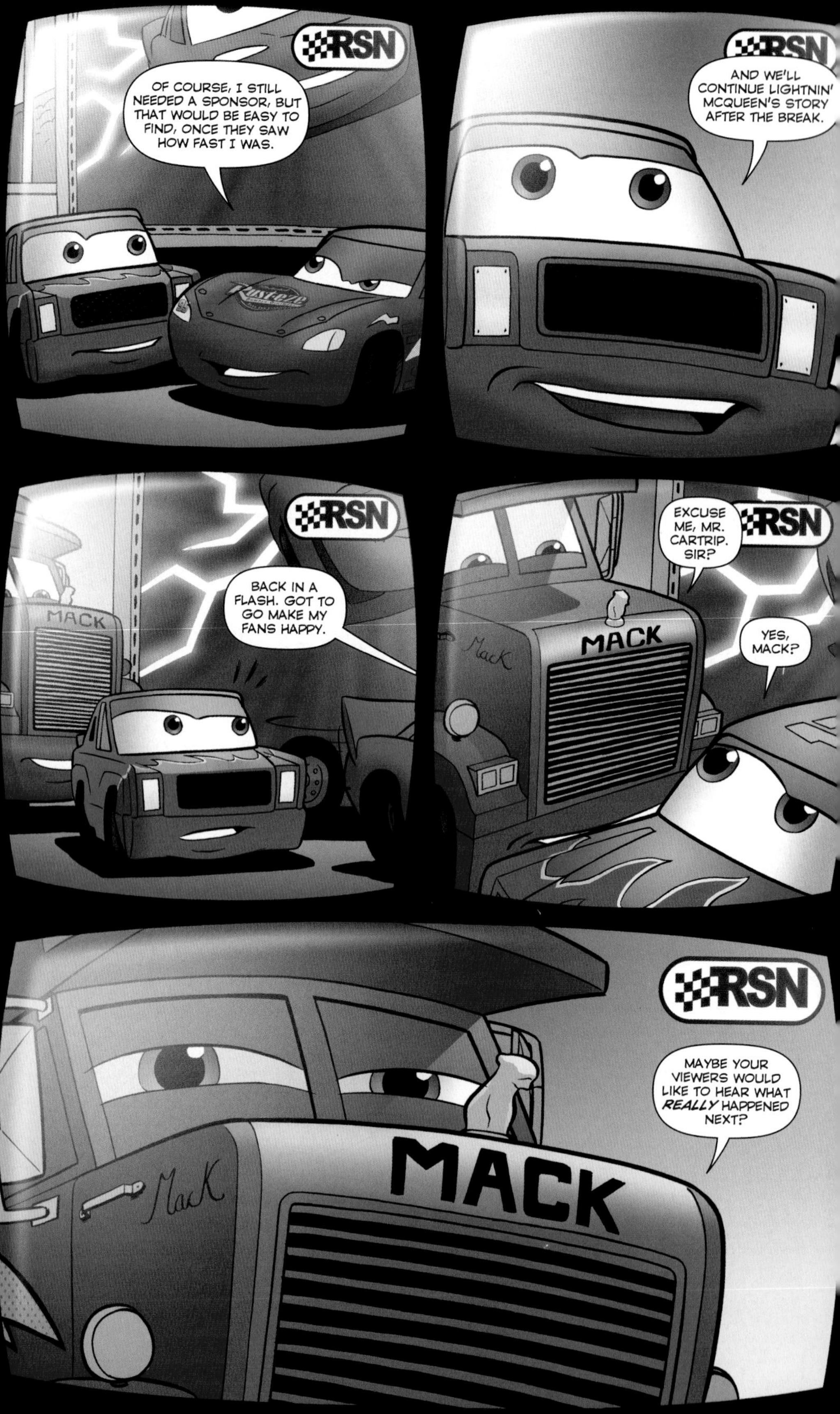
RSN
OF COURSE, I STILL NEEDED A SPONSOR, BUT THAT WOULD BE EASY TO FIND, ONCE THEY SAW HOW FAST I WAS.
RSN
AND WE'LL CONTINUE LIGHTNIN' MCQUEEN'S STORY AFTER THE BREAK.
RSN
MACK
BACK IN A FLASH. GOT TO GO MAKE MY FANS HAPPY.
EXCUSE ME, MR. CARTRIP. SIR?
RSN
MACK
YES, MACK?
RSN
MAYBE YOUR VIEWERS WOULD LIKE TO HEAR WHAT *REALLY* HAPPENED NEXT?
MACK

Chapter Two

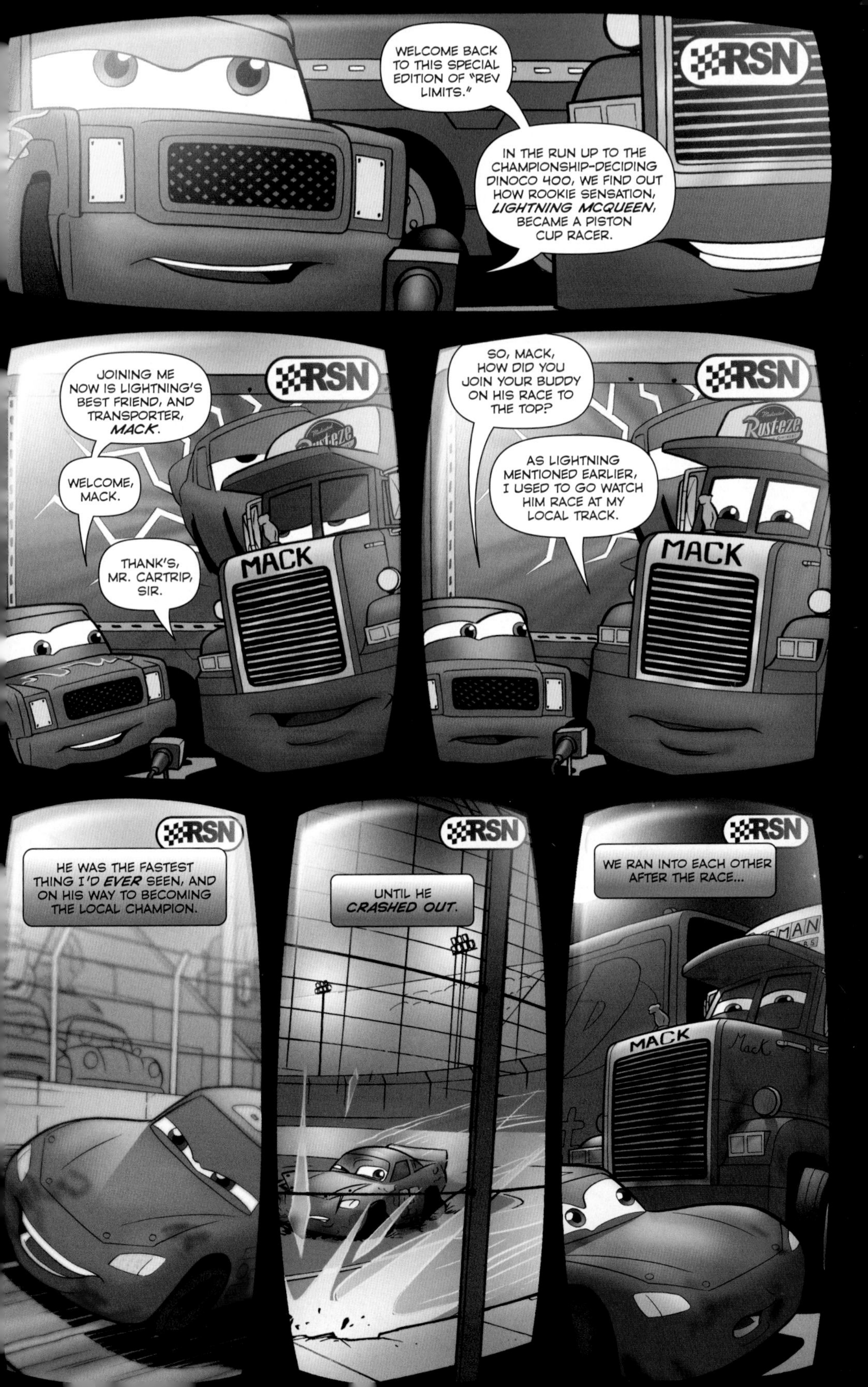
WELCOME BACK TO THIS SPECIAL EDITION OF "REV LIMITS."
IN THE RUN UP TO THE CHAMPIONSHIP-DECIDING DINOCO 400, WE FIND OUT HOW ROOKIE SENSATION, *LIGHTNING MCQUEEN*, BECAME A PISTON CUP RACER.
RSN
JOINING ME NOW IS LIGHTNING'S BEST FRIEND, AND TRANSPORTER, *MACK*.
WELCOME, MACK.
THANK'S, MR. CARTRIP, SIR.
MACK
SO, MACK, HOW DID YOU JOIN YOUR BUDDY ON HIS RACE TO THE TOP?
AS LIGHTNING MENTIONED EARLIER, I USED TO GO WATCH HIM RACE AT MY LOCAL TRACK.
HE WAS THE FASTEST THING I'D *EVER* SEEN, AND ON HIS WAY TO BECOMING THE LOCAL CHAMPION.
UNTIL HE *CRASHED OUT*.
WE RAN INTO EACH OTHER AFTER THE RACE...

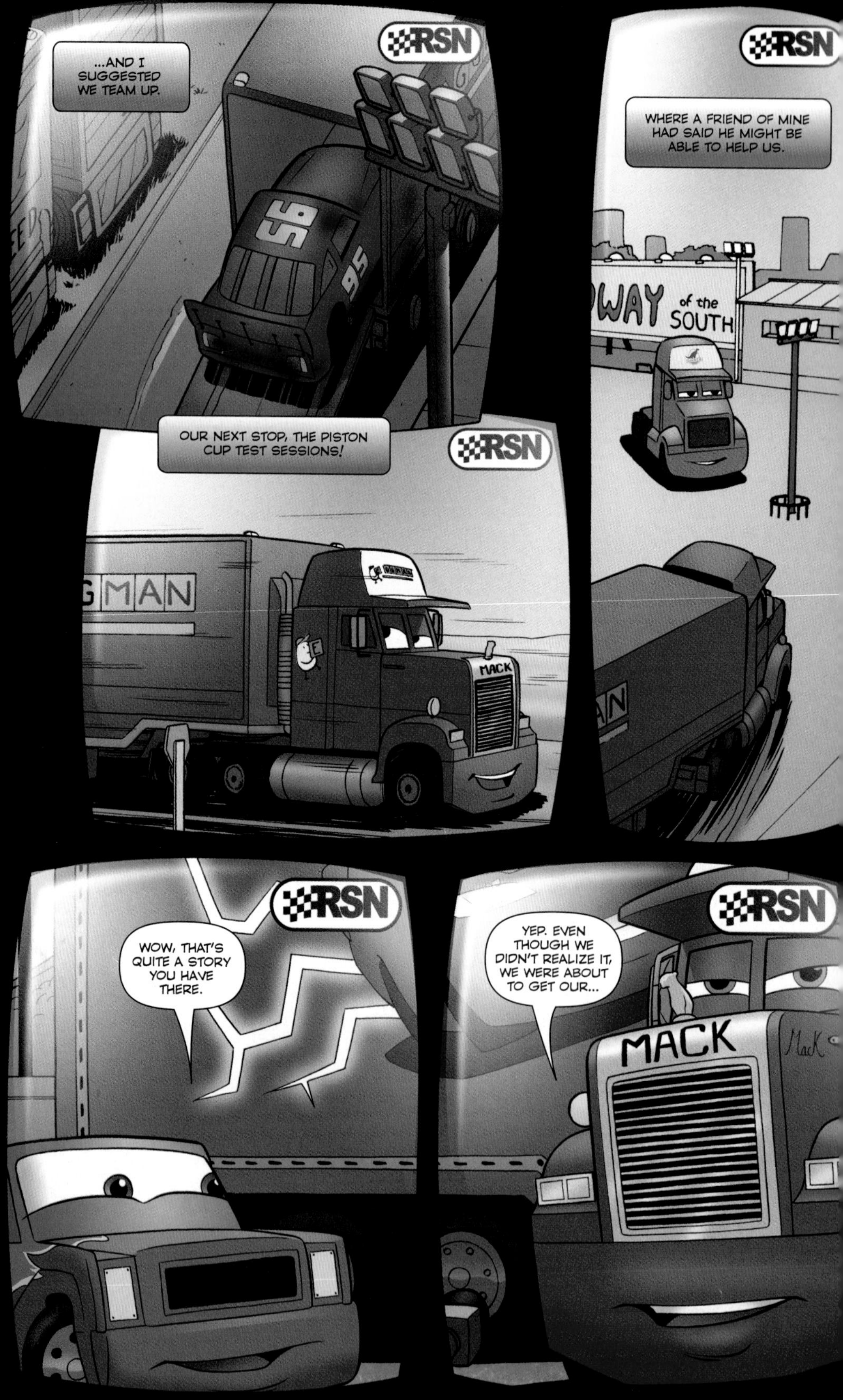

...AND I SUGGESTED WE TEAM UP.
OUR NEXT STOP, THE PISTON CUP TEST SESSIONS!
GMAN
MACK
WHERE A FRIEND OF MINE HAD SAID HE MIGHT BE ABLE TO HELP US.
WAY of the SOUTH
WOW, THAT'S QUITE A STORY YOU HAVE THERE.
YEP. EVEN THOUGH WE DIDN'T REALIZE IT, WE WERE ABOUT TO GET OUR...
MACK

"BIG BREAK!"

The Rookie Part 2

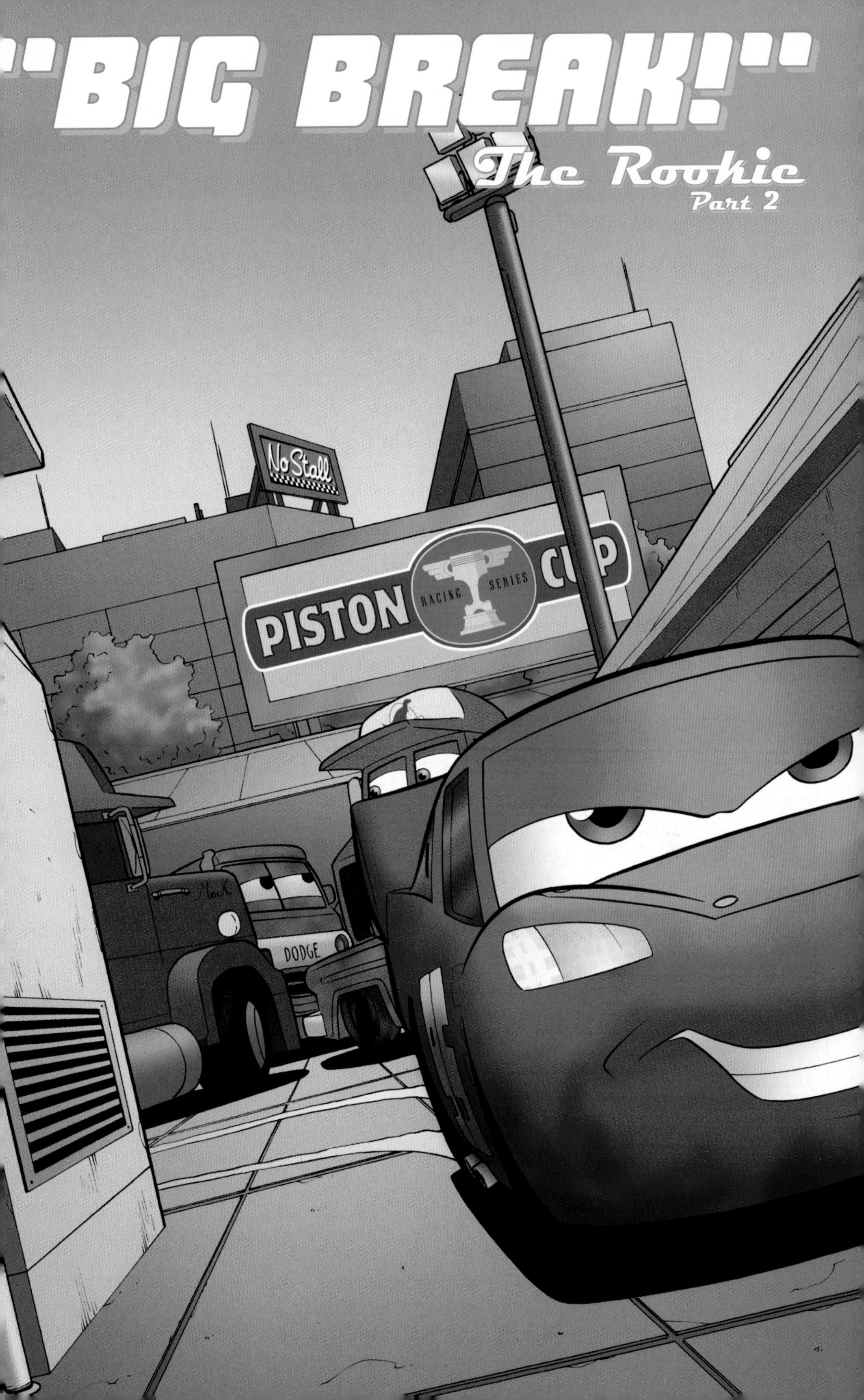

No Stall
PISTON CUP
RACING SERIES
Mack
DODGE

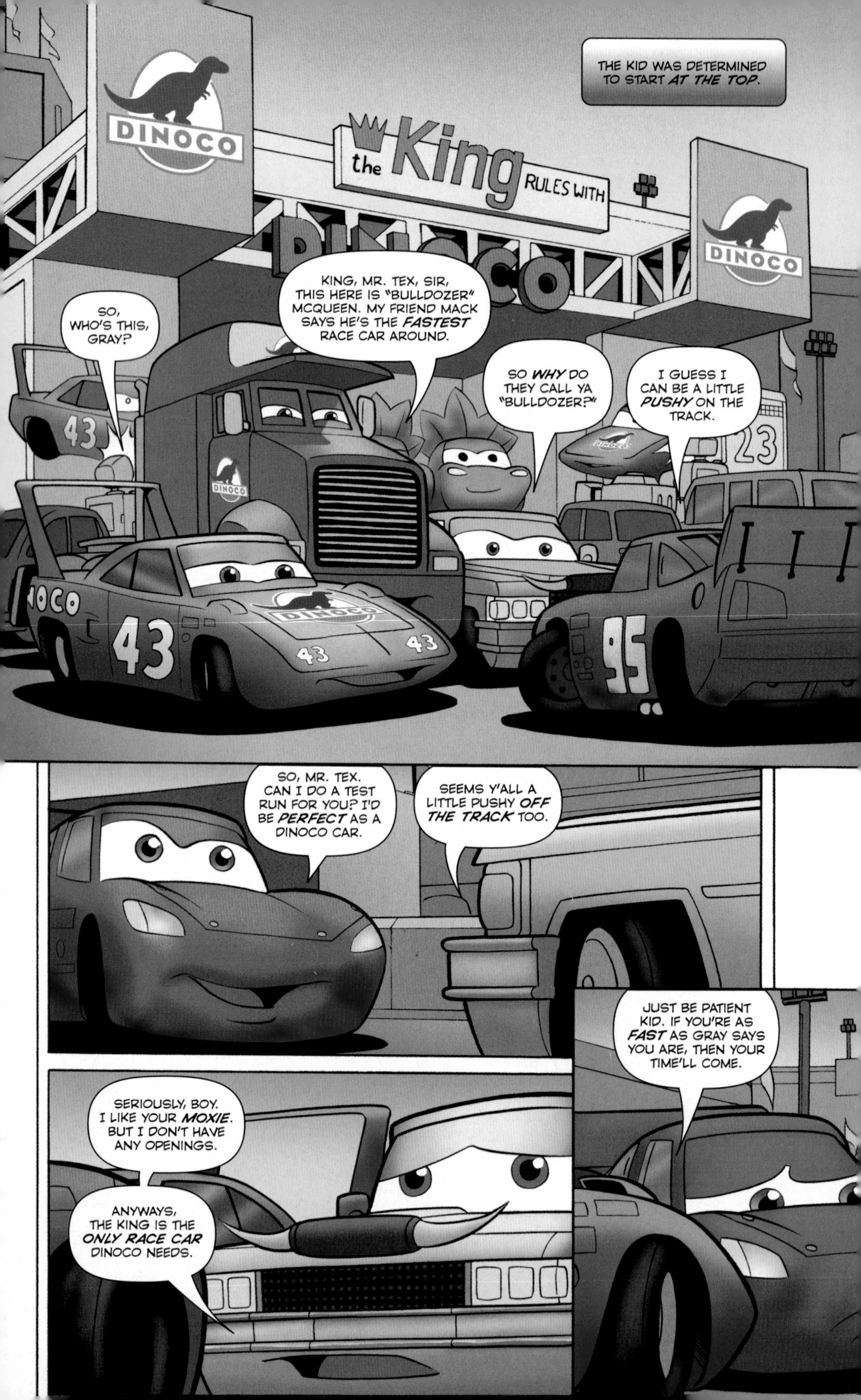
THE KID WAS DETERMINED TO START AT THE TOP.
DINOCO
the King RULES WITH
DINOCO
SO, WHO'S THIS, GRAY?
KING, MR. TEX, SIR, THIS HERE IS "BULLDOZER" MCQUEEN. MY FRIEND MACK SAYS HE'S THE FASTEST RACE CAR AROUND.
SO WHY DO THEY CALL YA "BULLDOZER?"
I GUESS I CAN BE A LITTLE PUSHY ON THE TRACK.
SO, MR. TEX. CAN I DO A TEST RUN FOR YOU? I'D BE PERFECT AS A DINOCO CAR.
SEEMS Y'ALL A LITTLE PUSHY OFF THE TRACK TOO.
SERIOUSLY, BOY. I LIKE YOUR MOXIE. BUT I DON'T HAVE ANY OPENINGS.
ANYWAYS, THE KING IS THE ONLY RACE CAR DINOCO NEEDS.
JUST BE PATIENT KID. IF YOU'RE AS FAST AS GRAY SAYS YOU ARE, THEN YOUR TIME'LL COME.

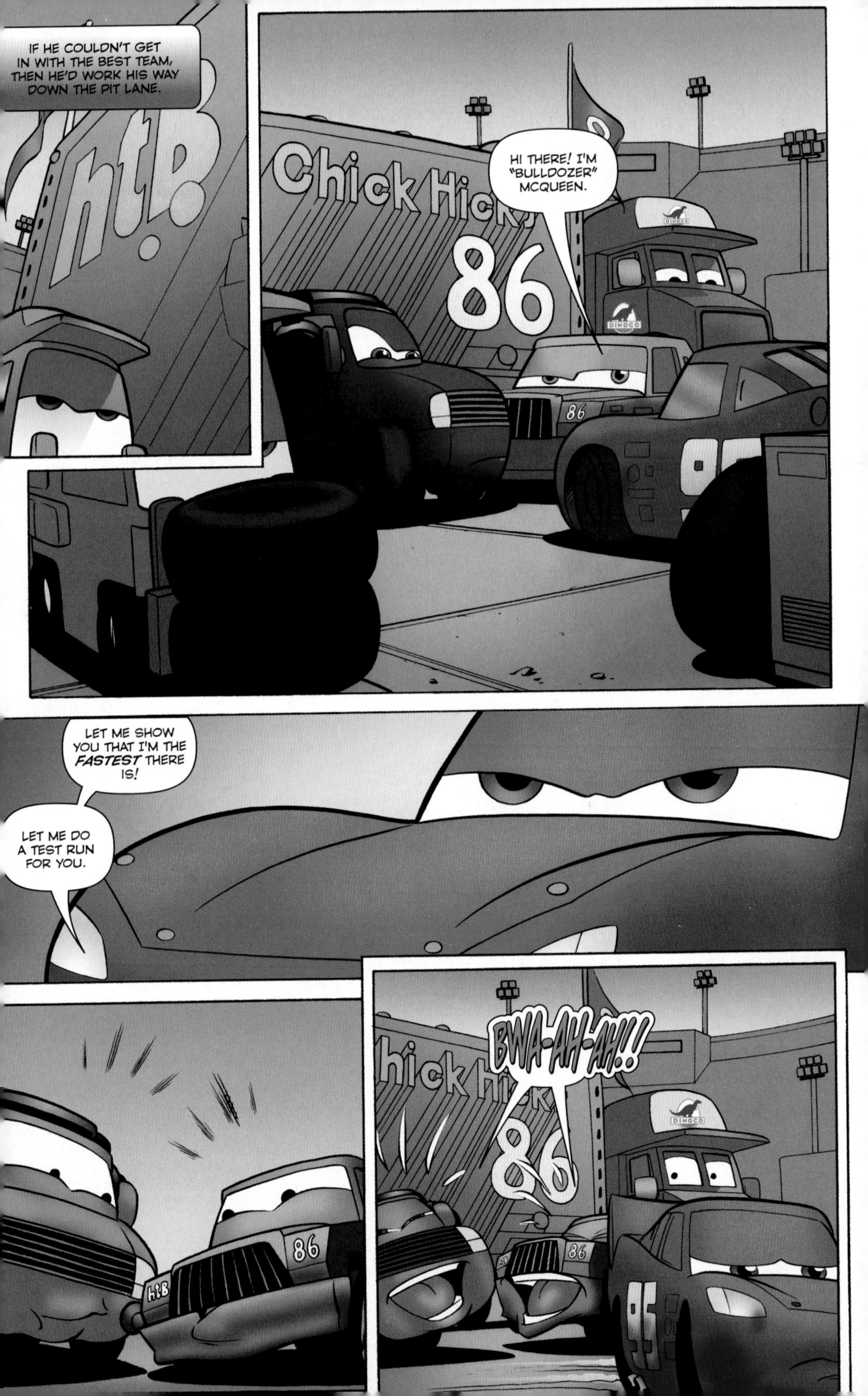
IF HE COULDN'T GET IN WITH THE BEST TEAM, THEN HE'D WORK HIS WAY DOWN THE PIT LANE.
HI THERE! I'M "BULLDOZER" MCQUEEN.
LET ME SHOW YOU THAT I'M THE *FASTEST* THERE IS!
LET ME DO A TEST RUN FOR YOU.
BWA-AH-AH!!

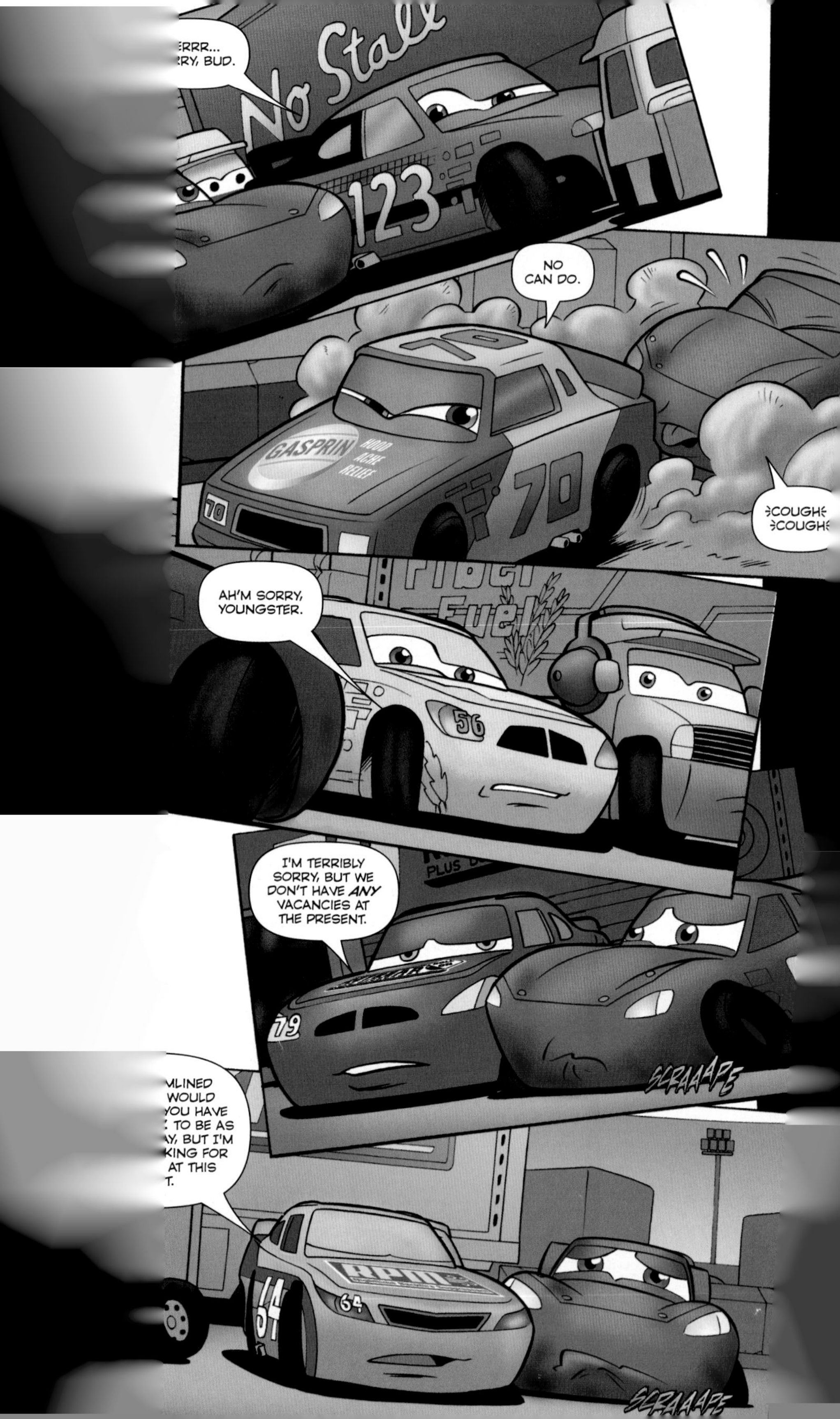

ERRR...
RY, BUD.
No Stall
123
NO CAN DO.
GASPRIN
HOOD ACHE RELIEF
70
COUGH COUGH
AH'M SORRY, YOUNGSTER.
56
I'M TERRIBLY SORRY, BUT WE DON'T HAVE *ANY* VACANCIES AT THE PRESENT.
79
SCRAAAPE
MLINED WOULD YOU HAVE TO BE AS AY, BUT I'M KING FOR AT THIS T.
RPM
64
SCRAAAPE

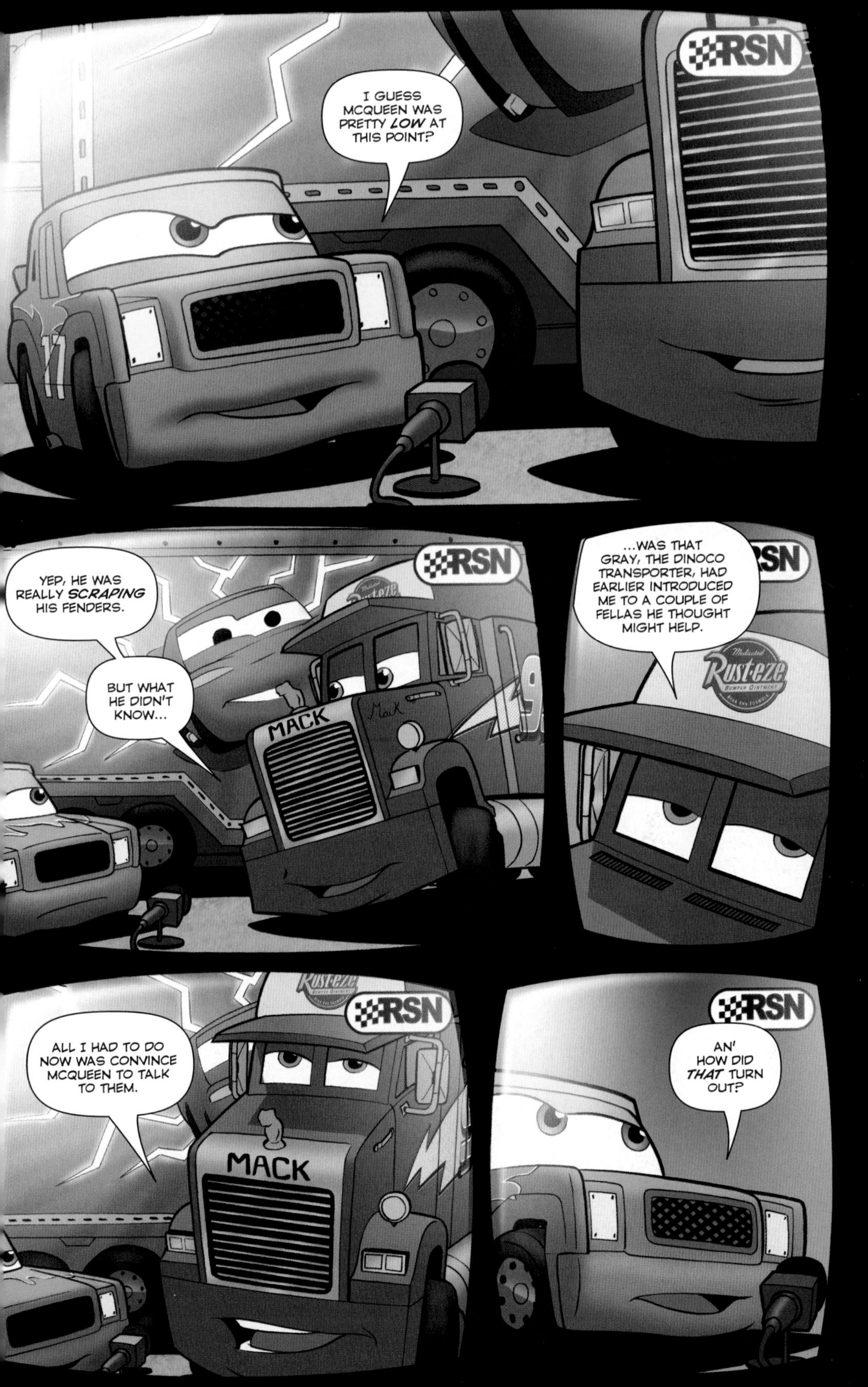
I GUESS MCQUEEN WAS PRETTY LOW AT THIS POINT?
RSN
YEP, HE WAS REALLY SCRAPING HIS FENDERS.
BUT WHAT HE DIDN'T KNOW...
MACK
...WAS THAT GRAY, THE DINOCO TRANSPORTER, HAD EARLIER INTRODUCED ME TO A COUPLE OF FELLAS HE THOUGHT MIGHT HELP.
Rust-eze
ALL I HAD TO DO NOW WAS CONVINCE MCQUEEN TO TALK TO THEM.
MACK
AN' HOW DID THAT TURN OUT?

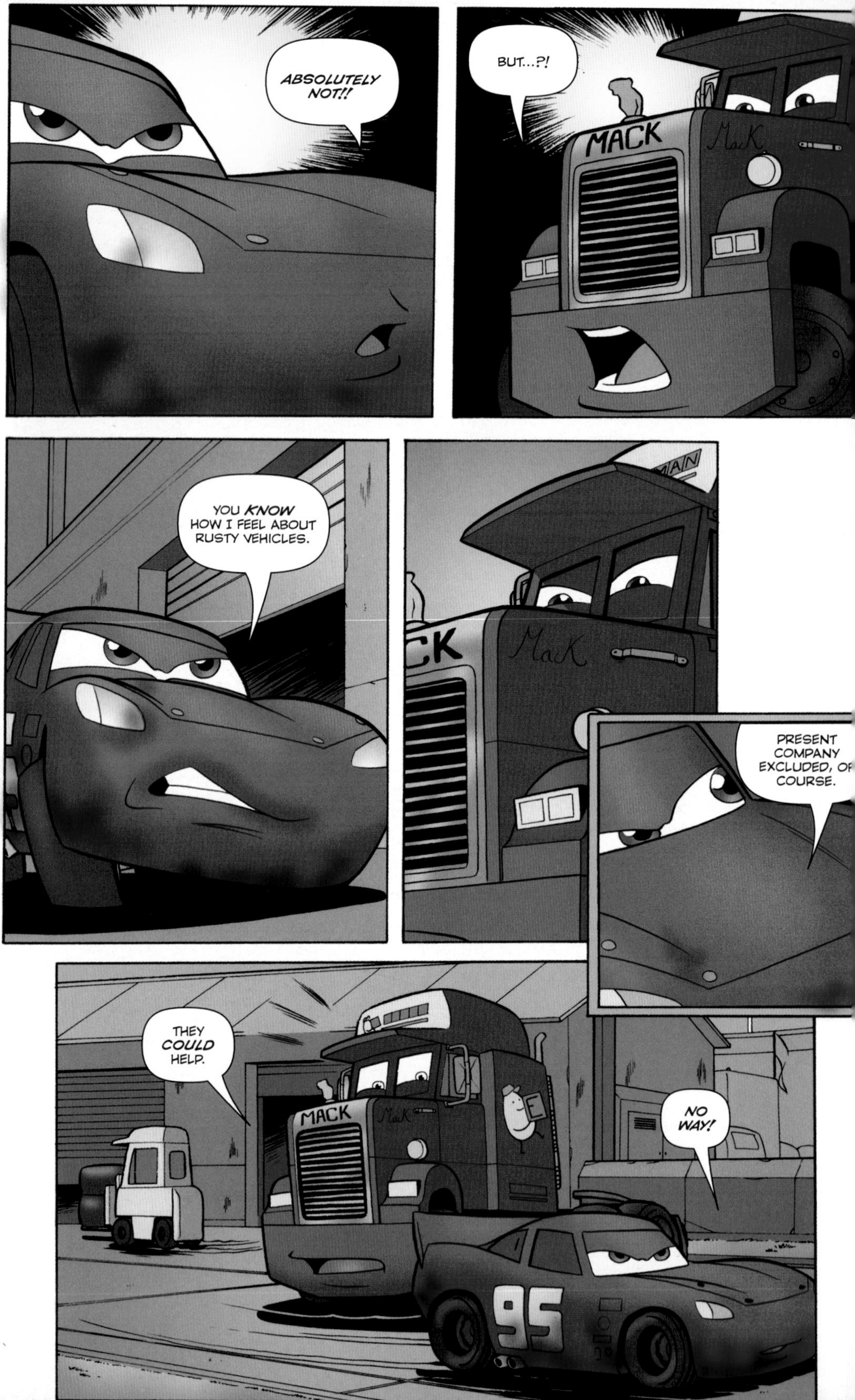
ABSOLUTELY NOT!!
BUT...?!
YOU *KNOW* HOW I FEEL ABOUT RUSTY VEHICLES.
PRESENT COMPANY EXCLUDED, OF COURSE.
THEY *COULD* HELP.
NO WAY!

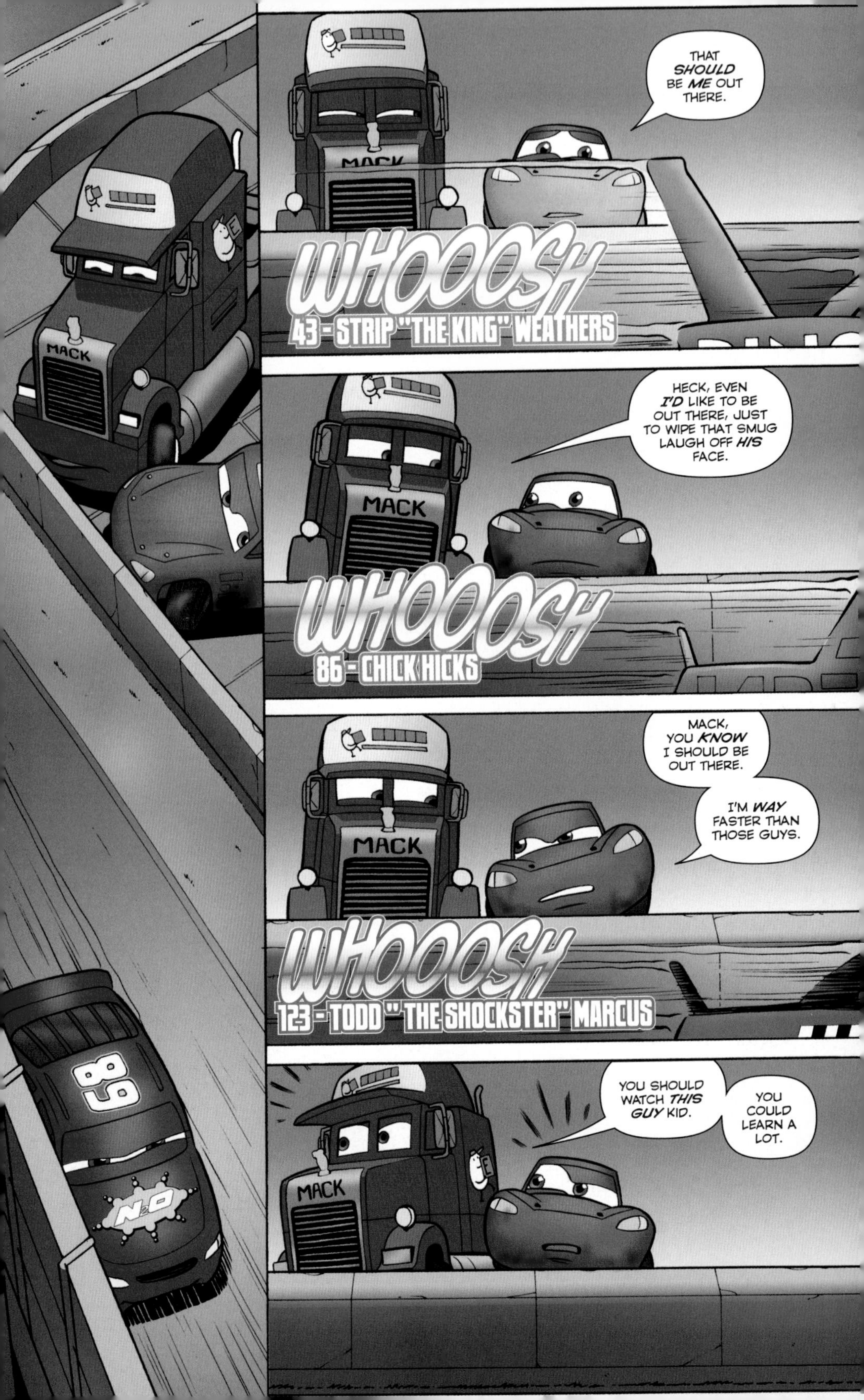
THAT SHOULD BE ME OUT THERE.
WHOOOSH
43 - STRIP "THE KING" WEATHERS
HECK, EVEN I'D LIKE TO BE OUT THERE, JUST TO WIPE THAT SMUG LAUGH OFF HIS FACE.
WHOOOSH
86 - CHICK HICKS
MACK, YOU KNOW I SHOULD BE OUT THERE.
I'M WAY FASTER THAN THOSE GUYS.
WHOOOSH
123 - TODD "THE SHOCKSTER" MARCUS
YOU SHOULD WATCH THIS GUY KID.
YOU COULD LEARN A LOT.
MACK
MACK
MACK
MACK
MACK
86
N2O

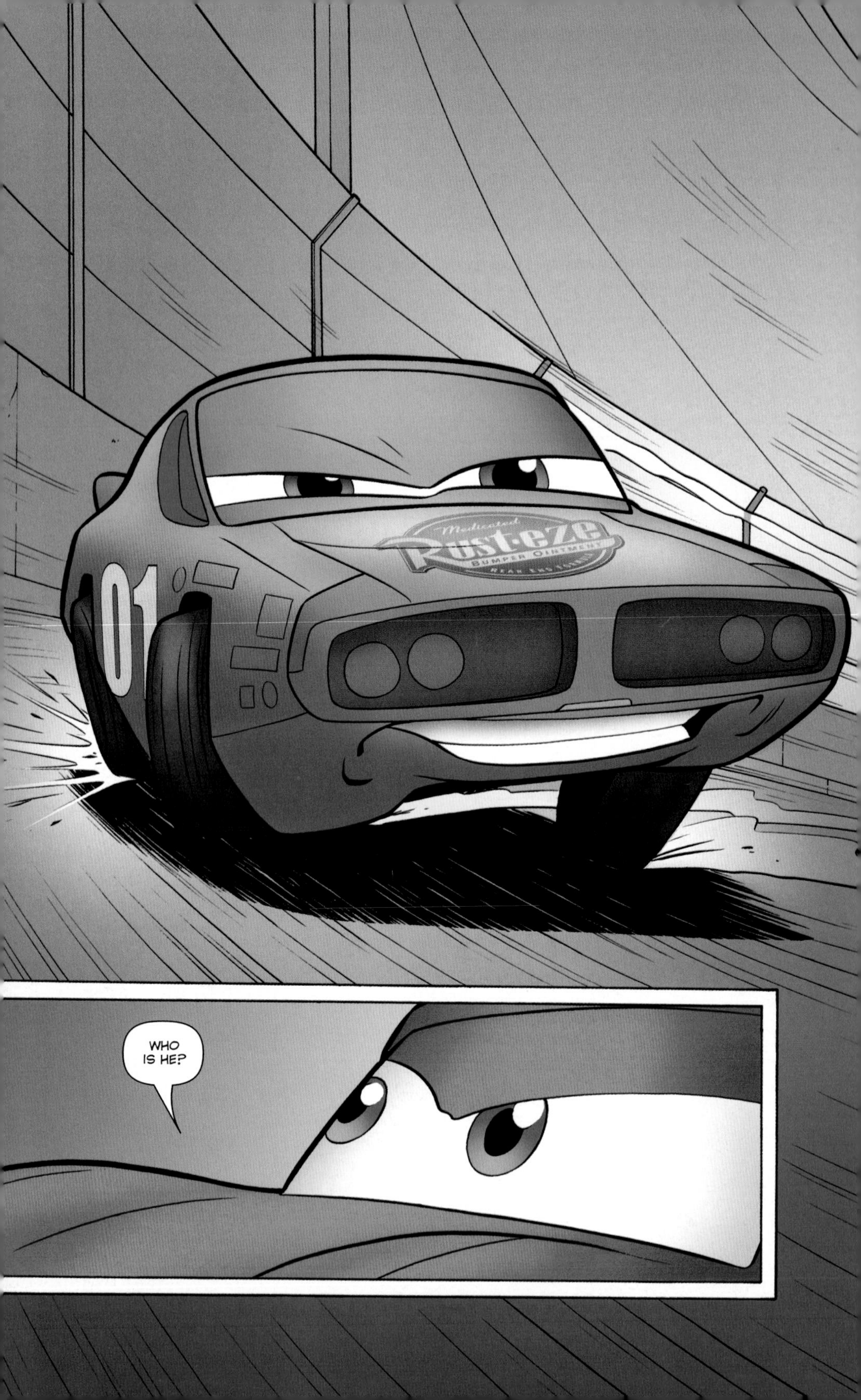
01
Medicated
Rust·eze
BUMPER OINTMENT
WHO IS HE?

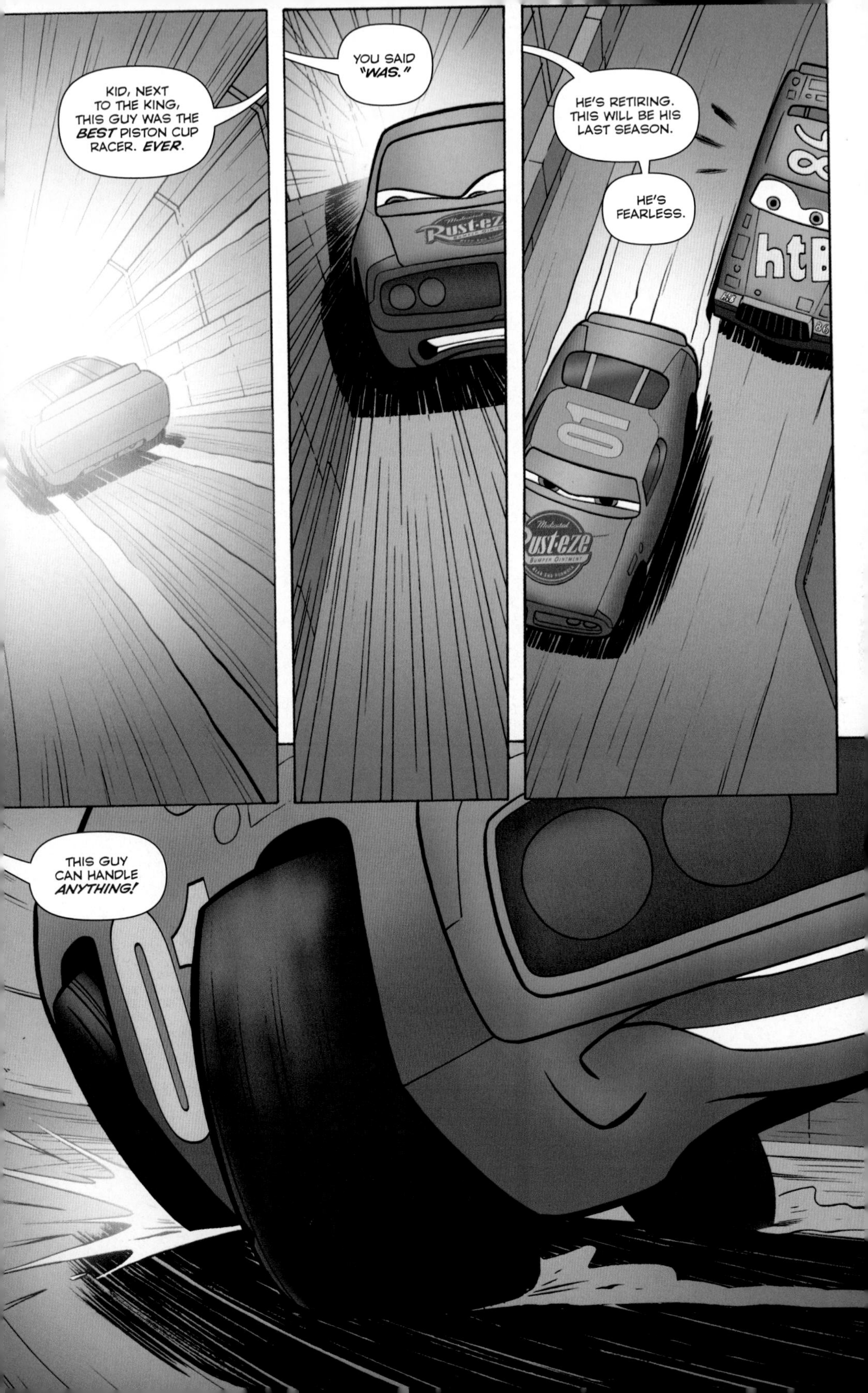
KID, NEXT TO THE KING, THIS GUY WAS THE BEST PISTON CUP RACER. EVER.
YOU SAID "WAS."
HE'S RETIRING. THIS WILL BE HIS LAST SEASON.
HE'S FEARLESS.
THIS GUY CAN HANDLE ANYTHING!

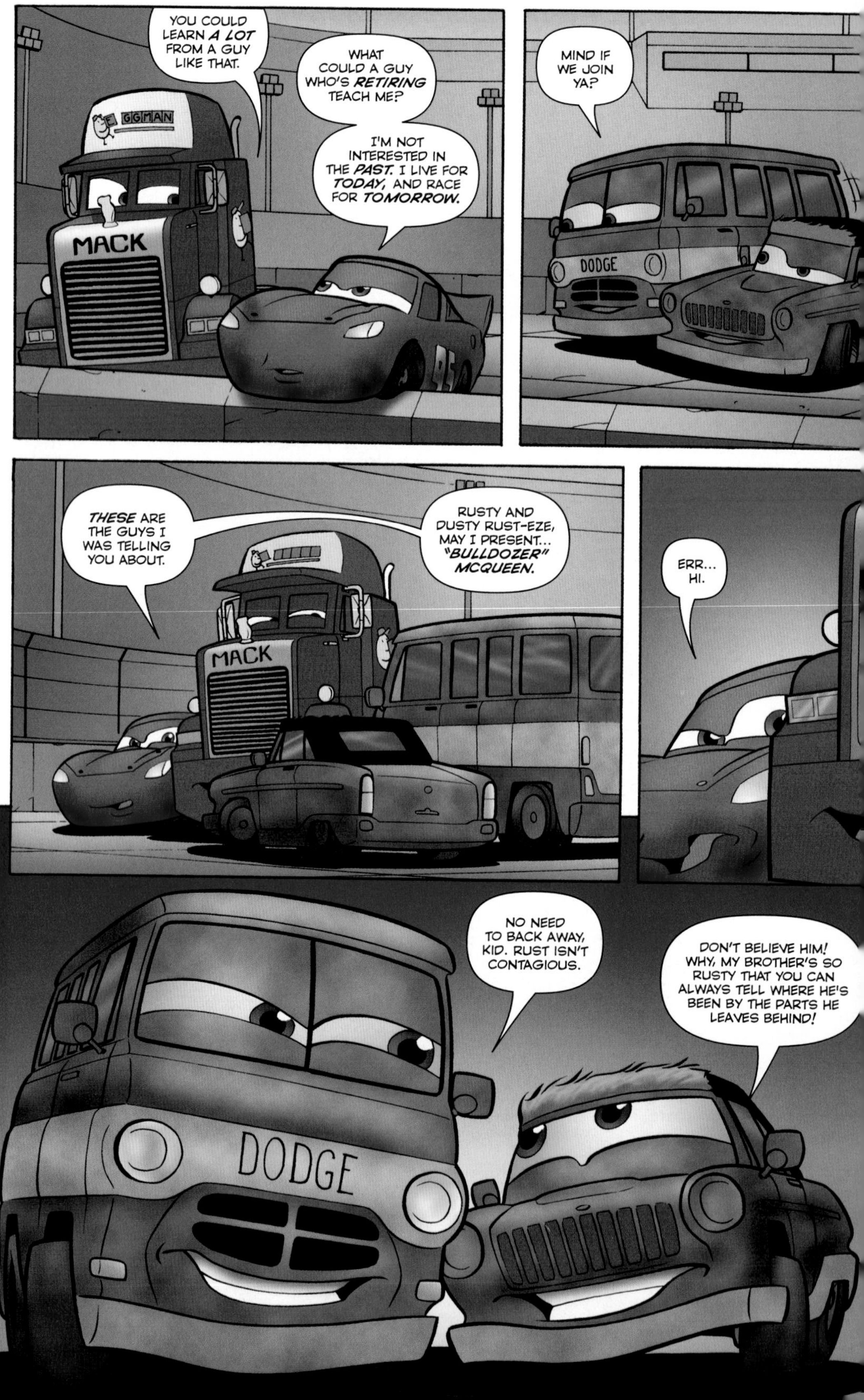
YOU COULD LEARN A LOT FROM A GUY LIKE THAT.
WHAT COULD A GUY WHO'S RETIRING TEACH ME?
I'M NOT INTERESTED IN THE PAST. I LIVE FOR TODAY, AND RACE FOR TOMORROW.
MACK
MIND IF WE JOIN YA?
DODGE
THESE ARE THE GUYS I WAS TELLING YOU ABOUT.
RUSTY AND DUSTY RUST-EZE, MAY I PRESENT... "BULLDOZER" MCQUEEN.
MACK
ERR... HI.
NO NEED TO BACK AWAY, KID. RUST ISN'T CONTAGIOUS.
DON'T BELIEVE HIM! WHY, MY BROTHER'S SO RUSTY THAT YOU CAN ALWAYS TELL WHERE HE'S BEEN BY THE PARTS HE LEAVES BEHIND!
DODGE

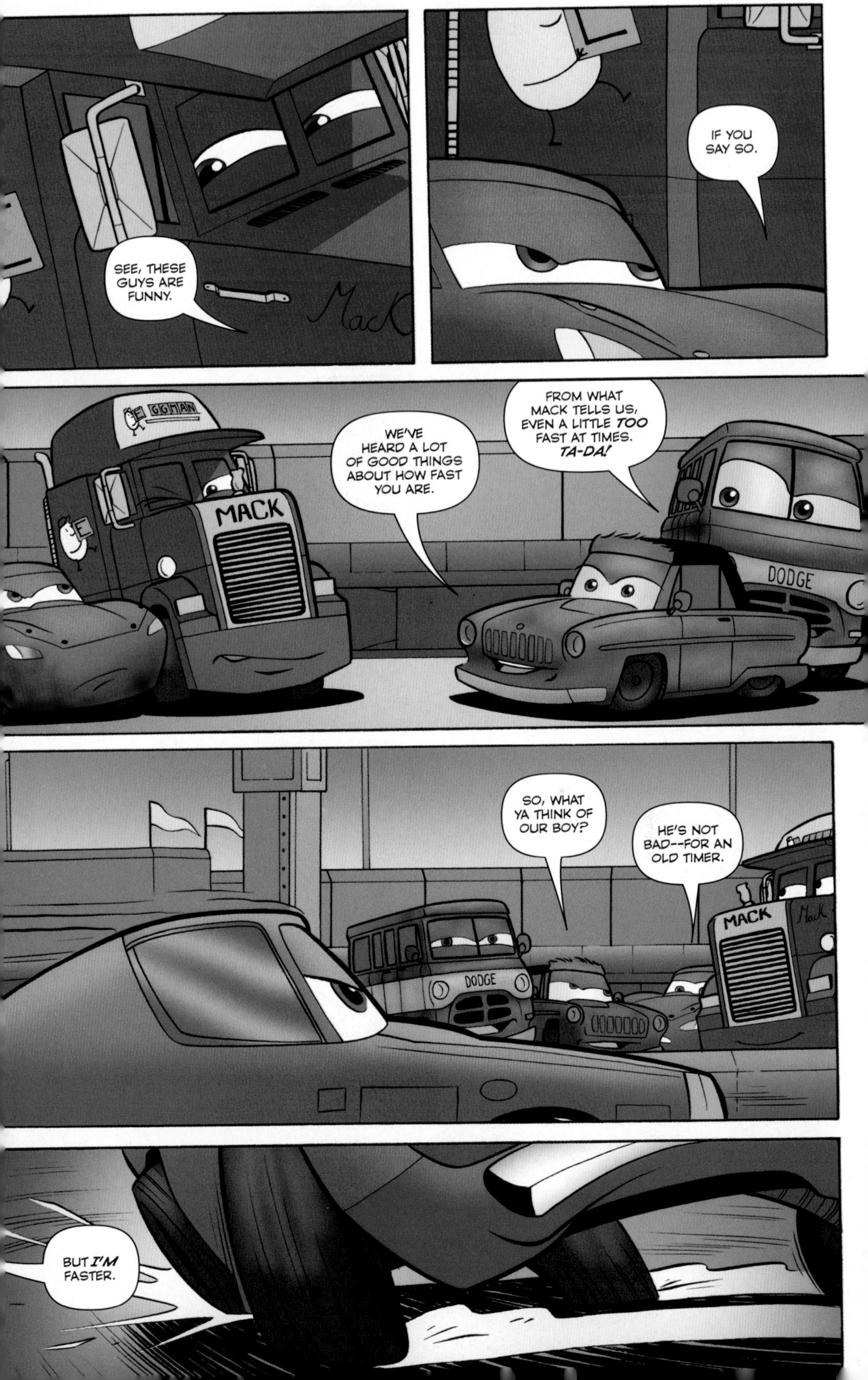
SEE, THESE GUYS ARE FUNNY.
Mack
IF YOU SAY SO.
EGGMAN
MACK
WE'VE HEARD A LOT OF GOOD THINGS ABOUT HOW FAST YOU ARE.
FROM WHAT MACK TELLS US, EVEN A LITTLE *TOO* FAST AT TIMES. *TA-DA!*
DODGE
SO, WHAT YA THINK OF OUR BOY?
HE'S NOT BAD--FOR AN OLD TIMER.
DODGE
MACK
BUT *I'M* FASTER.

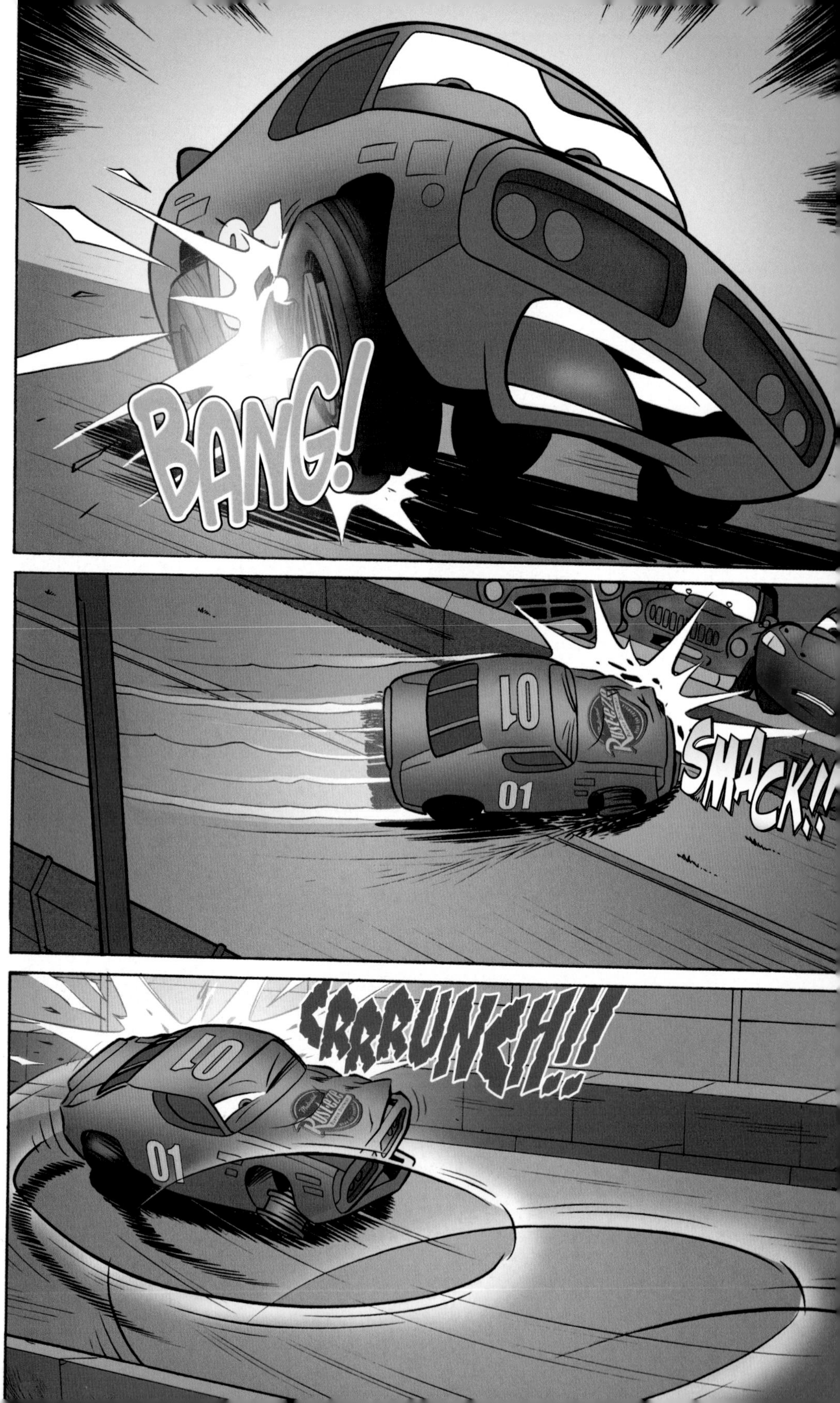
BANG!
SMACK!!
CRRRUNCH!!

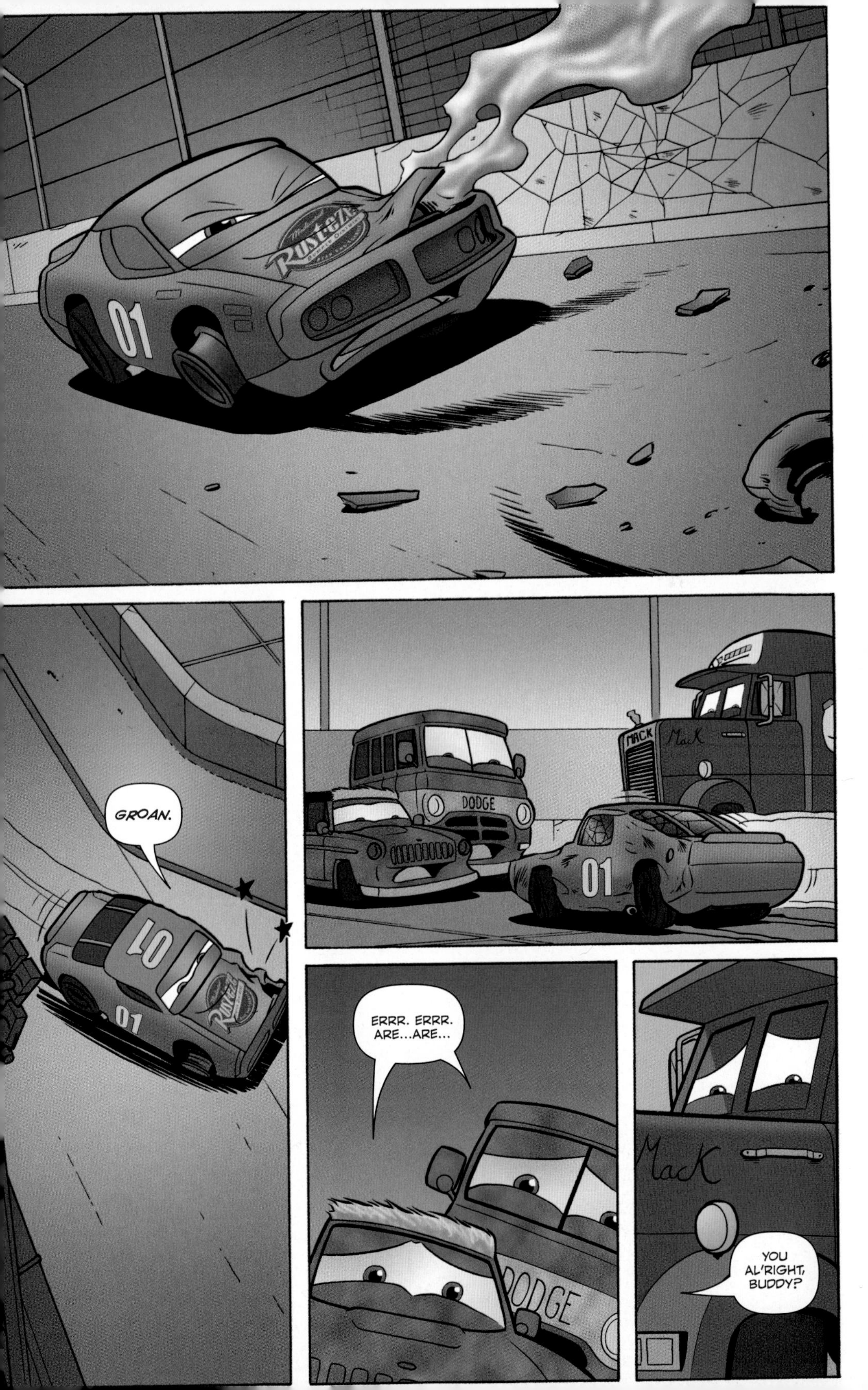
GROAN.
ERRR. ERRR. ARE...ARE...
YOU AL'RIGHT, BUDDY?

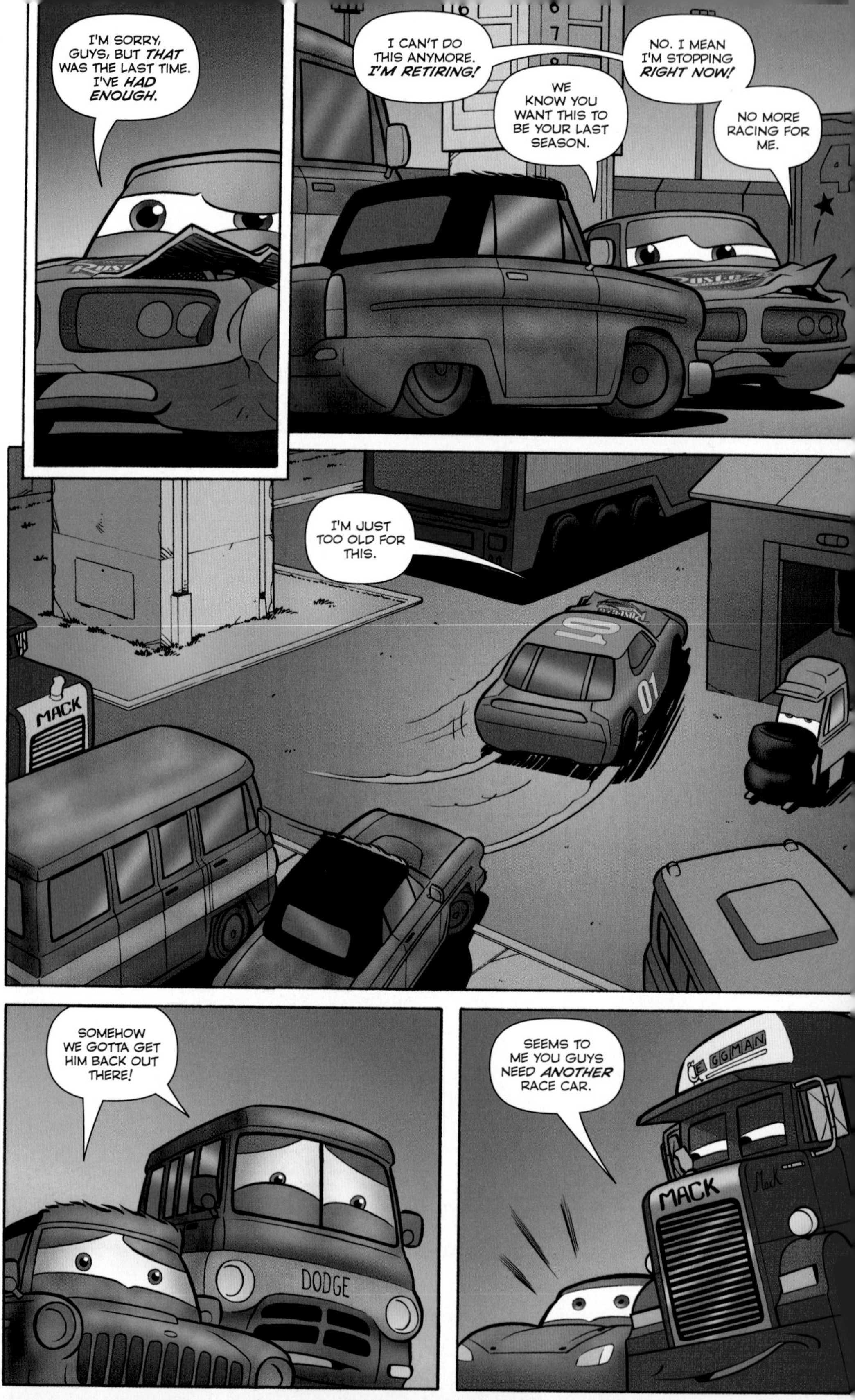
I'M SORRY, GUYS, BUT *THAT* WAS THE LAST TIME. I'VE *HAD ENOUGH.*
I CAN'T DO THIS ANYMORE. *I'M RETIRING!*
WE KNOW YOU WANT THIS TO BE YOUR LAST SEASON.
NO. I MEAN I'M STOPPING *RIGHT NOW!*
NO MORE RACING FOR ME.
I'M JUST TOO OLD FOR THIS.
MACK
01
SOMEHOW WE GOTTA GET HIM BACK OUT THERE!
DODGE
SEEMS TO ME YOU GUYS NEED *ANOTHER* RACE CAR.
EGGMAN
MACK

GO ON.

BUT, MACK. RUSTY CARS? REALLY?

IT'S YOUR CHANCE.

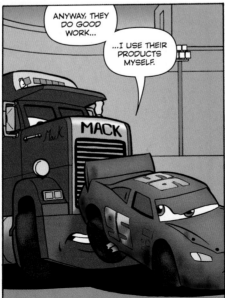

ANYWAY, THEY DO GOOD WORK...

...I USE THEIR PRODUCTS MYSELF.

WHY DOESN'T *THAT* SURPRISE ME?

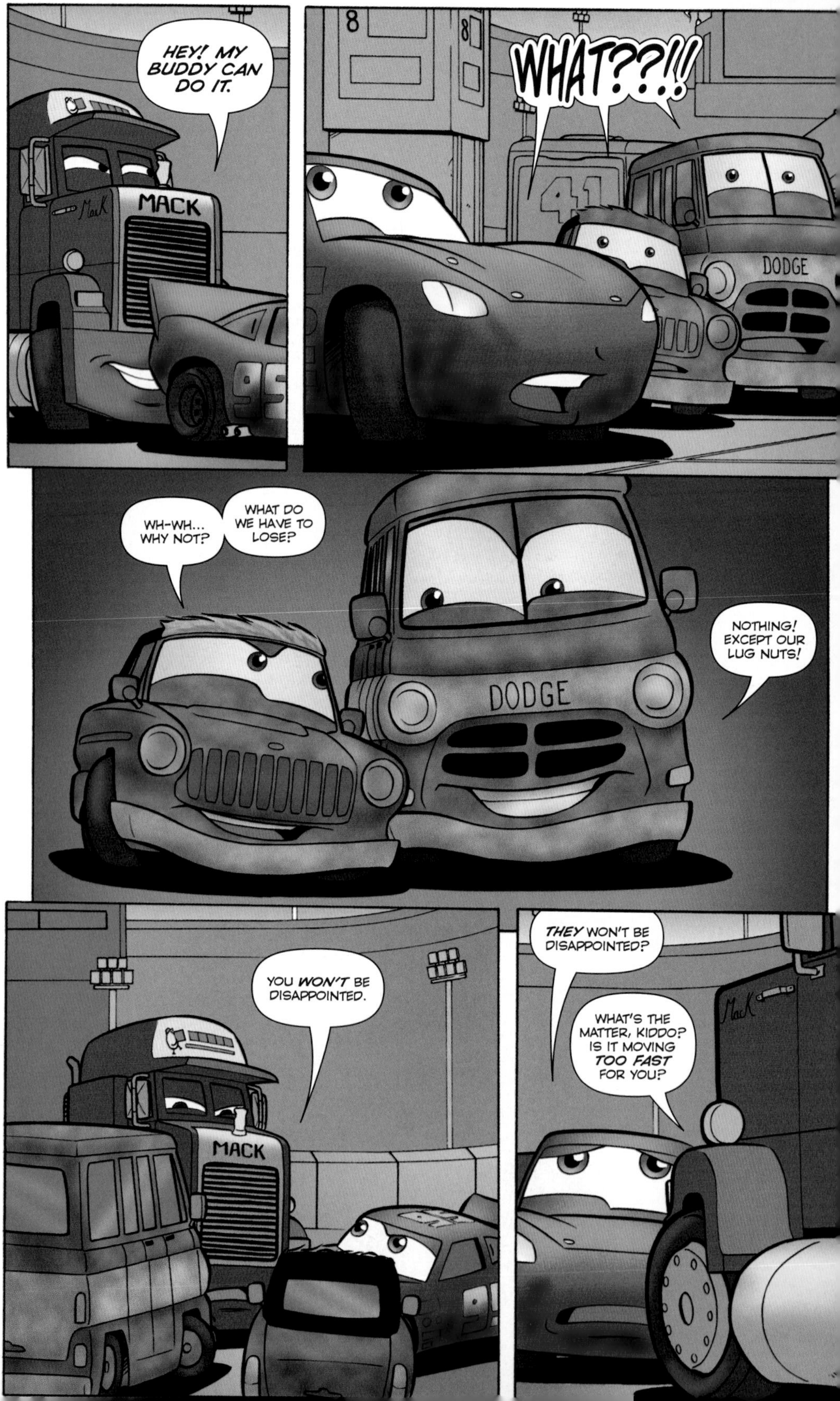
HEY! MY BUDDY CAN DO IT.
WHAT??!!
WH-WH... WHY NOT?
WHAT DO WE HAVE TO LOSE?
NOTHING! EXCEPT OUR LUG NUTS!
YOU WON'T BE DISAPPOINTED.
THEY WON'T BE DISAPPOINTED?
WHAT'S THE MATTER, KIDDO? IS IT MOVING TOO FAST FOR YOU?

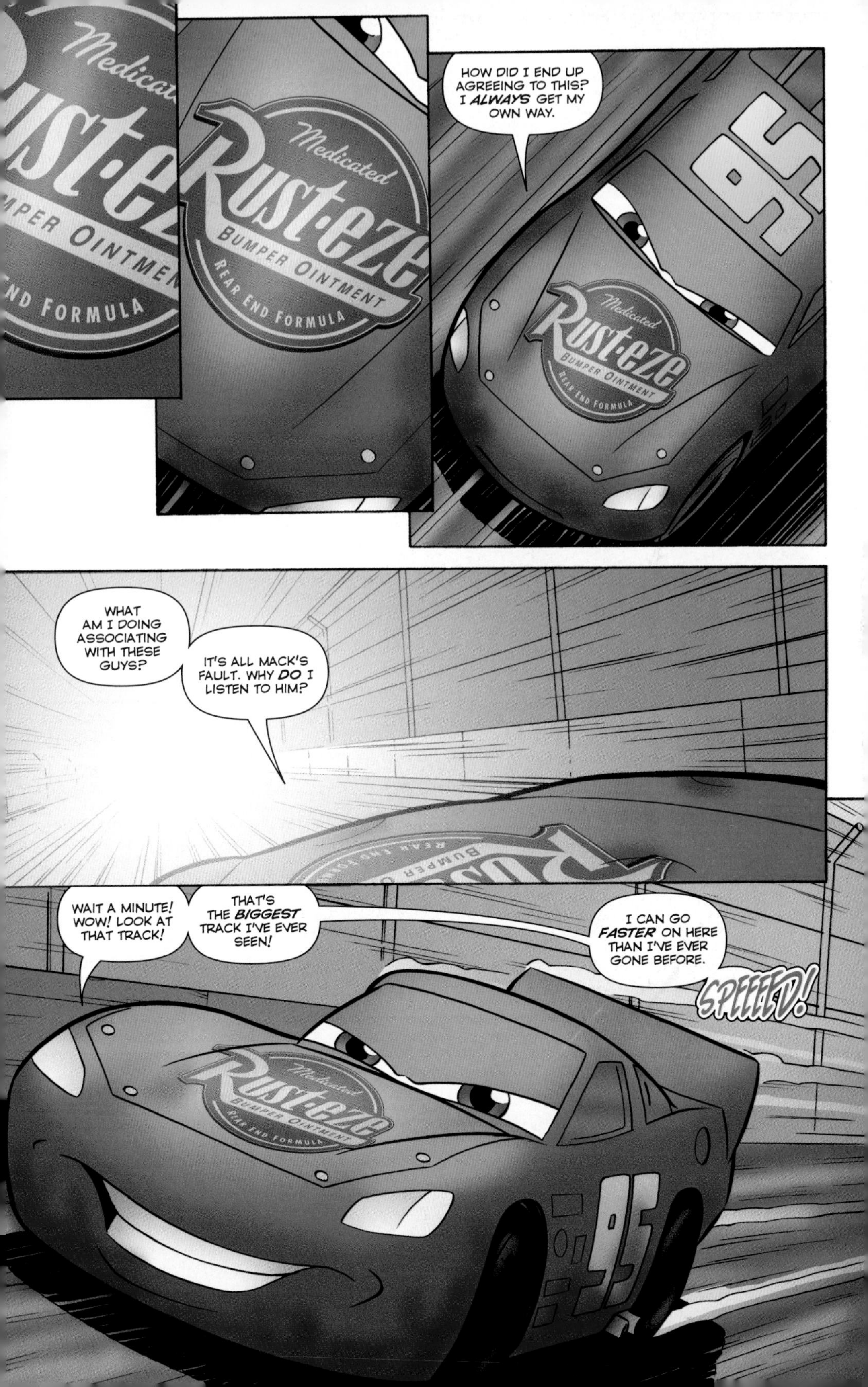

Medicated
Rust-eze
Bumper Ointment
Rear End Formula
HOW DID I END UP AGREEING TO THIS? I ALWAYS GET MY OWN WAY.
WHAT AM I DOING ASSOCIATING WITH THESE GUYS?
IT'S ALL MACK'S FAULT. WHY DO I LISTEN TO HIM?
WAIT A MINUTE! WOW! LOOK AT THAT TRACK!
THAT'S THE BIGGEST TRACK I'VE EVER SEEN!
I CAN GO FASTER ON HERE THAN I'VE EVER GONE BEFORE.
SPEEEED!

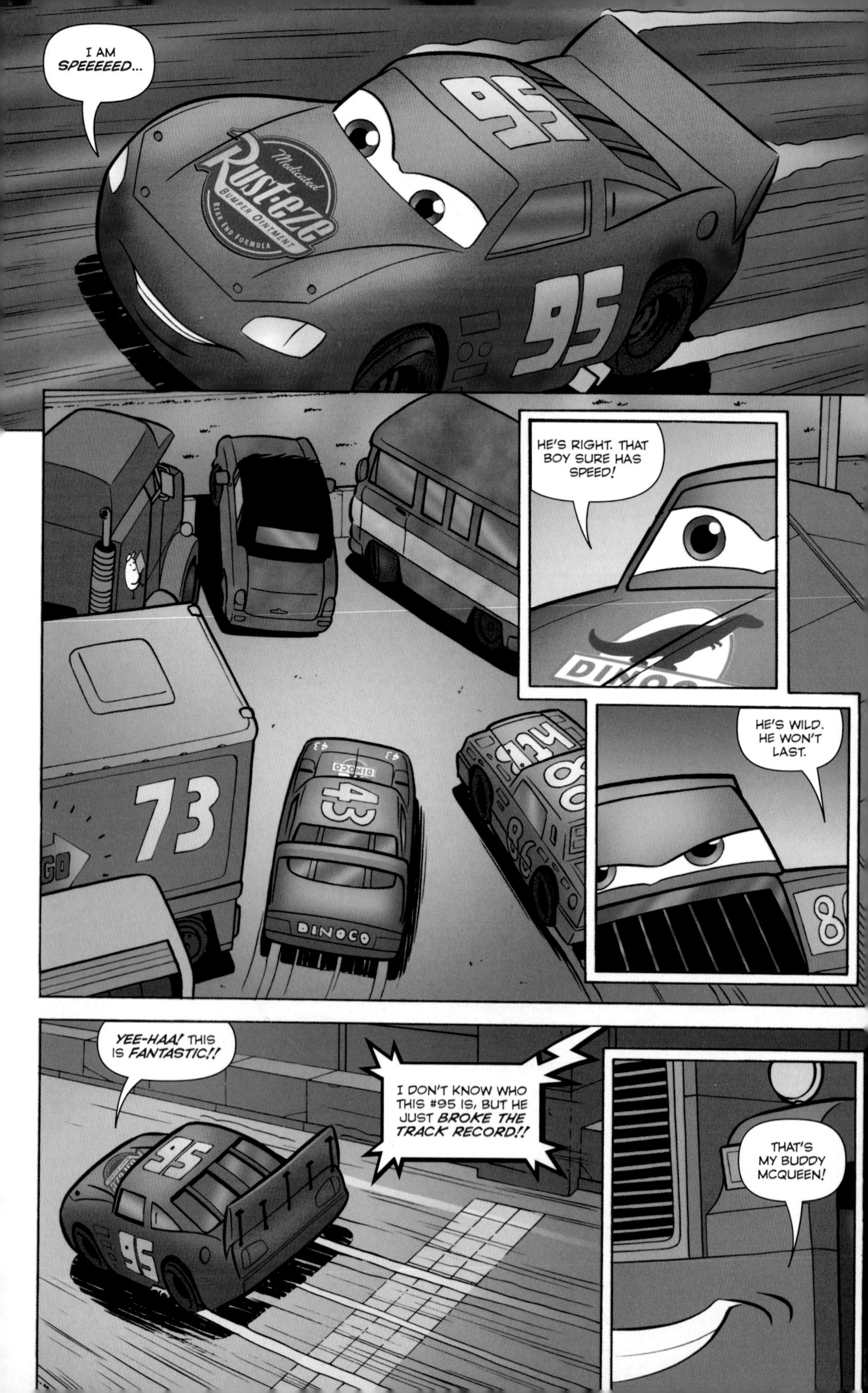

I AM SPEEEEED...
HE'S RIGHT. THAT BOY SURE HAS SPEED!
HE'S WILD. HE WON'T LAST.
YEE-HAA! THIS IS FANTASTIC!!
I DON'T KNOW WHO THIS #95 IS, BUT HE JUST BROKE THE TRACK RECORD!!
THAT'S MY BUDDY MCQUEEN!

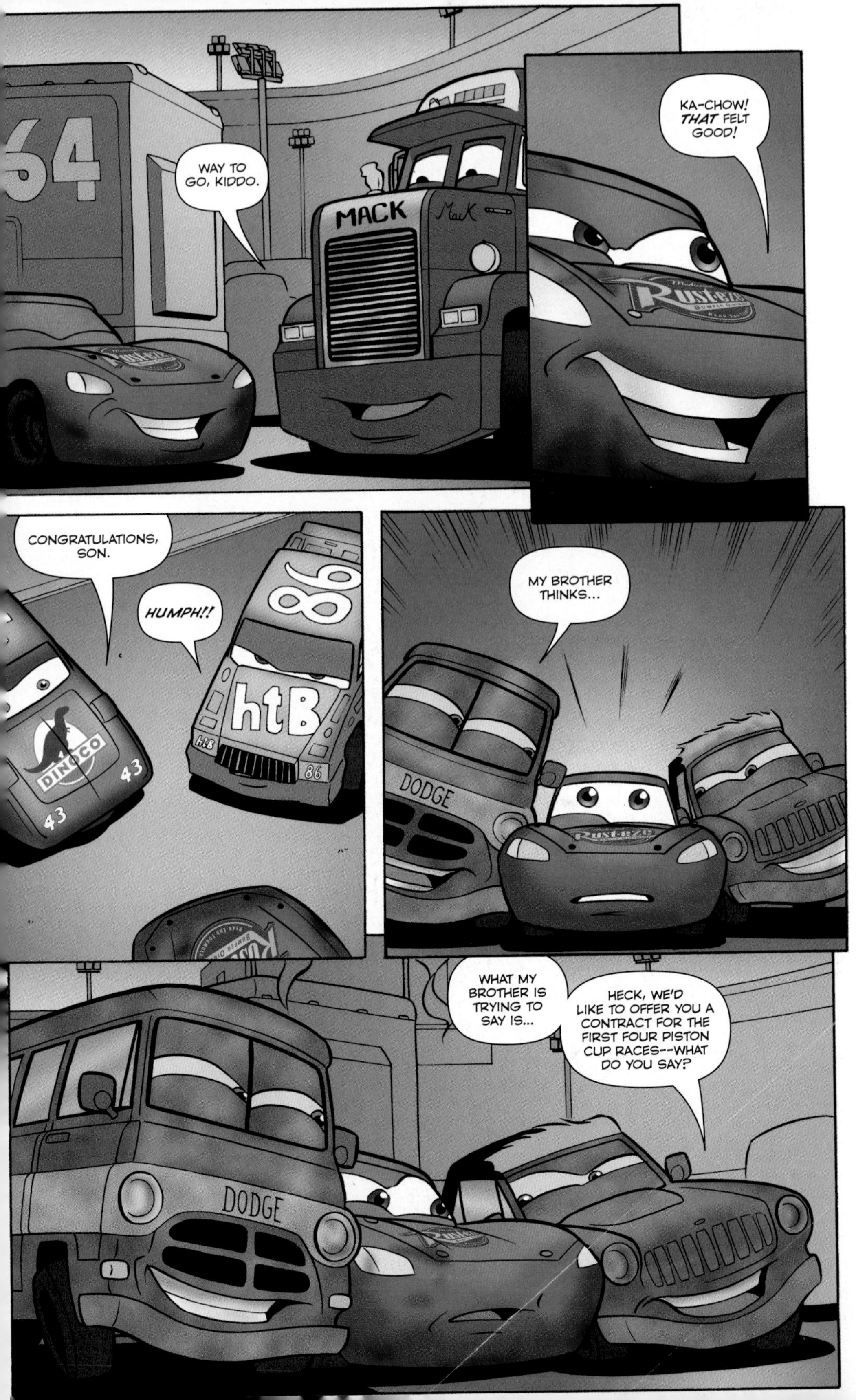
WAY TO GO, KIDDO.
MACK
KA-CHOW! *THAT* FELT GOOD!
CONGRATULATIONS, SON.
HUMPH!!
MY BROTHER THINKS...
WHAT MY BROTHER IS TRYING TO SAY IS...
HECK, WE'D LIKE TO OFFER YOU A CONTRACT FOR THE FIRST FOUR PISTON CUP RACES--WHAT DO YOU SAY?

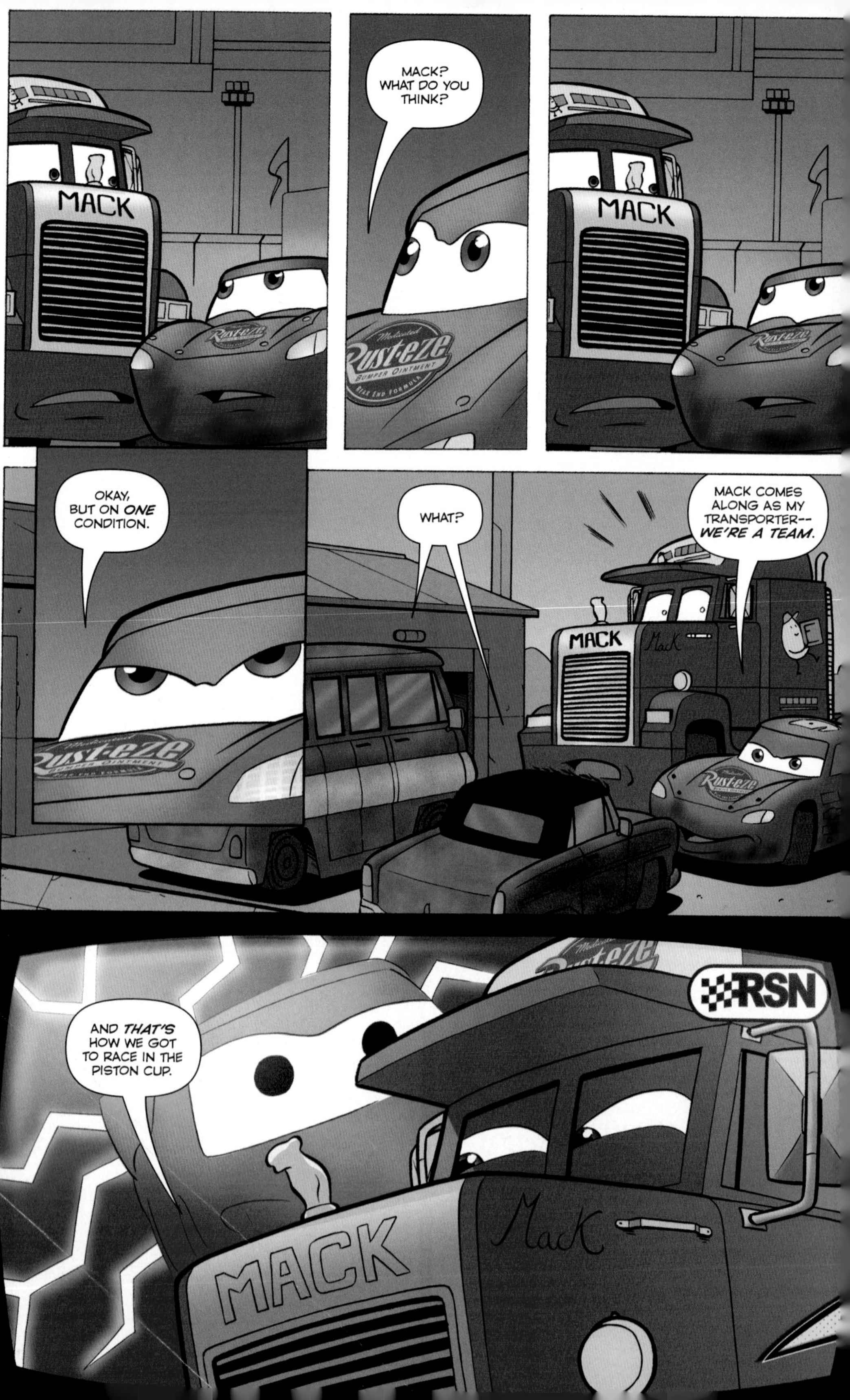
MACK
MACK? WHAT DO YOU THINK?
Motorated Rust-eze Bumper Ointment Rear End Formula
MACK
OKAY, BUT ON *ONE* CONDITION.
WHAT?
MACK COMES ALONG AS MY TRANSPORTER-- *WE'RE A TEAM.*
MACK
AND *THAT'S* HOW WE GOT TO RACE IN THE PISTON CUP.
RSN
MACK
Mack

Chapter Three

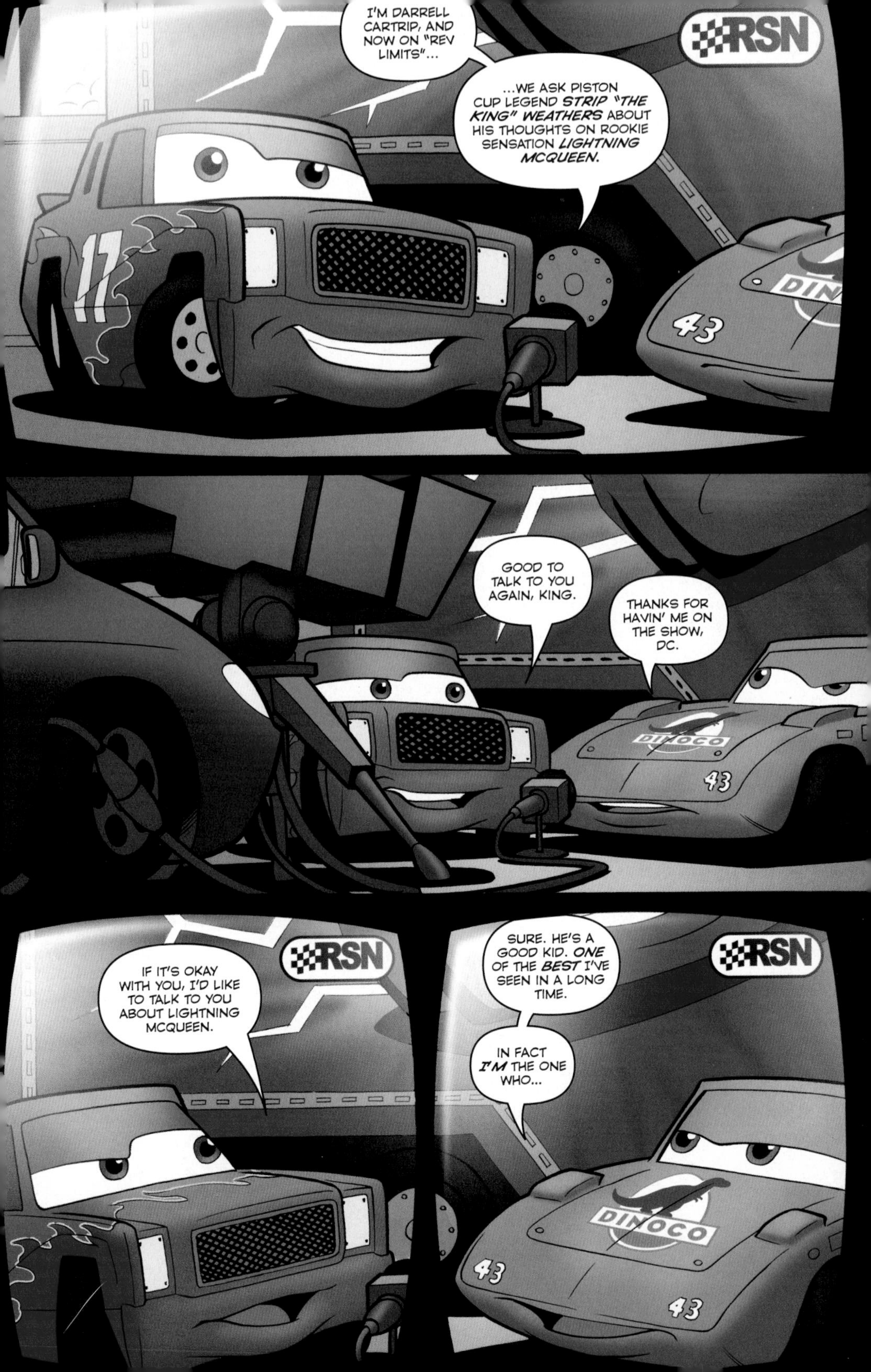
RSN
I'M DARRELL CARTRIP, AND NOW ON "REV LIMITS"...
...WE ASK PISTON CUP LEGEND *STRIP "THE KING" WEATHERS* ABOUT HIS THOUGHTS ON ROOKIE SENSATION *LIGHTNING MCQUEEN.*
GOOD TO TALK TO YOU AGAIN, KING.
THANKS FOR HAVIN' ME ON THE SHOW, DC.
RSN
IF IT'S OKAY WITH YOU, I'D LIKE TO TALK TO YOU ABOUT LIGHTNING MCQUEEN.
RSN
SURE. HE'S A GOOD KID. *ONE* OF THE *BEST* I'VE SEEN IN A LONG TIME.
IN FACT *I'M* THE ONE WHO...

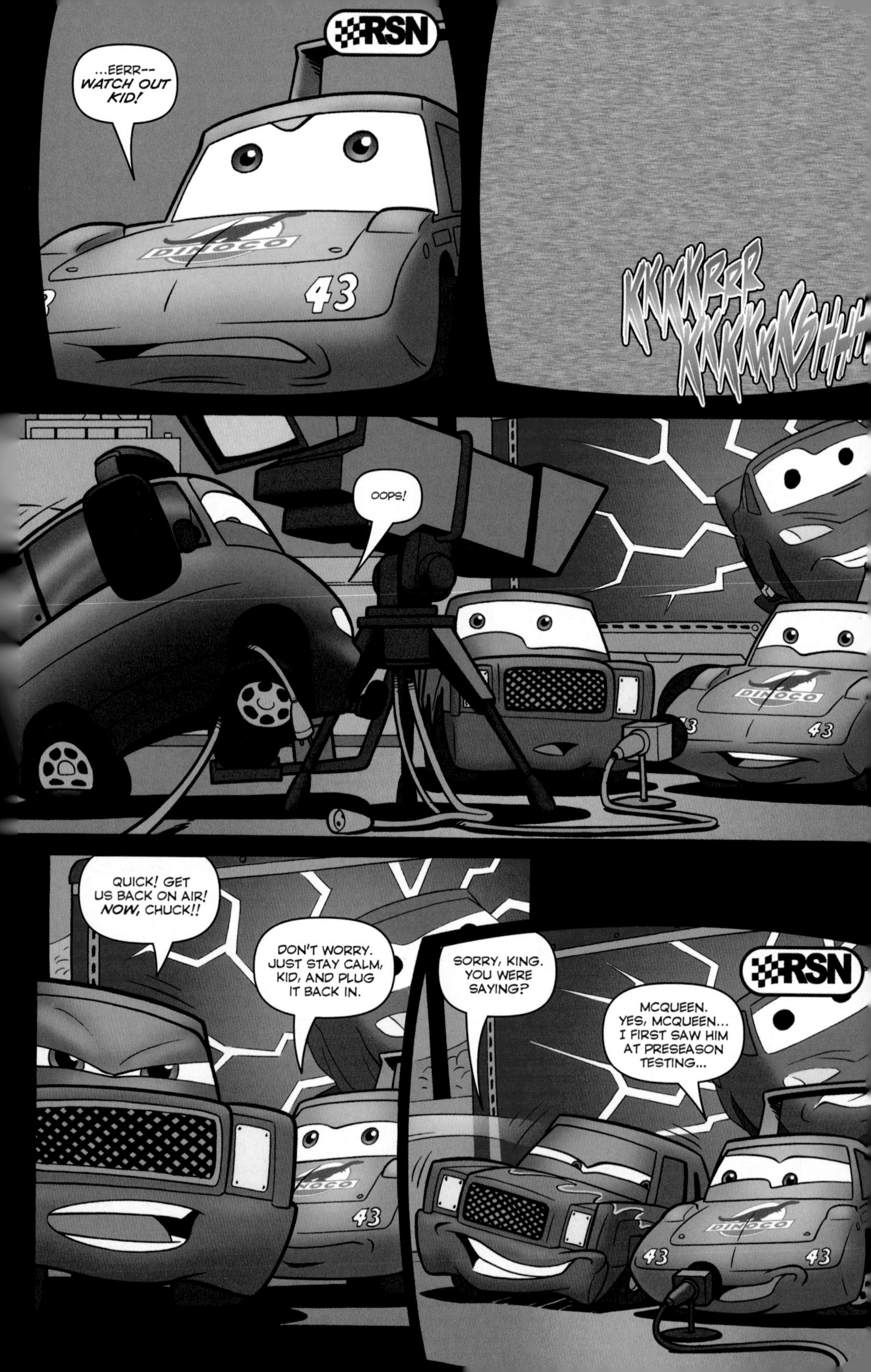
RSN
...EERR--
WATCH OUT
KID!
KKKKRRR
KKKKKKSHHH
OOPS!
QUICK! GET
US BACK ON AIR!
NOW, CHUCK!!
DON'T WORRY.
JUST STAY CALM,
KID, AND PLUG
IT BACK IN.
SORRY, KING.
YOU WERE
SAYING?
RSN
MCQUEEN.
YES, MCQUEEN...
I FIRST SAW HIM
AT PRESEASON
TESTING...

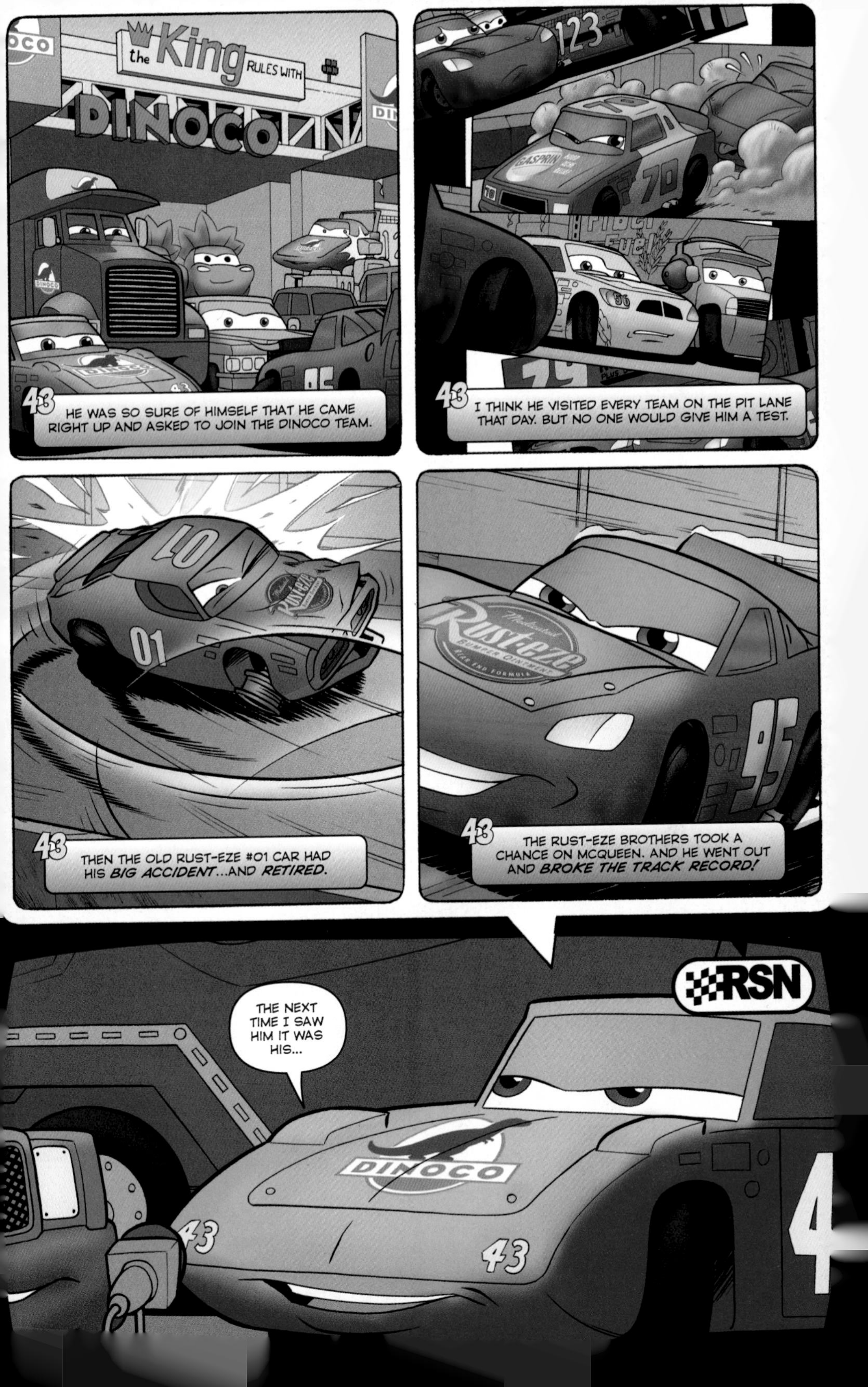
the King RULES WITH
DINOCO
HE WAS SO SURE OF HIMSELF THAT HE CAME RIGHT UP AND ASKED TO JOIN THE DINOCO TEAM.
I THINK HE VISITED EVERY TEAM ON THE PIT LANE THAT DAY. BUT NO ONE WOULD GIVE HIM A TEST.
THEN THE OLD RUST-EZE #01 CAR HAD HIS BIG ACCIDENT...AND RETIRED.
THE RUST-EZE BROTHERS TOOK A CHANCE ON MCQUEEN. AND HE WENT OUT AND BROKE THE TRACK RECORD!
RSN
THE NEXT TIME I SAW HIM IT WAS HIS...

“FIRST RACE!”

The Rookie Part 3

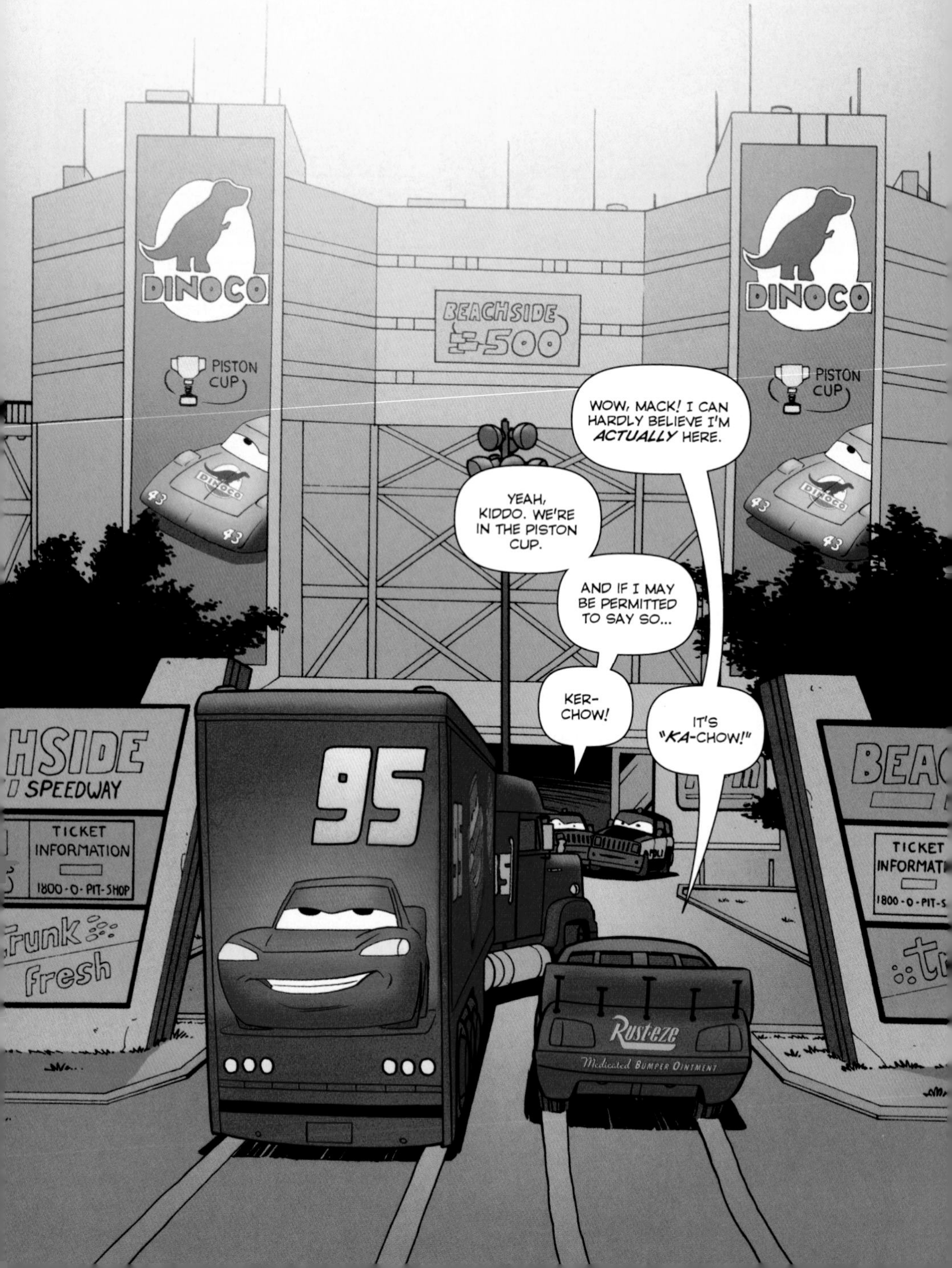
DINOCO
PISTON CUP
BEACHSIDE 500
DINOCO
PISTON CUP
WOW, MACK! I CAN HARDLY BELIEVE I'M *ACTUALLY* HERE.
YEAH, KIDDO. WE'RE IN THE PISTON CUP.
AND IF I MAY BE PERMITTED TO SAY SO...
KER-CHOW!
IT'S "*KA*-CHOW!"
HSIDE
SPEEDWAY
TICKET INFORMATION
1800-O-PIT-SHOP
Trunk Fresh
95
Rust-eze
Medicated Bumper Ointment
BEAC
TICKET INFORMAT
1800-O-PIT-S

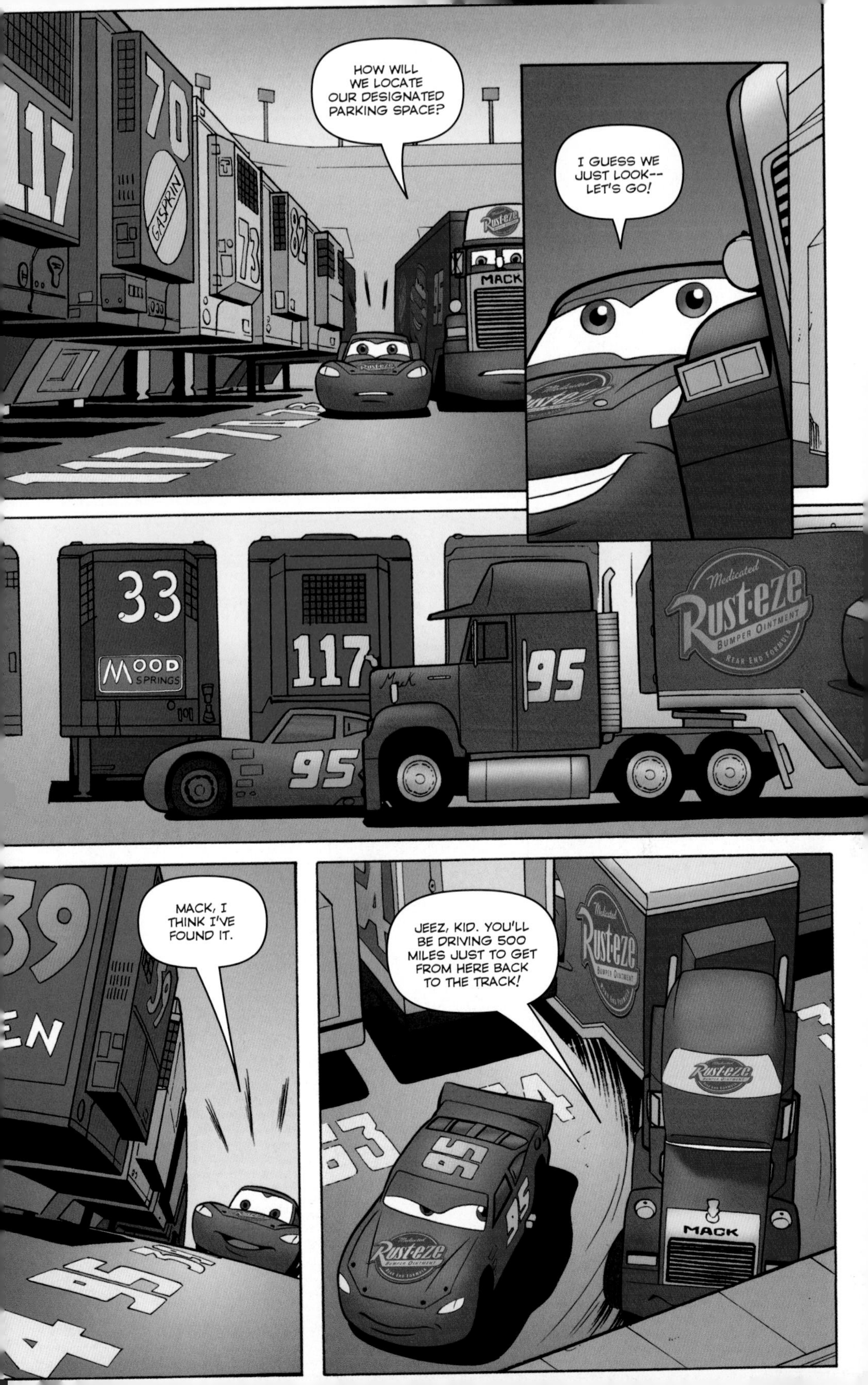
HOW WILL WE LOCATE OUR DESIGNATED PARKING SPACE?
I GUESS WE JUST LOOK-- LET'S GO!
MACK, I THINK I'VE FOUND IT.
JEEZ, KID. YOU'LL BE DRIVING 500 MILES JUST TO GET FROM HERE BACK TO THE TRACK!

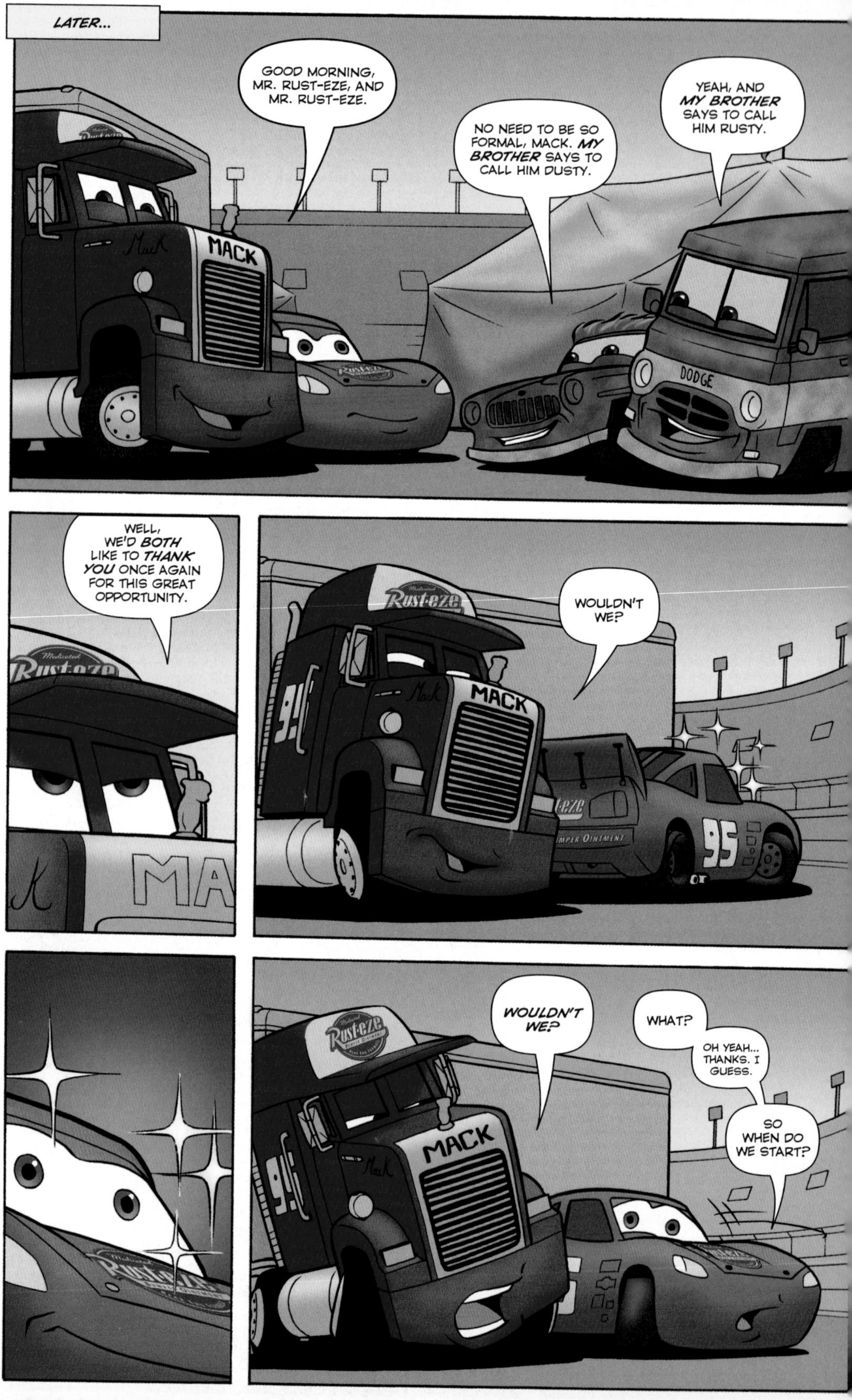
LATER...
GOOD MORNING, MR. RUST-EZE, AND MR. RUST-EZE.
NO NEED TO BE SO FORMAL, MACK. MY BROTHER SAYS TO CALL HIM DUSTY.
YEAH, AND MY BROTHER SAYS TO CALL HIM RUSTY.
WELL, WE'D BOTH LIKE TO THANK YOU ONCE AGAIN FOR THIS GREAT OPPORTUNITY.
WOULDN'T WE?
WOULDN'T WE?
WHAT?
OH YEAH... THANKS. I GUESS.
SO WHEN DO WE START?

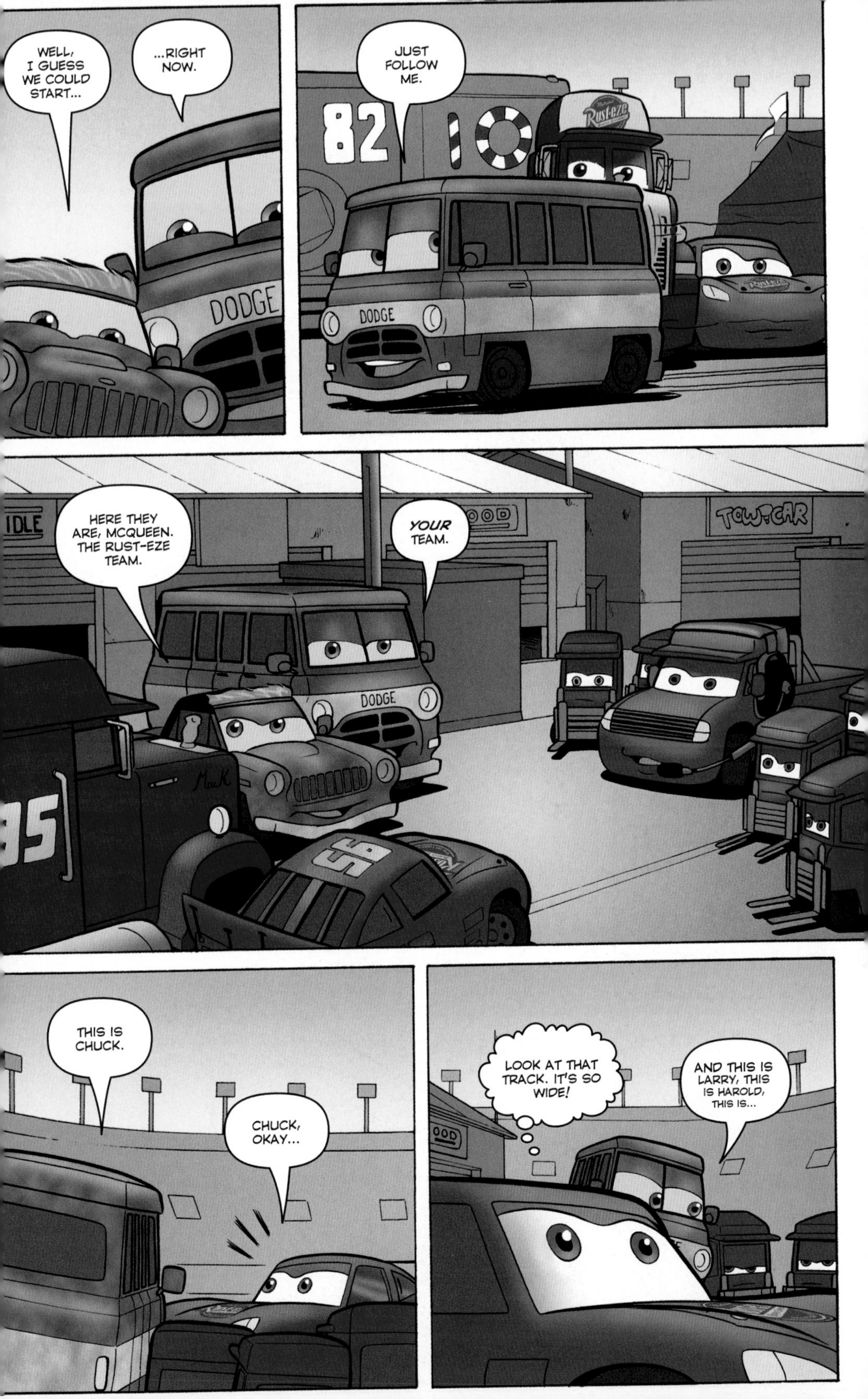
WELL, I GUESS WE COULD START...
...RIGHT NOW.
DODGE
82
Rust-eze
JUST FOLLOW ME.
DODGE
IDLE
HERE THEY ARE, MCQUEEN. THE RUST-EZE TEAM.
YOUR TEAM.
TOW CAR
DODGE
95
THIS IS CHUCK.
CHUCK, OKAY...
LOOK AT THAT TRACK. IT'S SO WIDE!
AND THIS IS LARRY, THIS IS HAROLD, THIS IS...

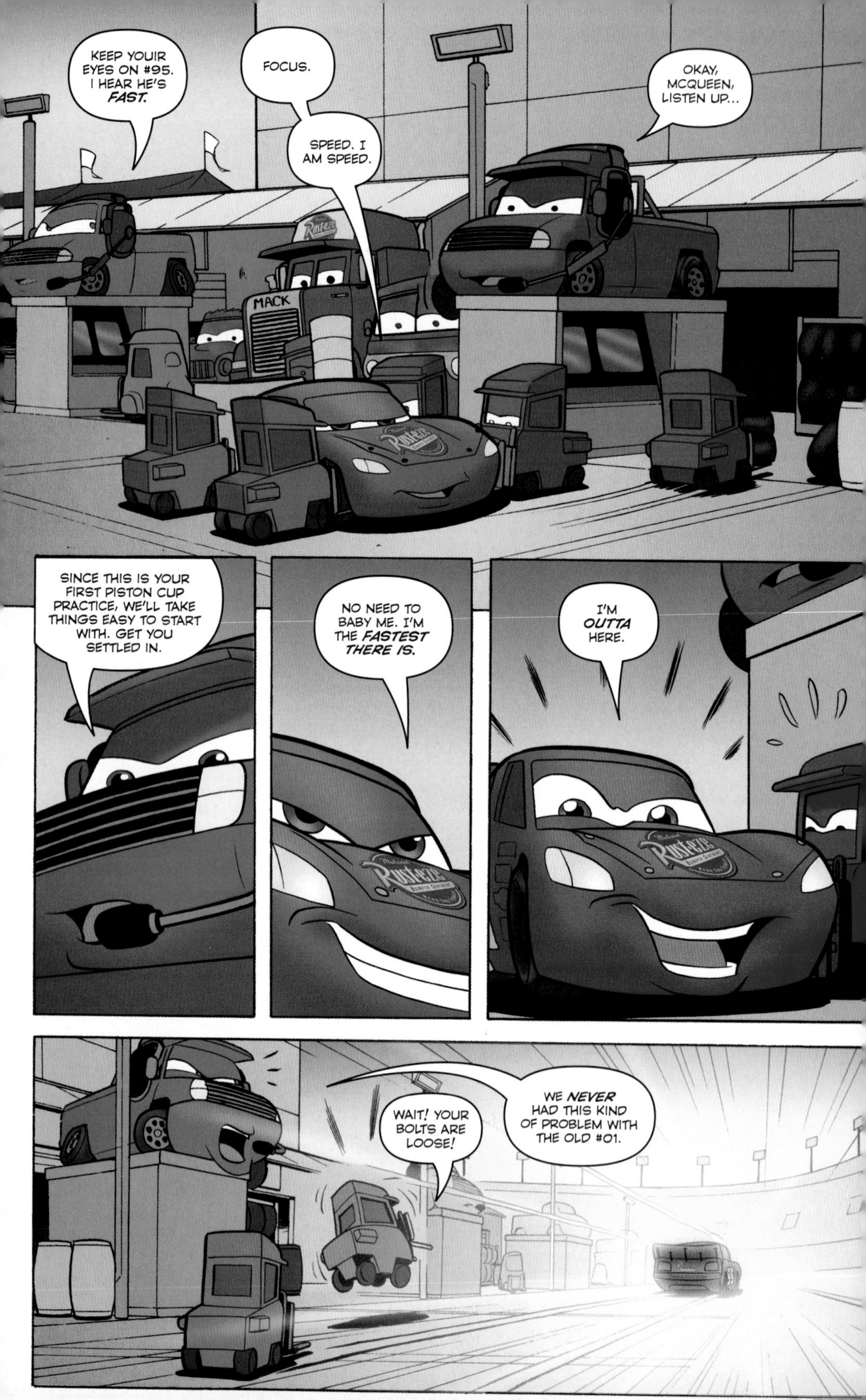
KEEP YOUIR EYES ON #95. I HEAR HE'S *FAST.*
FOCUS.
SPEED. I AM SPEED.
OKAY, MCQUEEN, LISTEN UP...
MACK
SINCE THIS IS YOUR FIRST PISTON CUP PRACTICE, WE'LL TAKE THINGS EASY TO START WITH. GET YOU SETTLED IN.
NO NEED TO BABY ME. I'M THE *FASTEST THERE IS.*
I'M *OUTTA* HERE.
WAIT! YOUR BOLTS ARE LOOSE!
WE *NEVER* HAD THIS KIND OF PROBLEM WITH THE OLD #01.

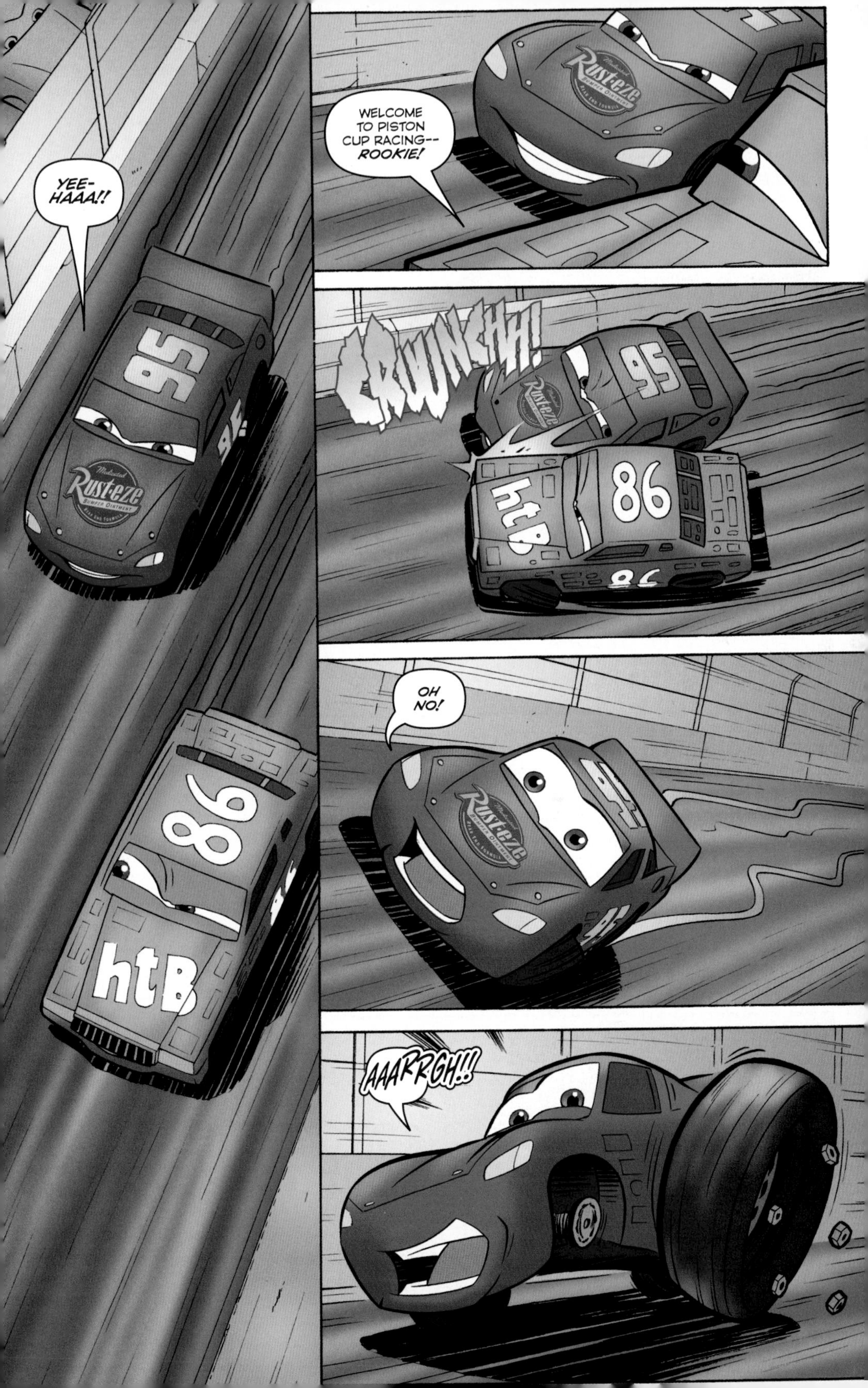
YEE-
HAAA!!
WELCOME TO PISTON CUP RACING-- ROOKIE!
CRUNCHH!
OH NO!
AAARRGH!!

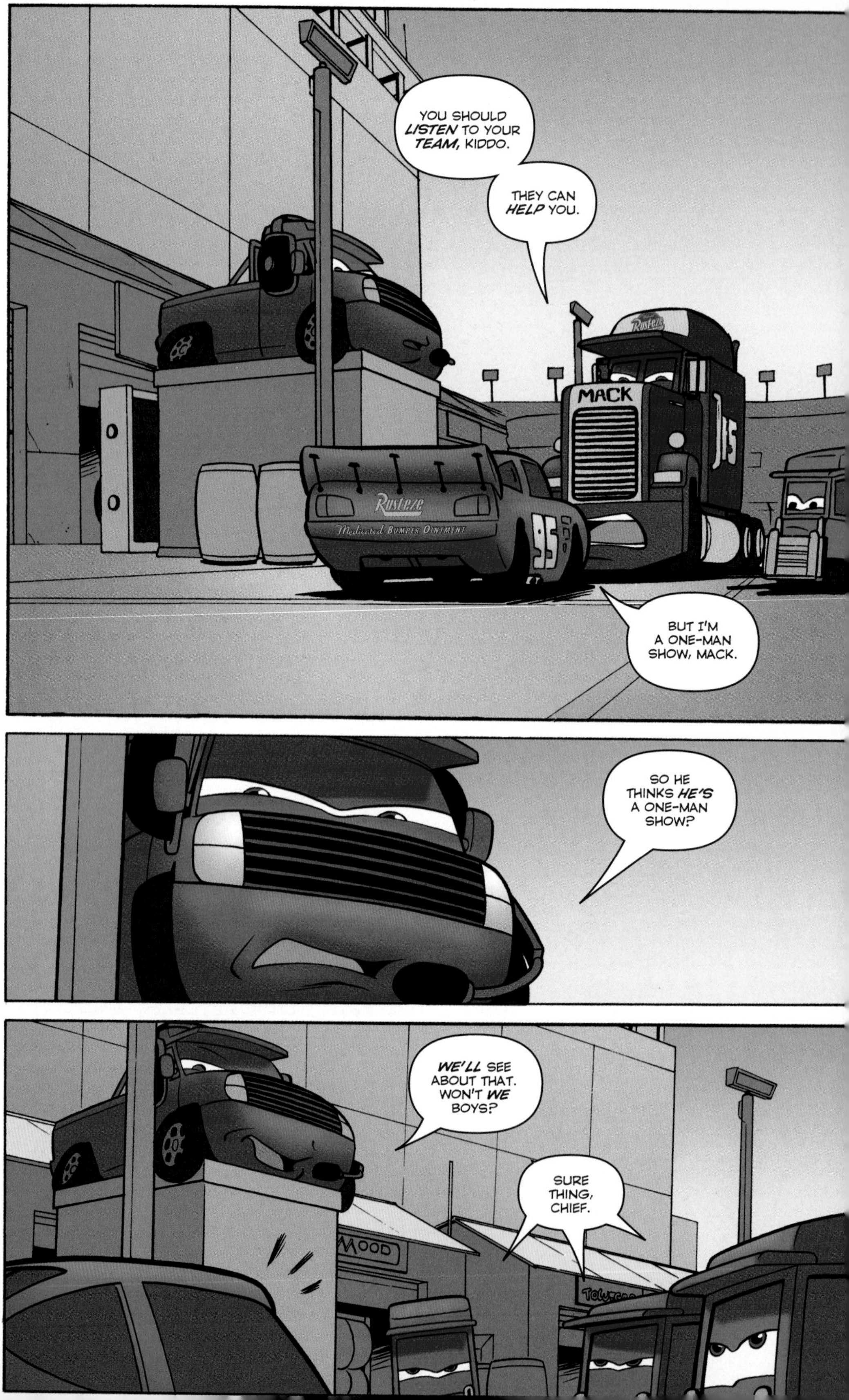
YOU SHOULD *LISTEN* TO YOUR *TEAM,* KIDDO.
THEY CAN *HELP* YOU.
BUT I'M A ONE-MAN SHOW, MACK.
SO HE THINKS *HE'S* A ONE-MAN SHOW?
WE'LL SEE ABOUT THAT. WON'T *WE* BOYS?
SURE THING, CHIEF.

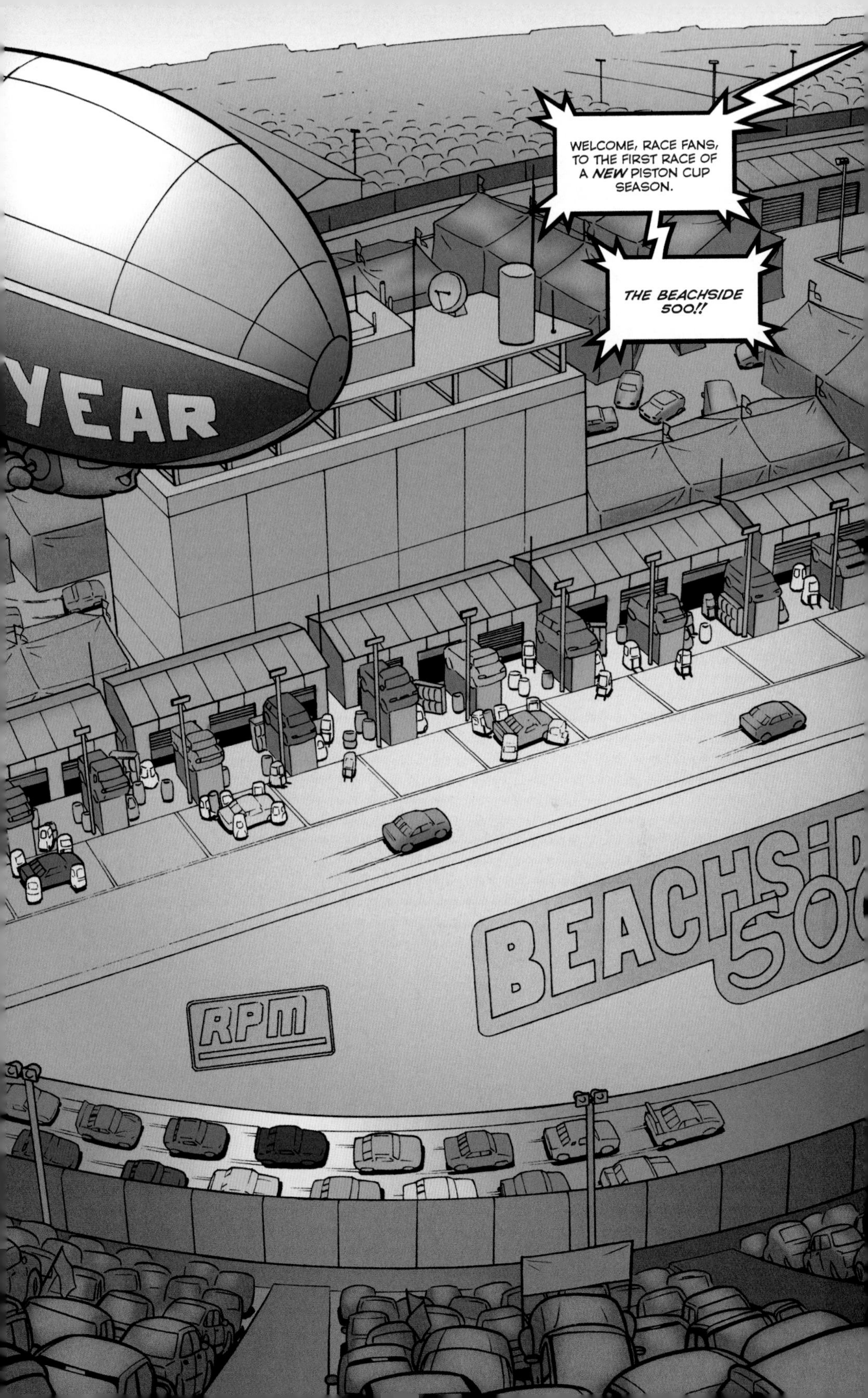
WELCOME, RACE FANS, TO THE FIRST RACE OF A *NEW* PISTON CUP SEASON.
THE BEACHSIDE 500!!
YEAR
BEACHSIDE 500
RPM

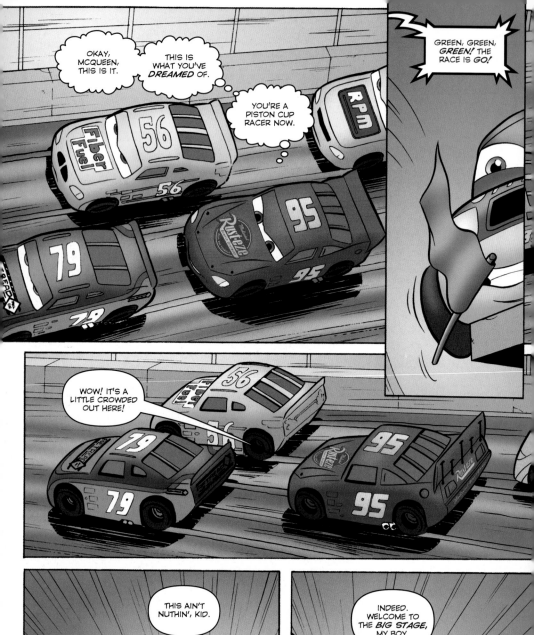

OKAY, MCQUEEN, THIS IS IT.

THIS IS WHAT YOU'VE *DREAMED* OF.

YOU'RE A PISTON CUP RACER NOW.

GREEN, GREEN, *GREEN!* THE RACE IS *GO!*

WOW! IT'S A LITTLE CROWDED OUT HERE!

THIS AIN'T NUTHIN', KID.

INDEED. WELCOME TO THE *BIG STAGE*, MY BOY.

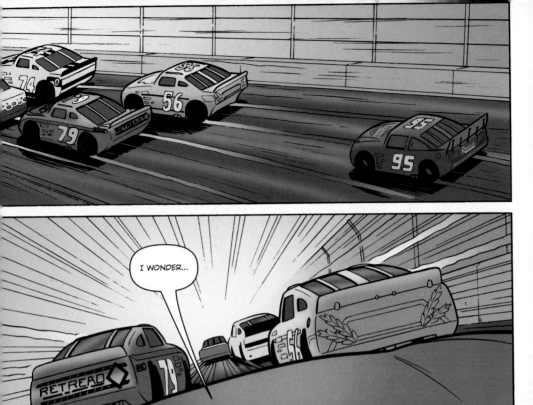

I WONDER...

NOT AGAIN!

IF YOU CAN'T GO THROUGH...

...GO AROUND.

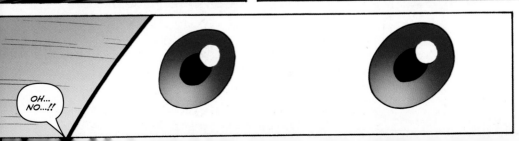

OH... NO...!!

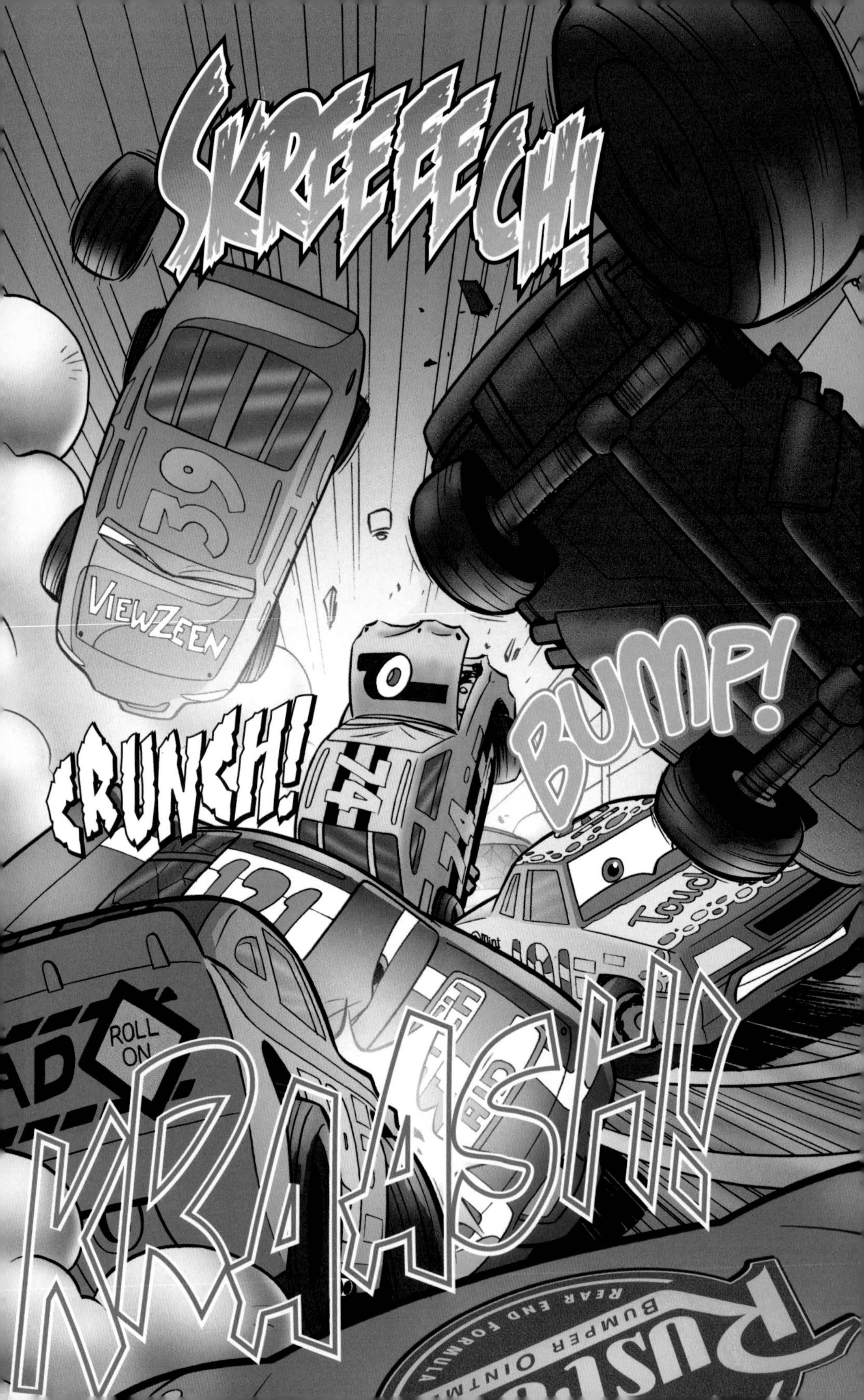
SKREEEECH!
ViewZeen
CRUNCH!
BUMP!
ROLL ON
KRAASH!
REAR END FORMULA

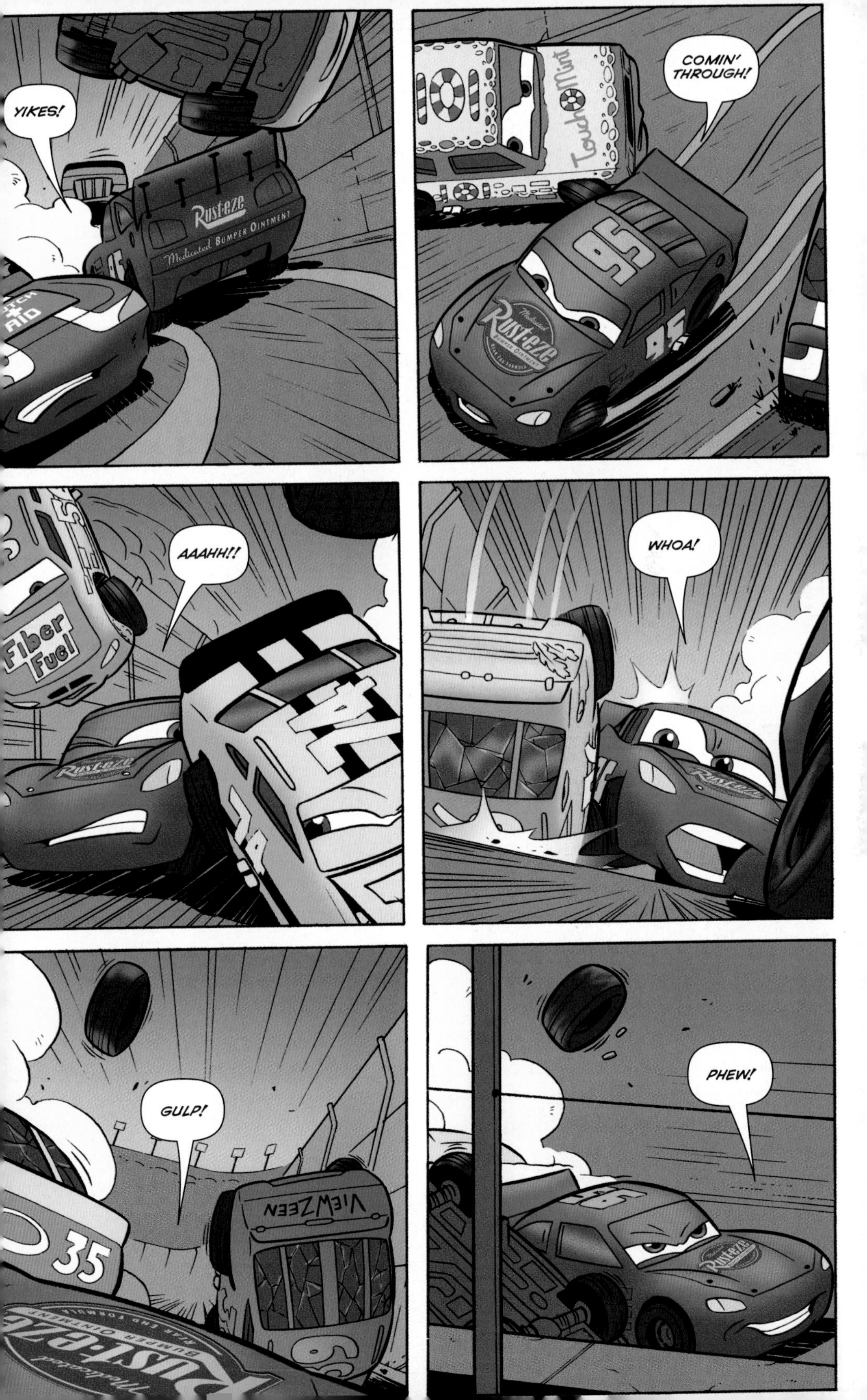

YIKES!
Rust-eze
Medicated BUMPER OINTMENT
Touch Mint
COMIN' THROUGH!
Fiber Fuel
AAAHH!!
WHOA!
GULP!
PHEW!

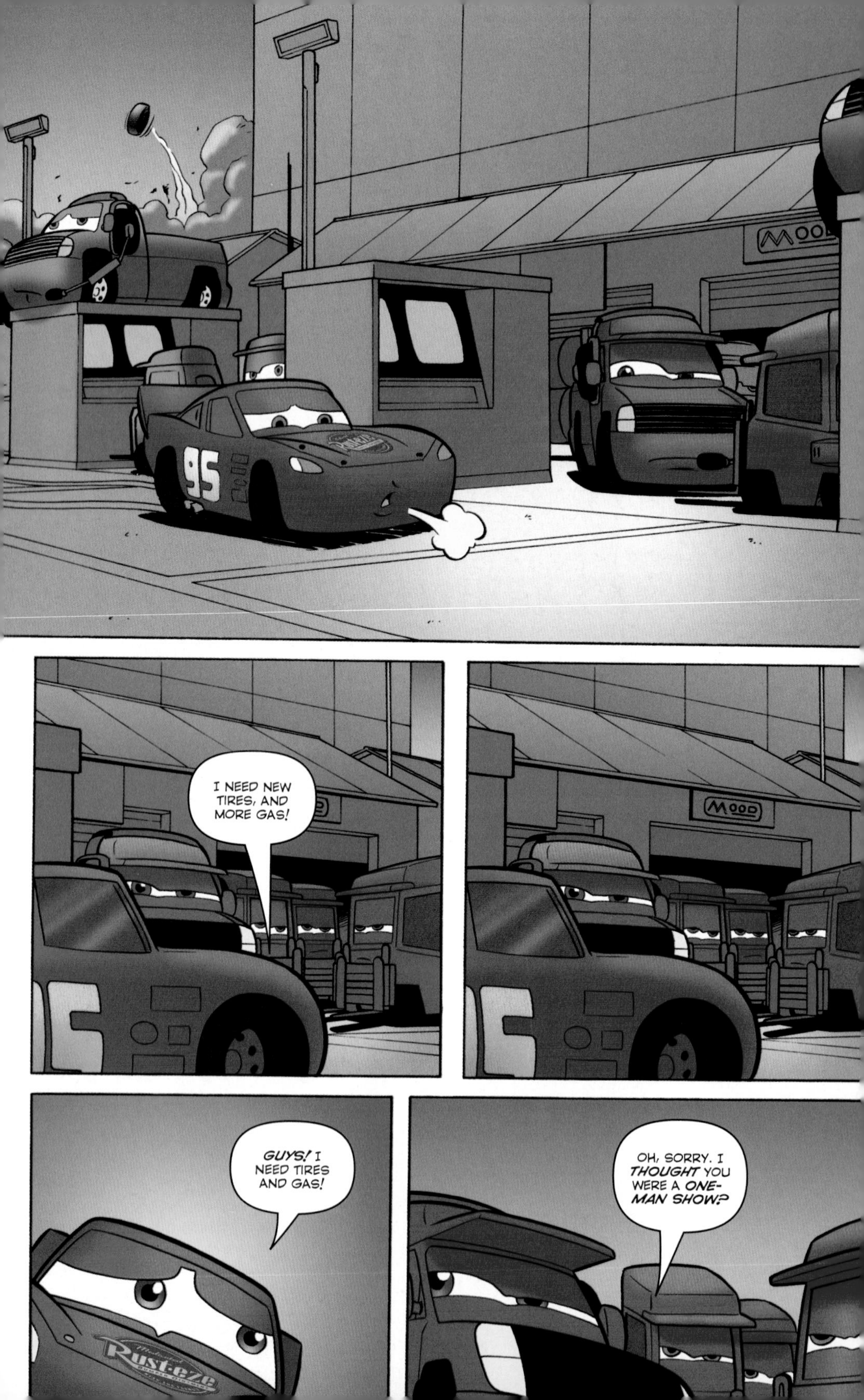
I NEED NEW TIRES, AND MORE GAS!
GUYS! I NEED TIRES AND GAS!
OH, SORRY. I THOUGHT YOU WERE A ONE-MAN SHOW?

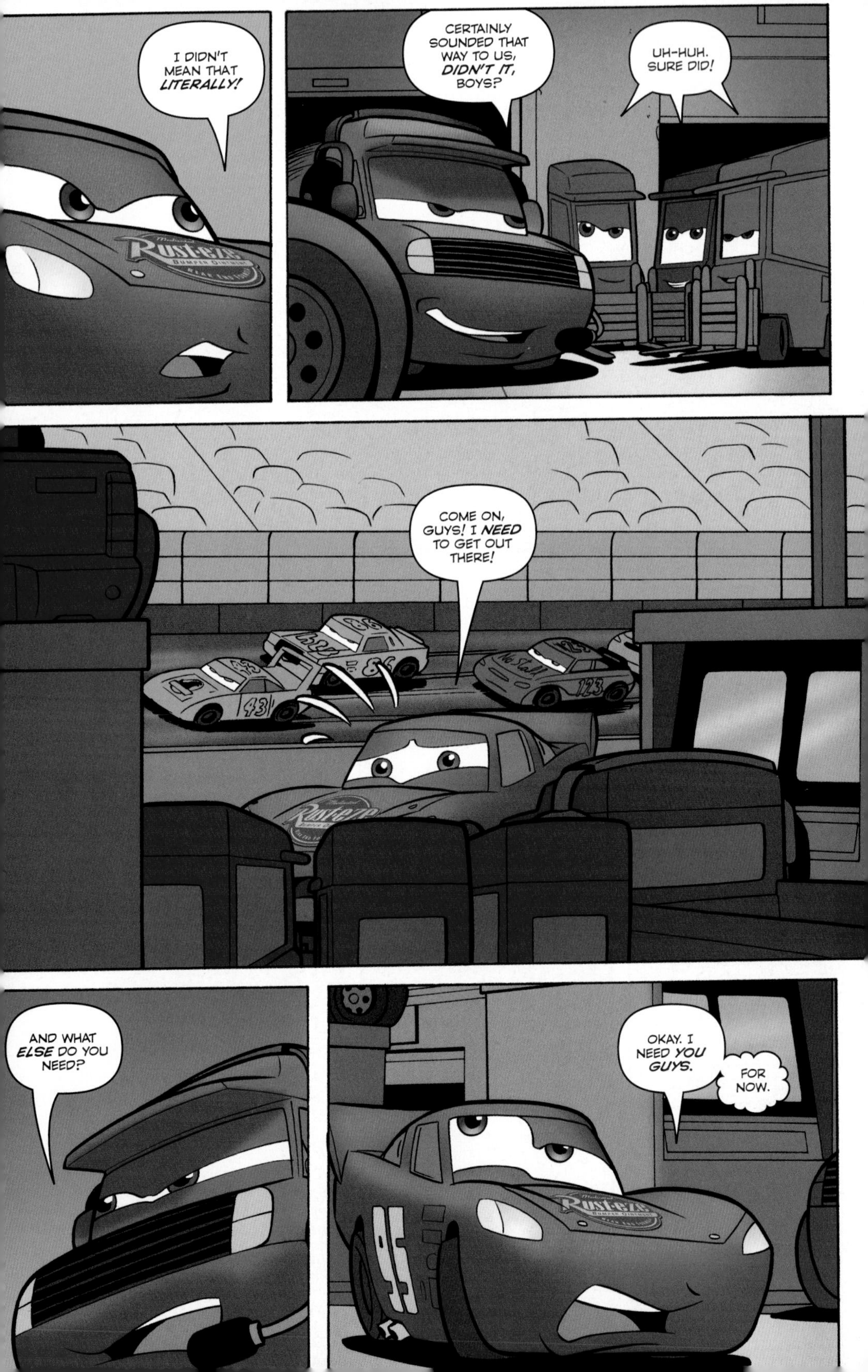
I DIDN'T MEAN THAT *LITERALLY!*
CERTAINLY SOUNDED THAT WAY TO US, *DIDN'T IT,* BOYS?
UH-HUH. SURE DID!
COME ON, GUYS! I *NEED* TO GET OUT THERE!
AND WHAT *ELSE* DO YOU NEED?
OKAY. I NEED *YOU GUYS.*
FOR NOW.

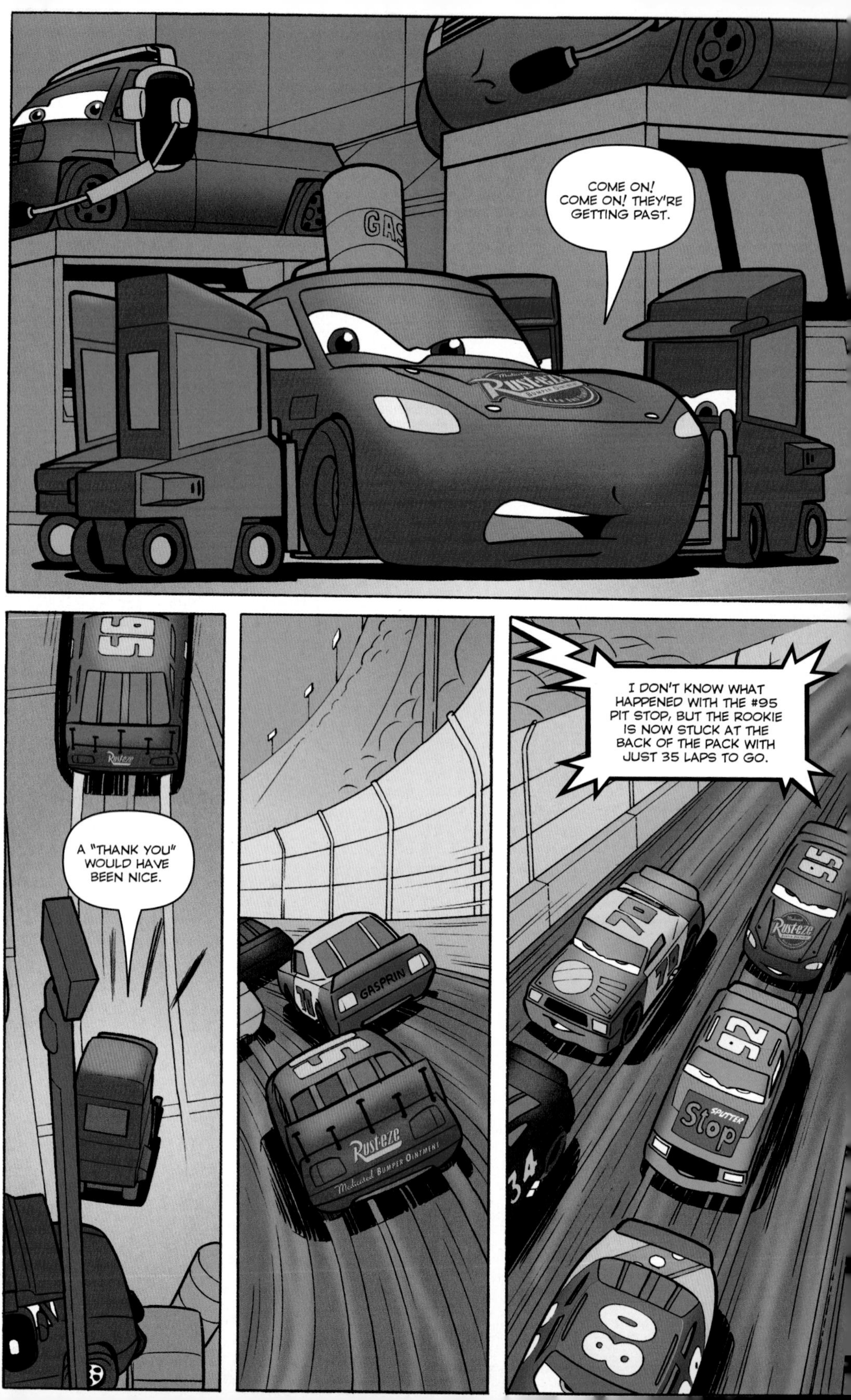
COME ON! COME ON! THEY'RE GETTING PAST.
A "THANK YOU" WOULD HAVE BEEN NICE.
GASPRIN
Rust-eze
Medicated BUMPER OINTMENT
I DON'T KNOW WHAT HAPPENED WITH THE #95 PIT STOP, BUT THE ROOKIE IS NOW STUCK AT THE BACK OF THE PACK WITH JUST 35 LAPS TO GO.
SPUTTER
Stop

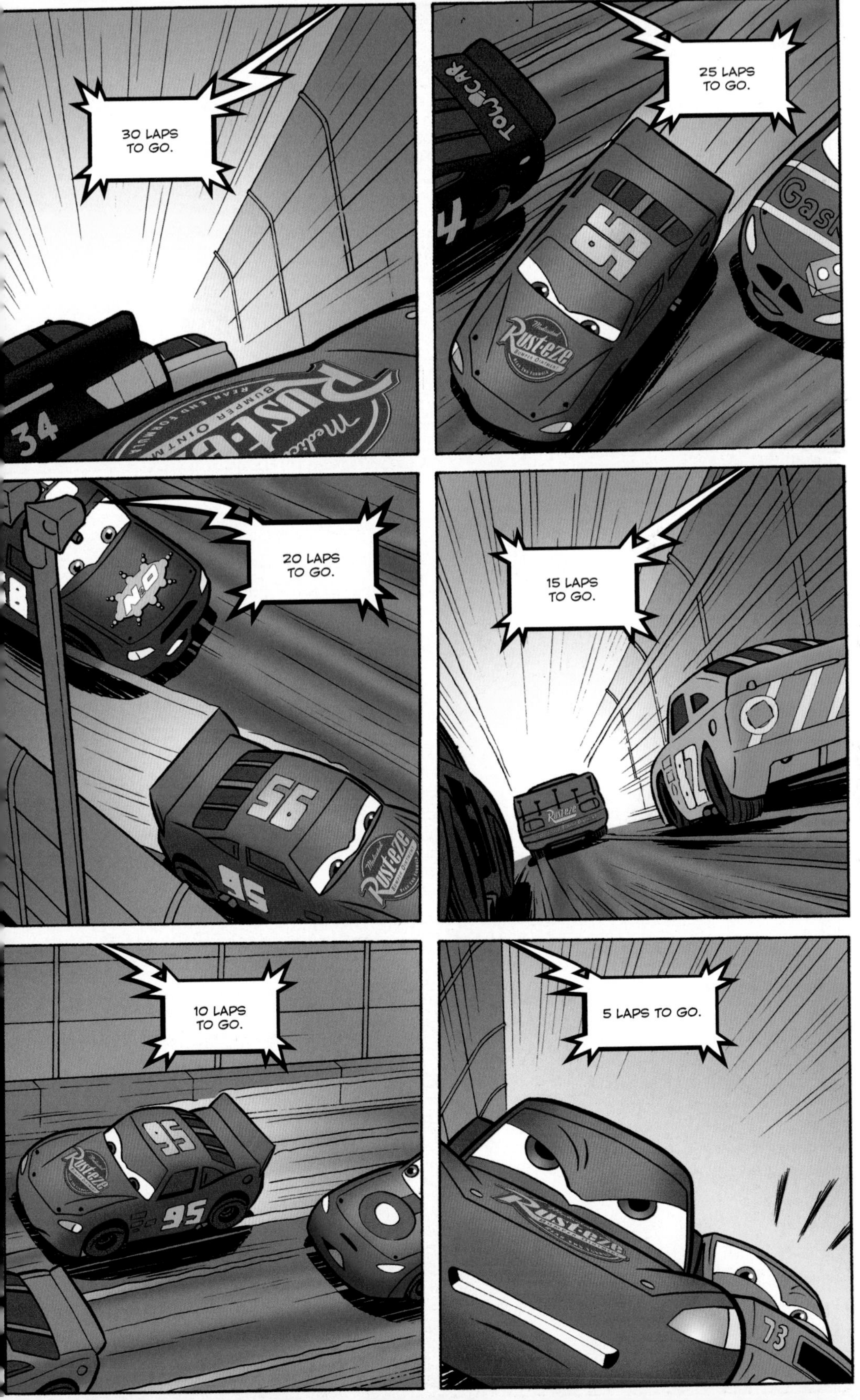
30 LAPS
TO GO.
25 LAPS
TO GO.
20 LAPS
TO GO.
15 LAPS
TO GO.
10 LAPS
TO GO.
5 LAPS TO GO.

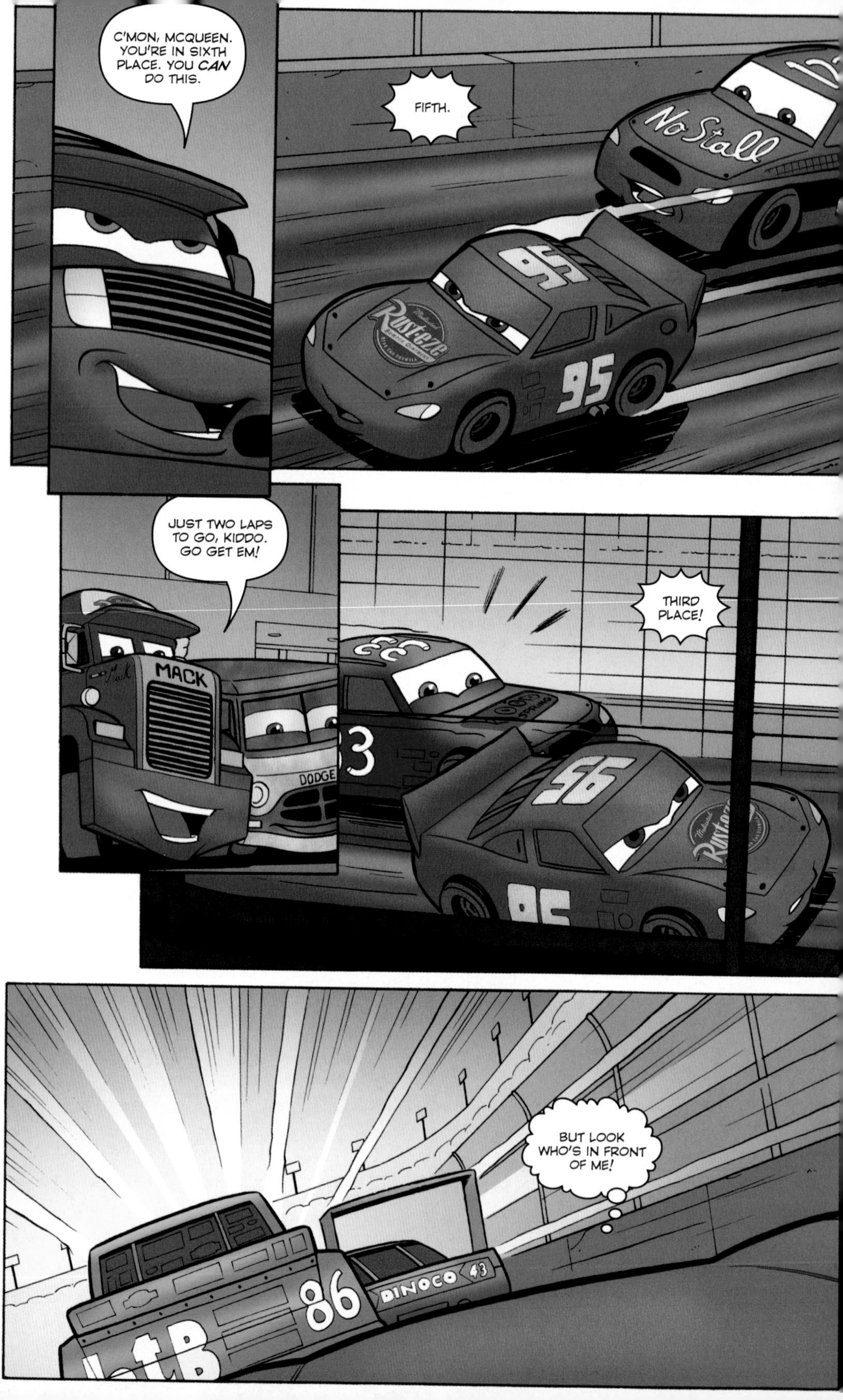
C'MON, MCQUEEN. YOU'RE IN SIXTH PLACE. YOU *CAN* DO THIS.
FIFTH.
No Stall
Rust-eze
95
JUST TWO LAPS TO GO, KIDDO. GO GET EM!
THIRD PLACE!
MACK
DODGE
95
BUT LOOK WHO'S IN FRONT OF ME!
86
DINOCO
43

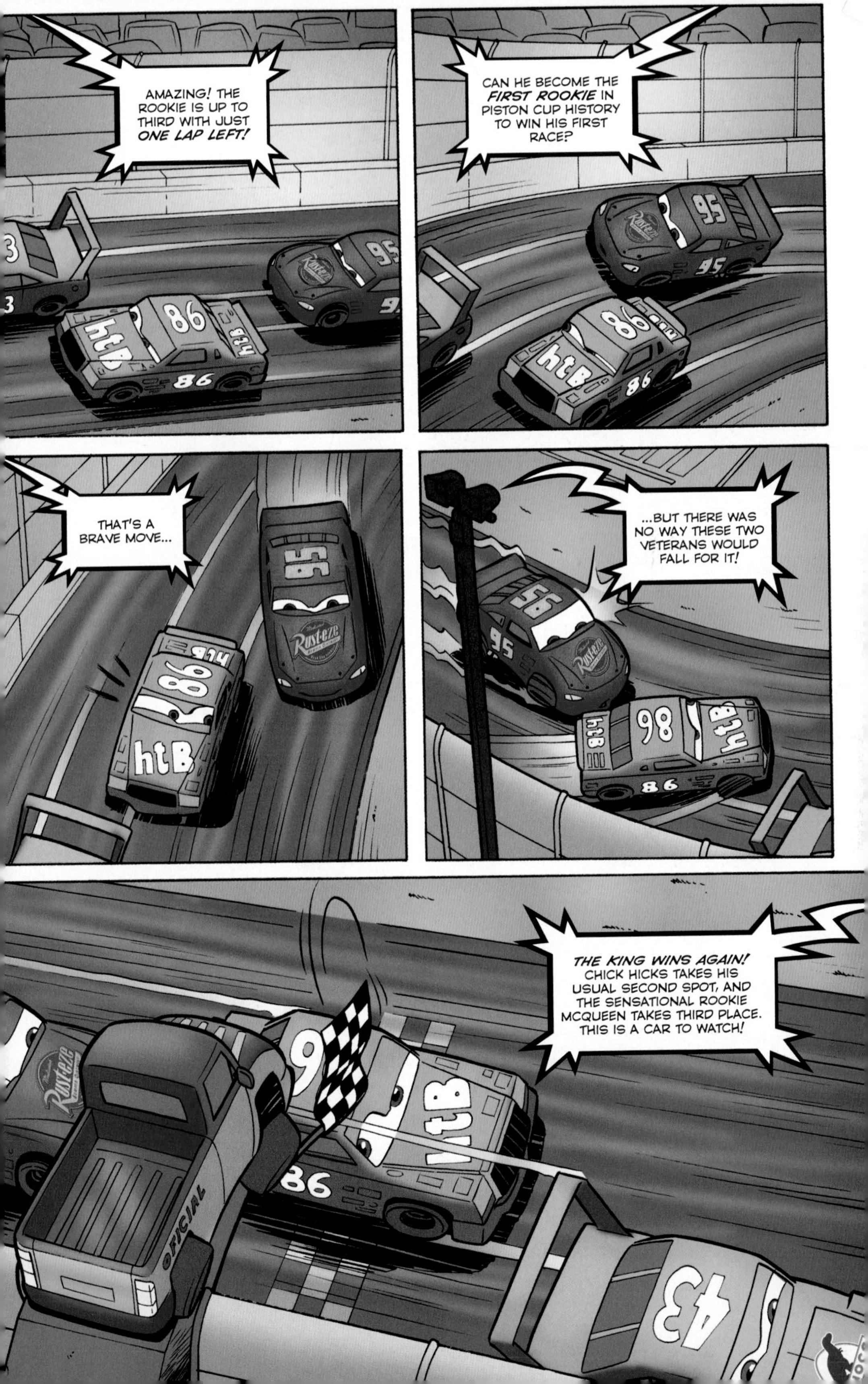

AMAZING! THE ROOKIE IS UP TO THIRD WITH JUST *ONE LAP LEFT!*
CAN HE BECOME THE ***FIRST ROOKIE*** IN PISTON CUP HISTORY TO WIN HIS FIRST RACE?
THAT'S A BRAVE MOVE...
...BUT THERE WAS NO WAY THESE TWO VETERANS WOULD FALL FOR IT!
THE KING WINS AGAIN! CHICK HICKS TAKES HIS USUAL SECOND SPOT, AND THE SENSATIONAL ROOKIE MCQUEEN TAKES THIRD PLACE. THIS IS A CAR TO WATCH!

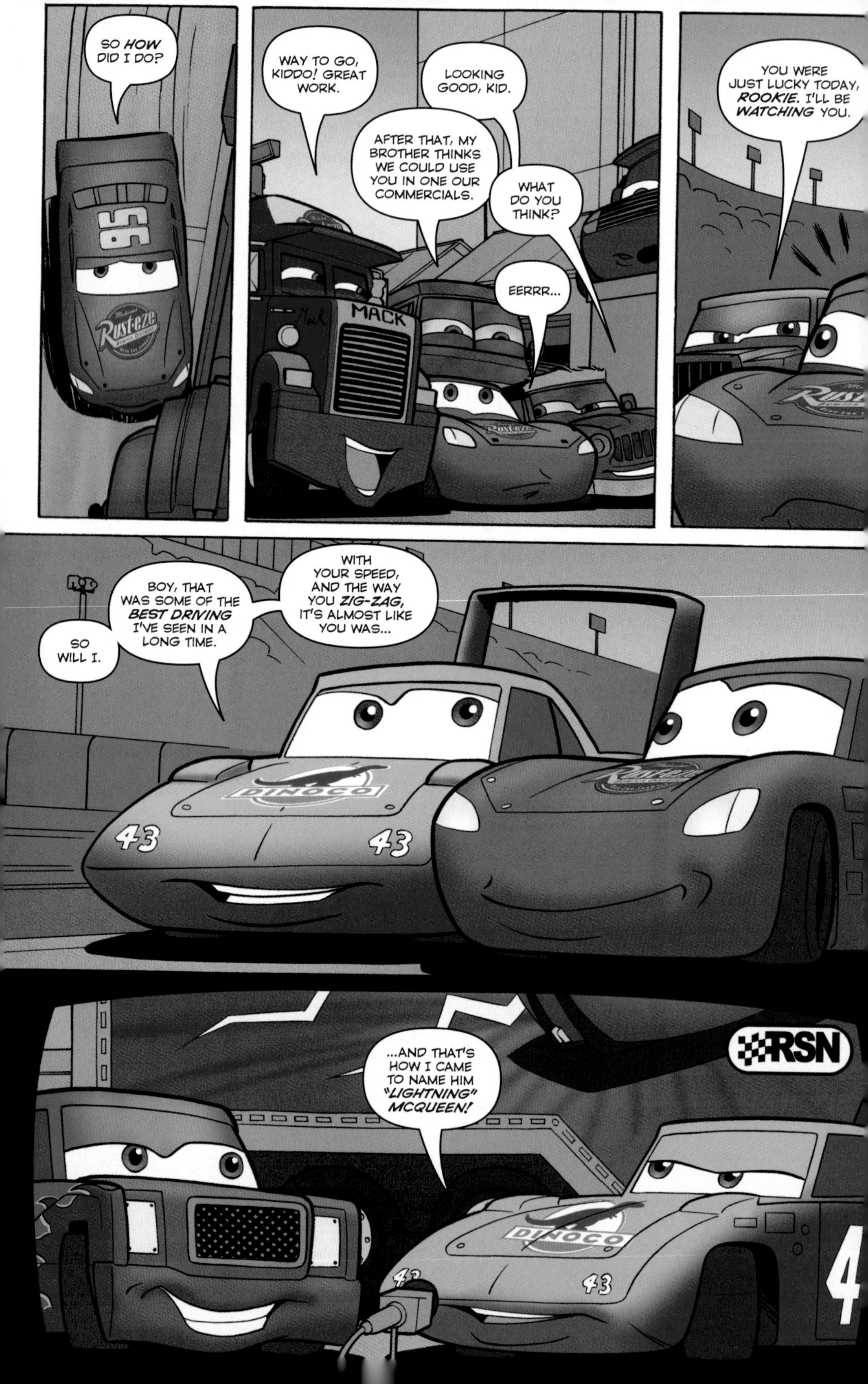
SO HOW DID I DO?
95
Rust-eze
WAY TO GO, KIDDO! GREAT WORK.
LOOKING GOOD, KID.
AFTER THAT, MY BROTHER THINKS WE COULD USE YOU IN ONE OUR COMMERCIALS.
WHAT DO YOU THINK?
MACK
EERRR...
YOU WERE JUST LUCKY TODAY, ROOKIE. I'LL BE WATCHING YOU.
SO WILL I.
BOY, THAT WAS SOME OF THE BEST DRIVING I'VE SEEN IN A LONG TIME.
WITH YOUR SPEED, AND THE WAY YOU ZIG-ZAG, IT'S ALMOST LIKE YOU WAS...
DINOCO
43
RSN
...AND THAT'S HOW I CAME TO NAME HIM "LIGHTNING" MCQUEEN!

Chapter Four

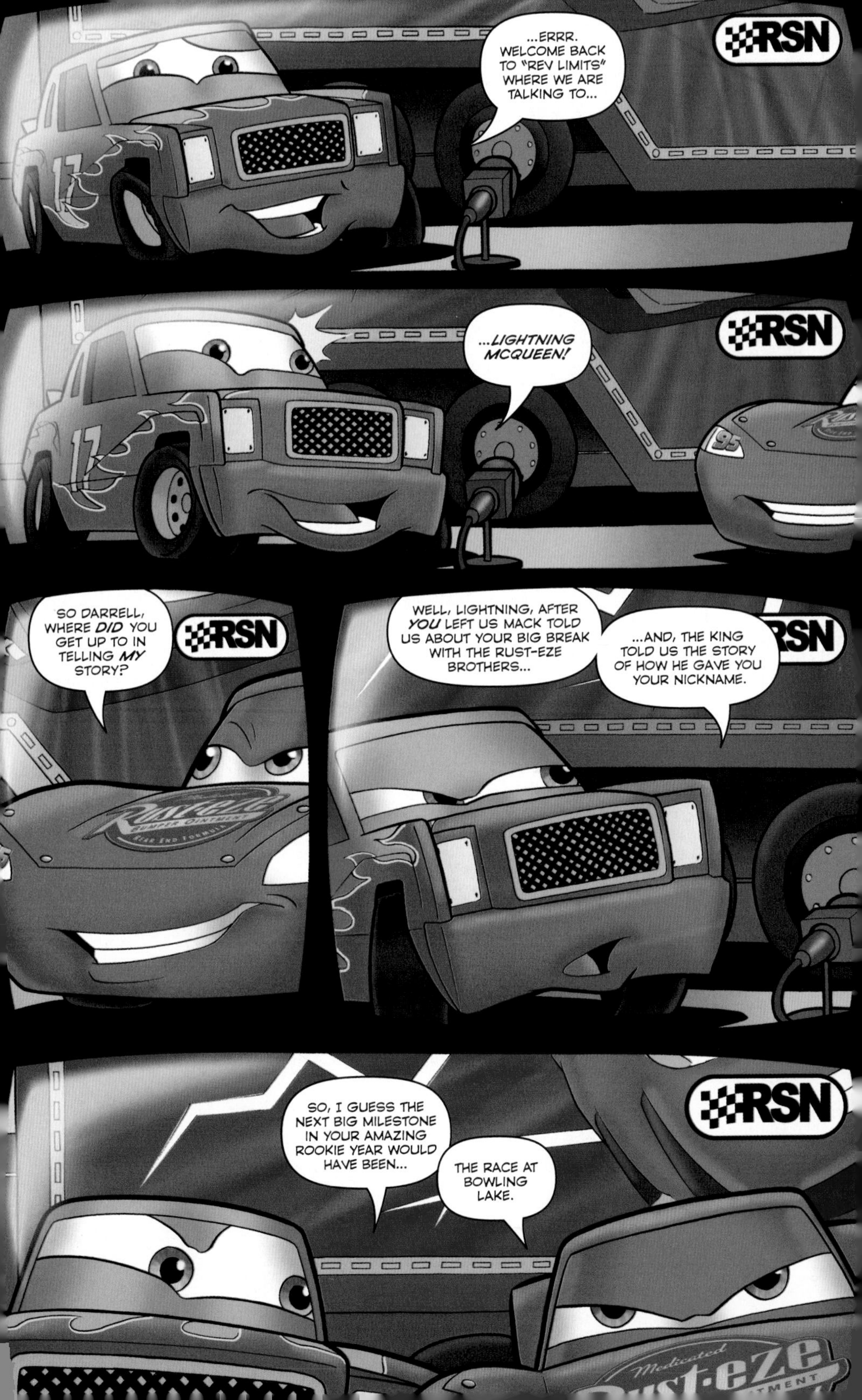
...ERRR. WELCOME BACK TO "REV LIMITS" WHERE WE ARE TALKING TO...
...LIGHTNING MCQUEEN!
SO DARRELL, WHERE DID YOU GET UP TO IN TELLING MY STORY?
WELL, LIGHTNING, AFTER YOU LEFT US MACK TOLD US ABOUT YOUR BIG BREAK WITH THE RUST-EZE BROTHERS...
...AND, THE KING TOLD US THE STORY OF HOW HE GAVE YOU YOUR NICKNAME.
SO, I GUESS THE NEXT BIG MILESTONE IN YOUR AMAZING ROOKIE YEAR WOULD HAVE BEEN...
THE RACE AT BOWLING LAKE.

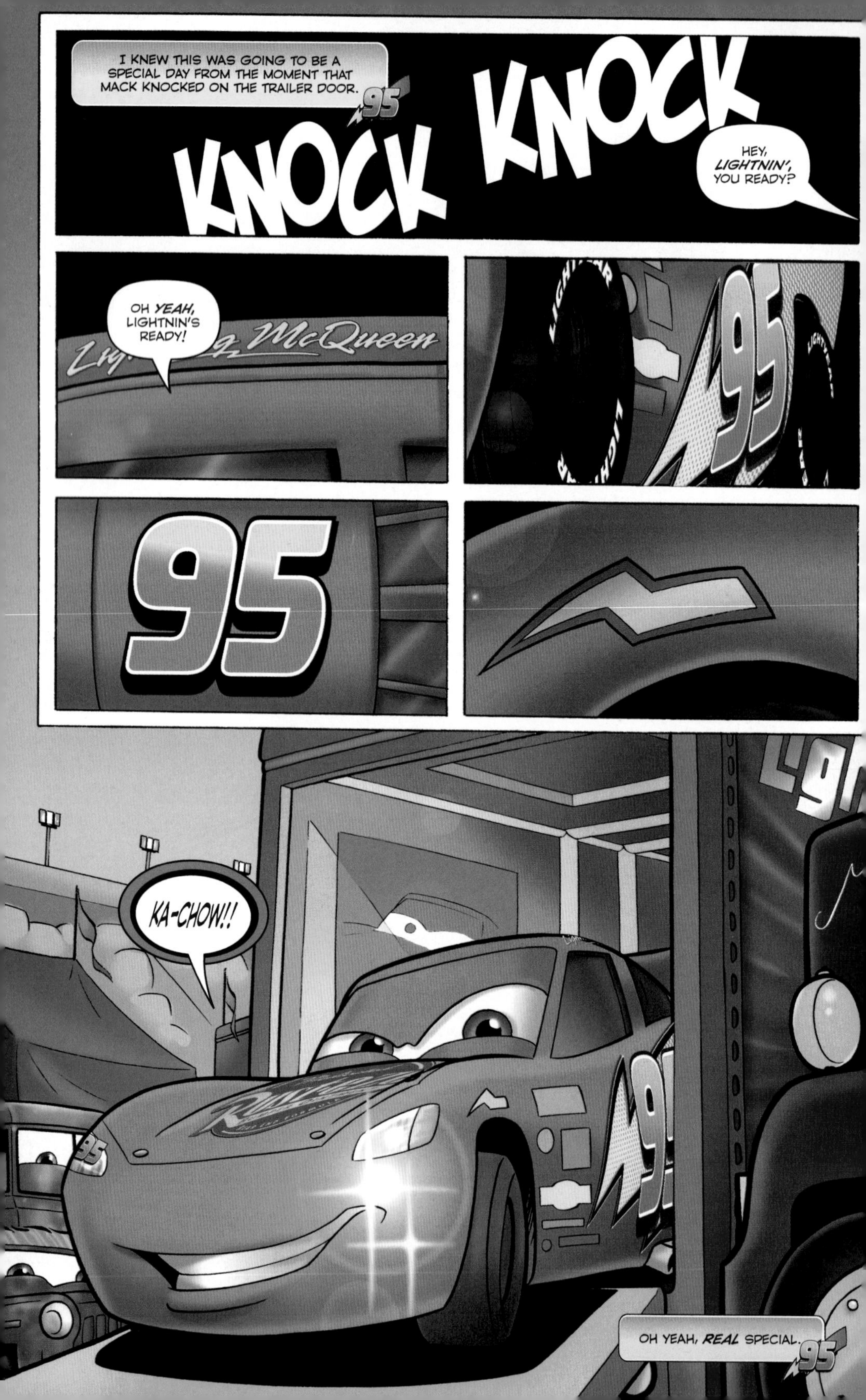
I KNEW THIS WAS GOING TO BE A SPECIAL DAY FROM THE MOMENT THAT MACK KNOCKED ON THE TRAILER DOOR.
KNOCK KNOCK
HEY, *LIGHTNIN'*, YOU READY?
OH *YEAH*, LIGHTNIN'S READY!
KA-CHOW!!
OH YEAH, ***REAL*** SPECIAL.

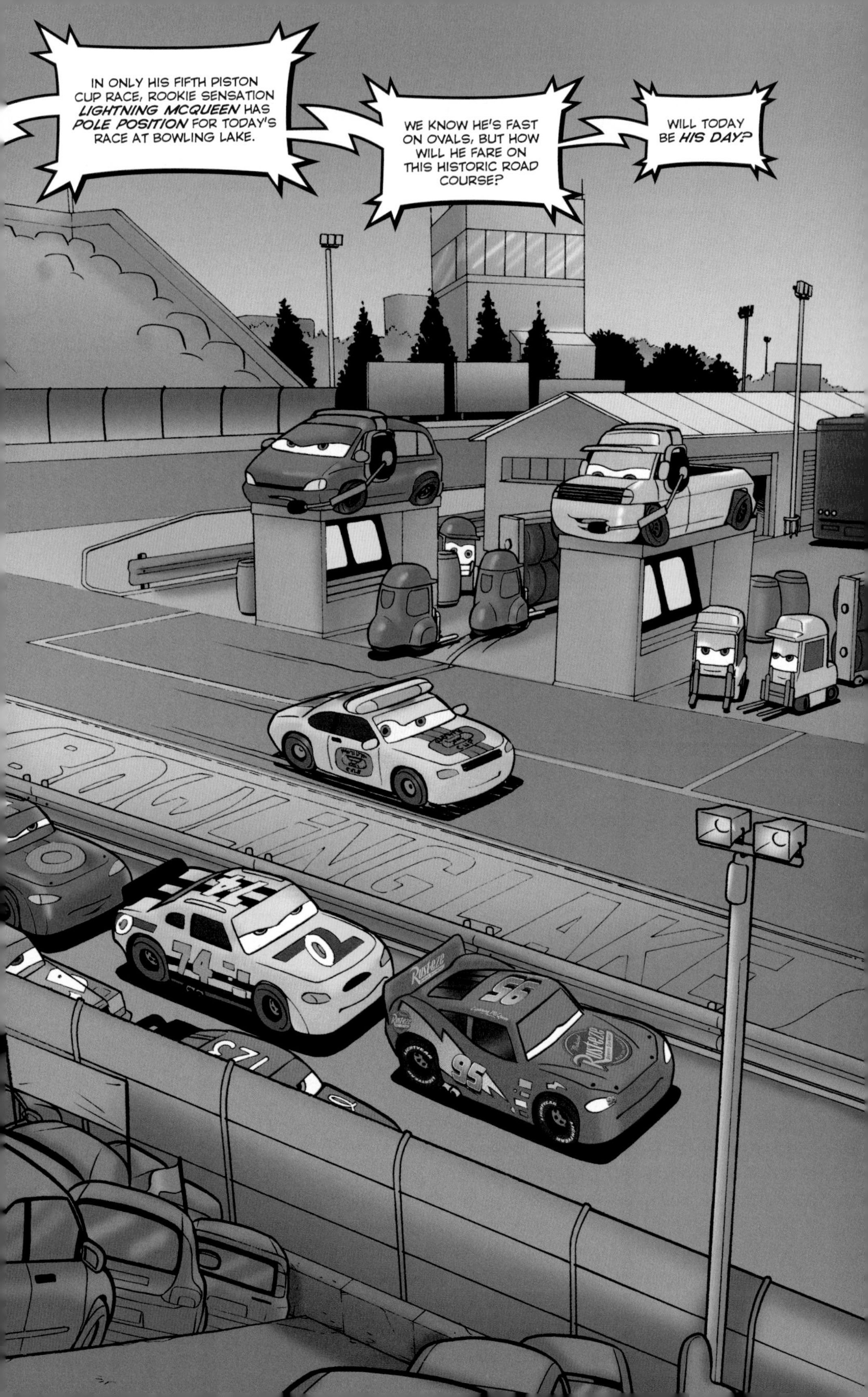
IN ONLY HIS FIFTH PISTON CUP RACE, ROOKIE SENSATION *LIGHTNING MCQUEEN* HAS *POLE POSITION* FOR TODAY'S RACE AT BOWLING LAKE.
WE KNOW HE'S FAST ON OVALS, BUT HOW WILL HE FARE ON THIS HISTORIC ROAD COURSE?
WILL TODAY BE *HIS DAY?*
BOWLING LAKE
74
95
123

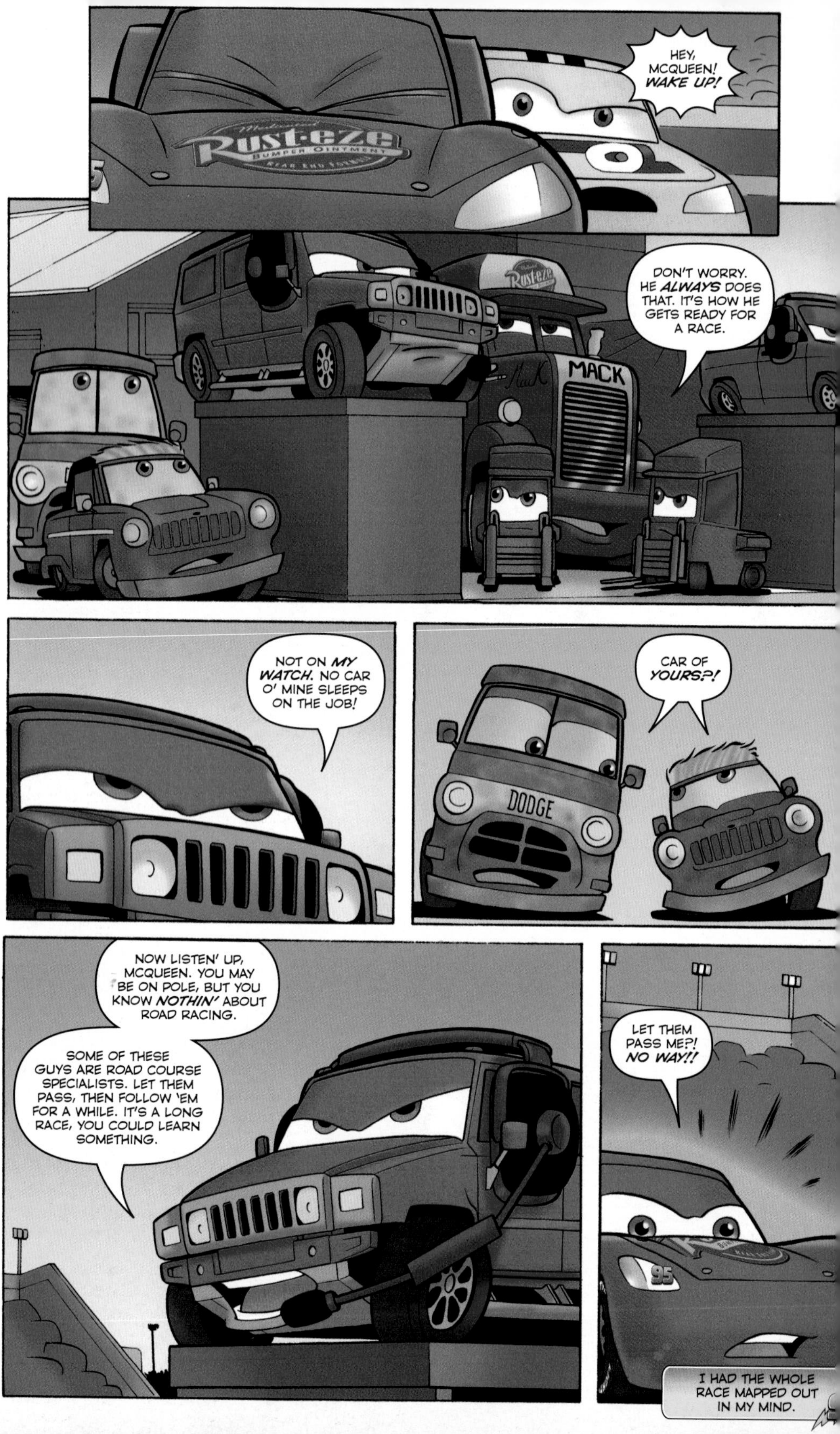
HEY, MCQUEEN! WAKE UP!
DON'T WORRY. HE ALWAYS DOES THAT. IT'S HOW HE GETS READY FOR A RACE.
MACK
NOT ON MY WATCH. NO CAR O' MINE SLEEPS ON THE JOB!
CAR OF YOURS?!
DODGE
NOW LISTEN' UP, MCQUEEN. YOU MAY BE ON POLE, BUT YOU KNOW NOTHIN' ABOUT ROAD RACING.
SOME OF THESE GUYS ARE ROAD COURSE SPECIALISTS. LET THEM PASS, THEN FOLLOW 'EM FOR A WHILE. IT'S A LONG RACE, YOU COULD LEARN SOMETHING.
LET THEM PASS ME?! NO WAY!!
I HAD THE WHOLE RACE MAPPED OUT IN MY MIND.

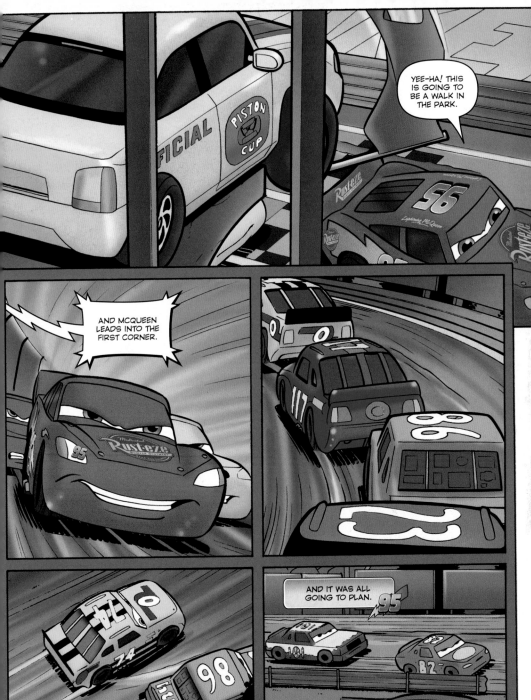

YEE-HA! THIS IS GOING TO BE A WALK IN THE PARK.

AND MCQUEEN LEADS INTO THE FIRST CORNER.

AND IT WAS ALL GOING TO PLAN.

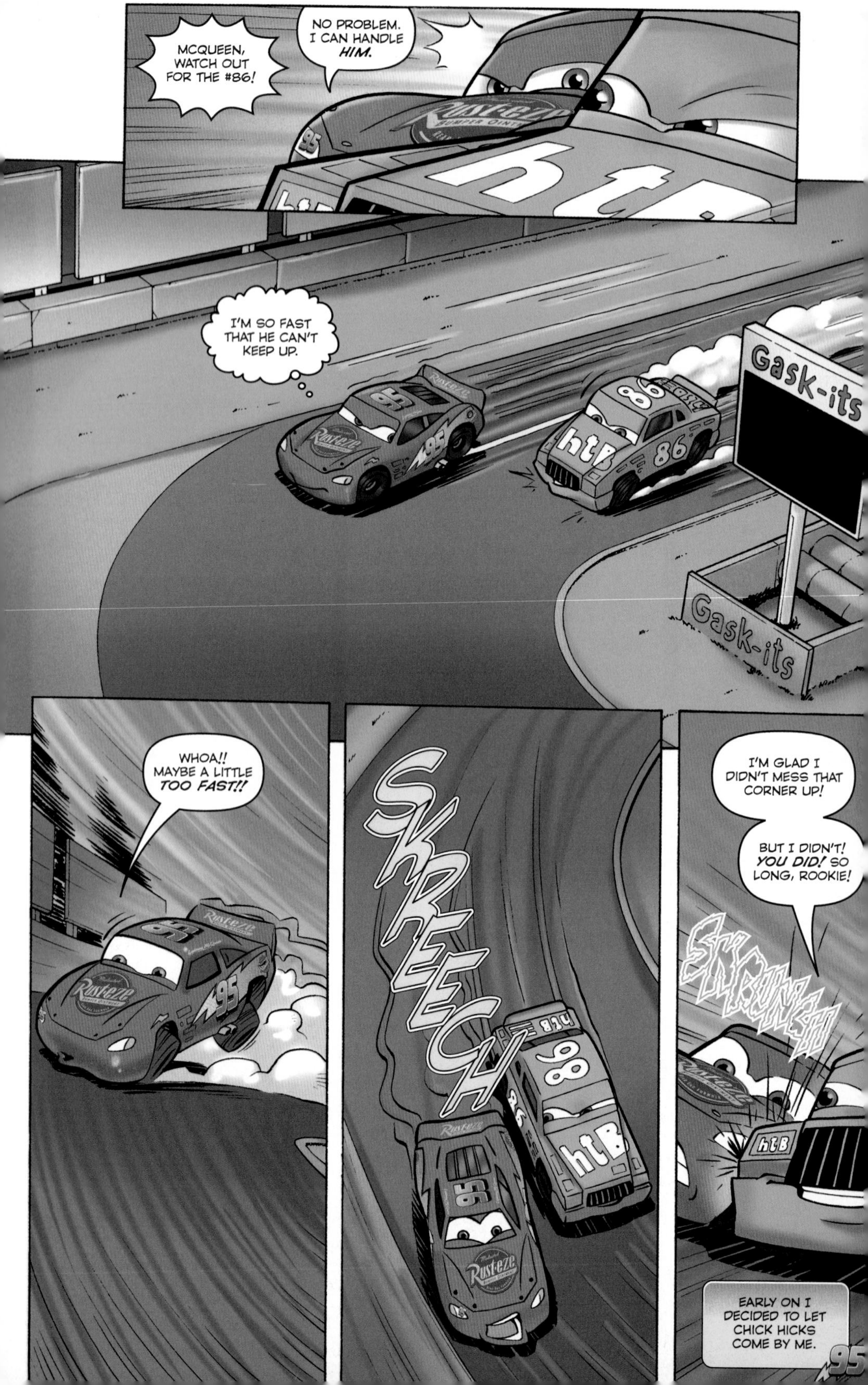

MCQUEEN, WATCH OUT FOR THE #86!
NO PROBLEM. I CAN HANDLE *HIM*.
I'M SO FAST THAT HE CAN'T KEEP UP.
Gask-its
Gask-its
WHOA!! MAYBE A LITTLE *TOO FAST!!*
SKREECH
I'M GLAD I DIDN'T MESS THAT CORNER UP!
BUT I DIDN'T! *YOU DID!* SO LONG, ROOKIE!
EARLY ON I DECIDED TO LET CHICK HICKS COME BY ME.

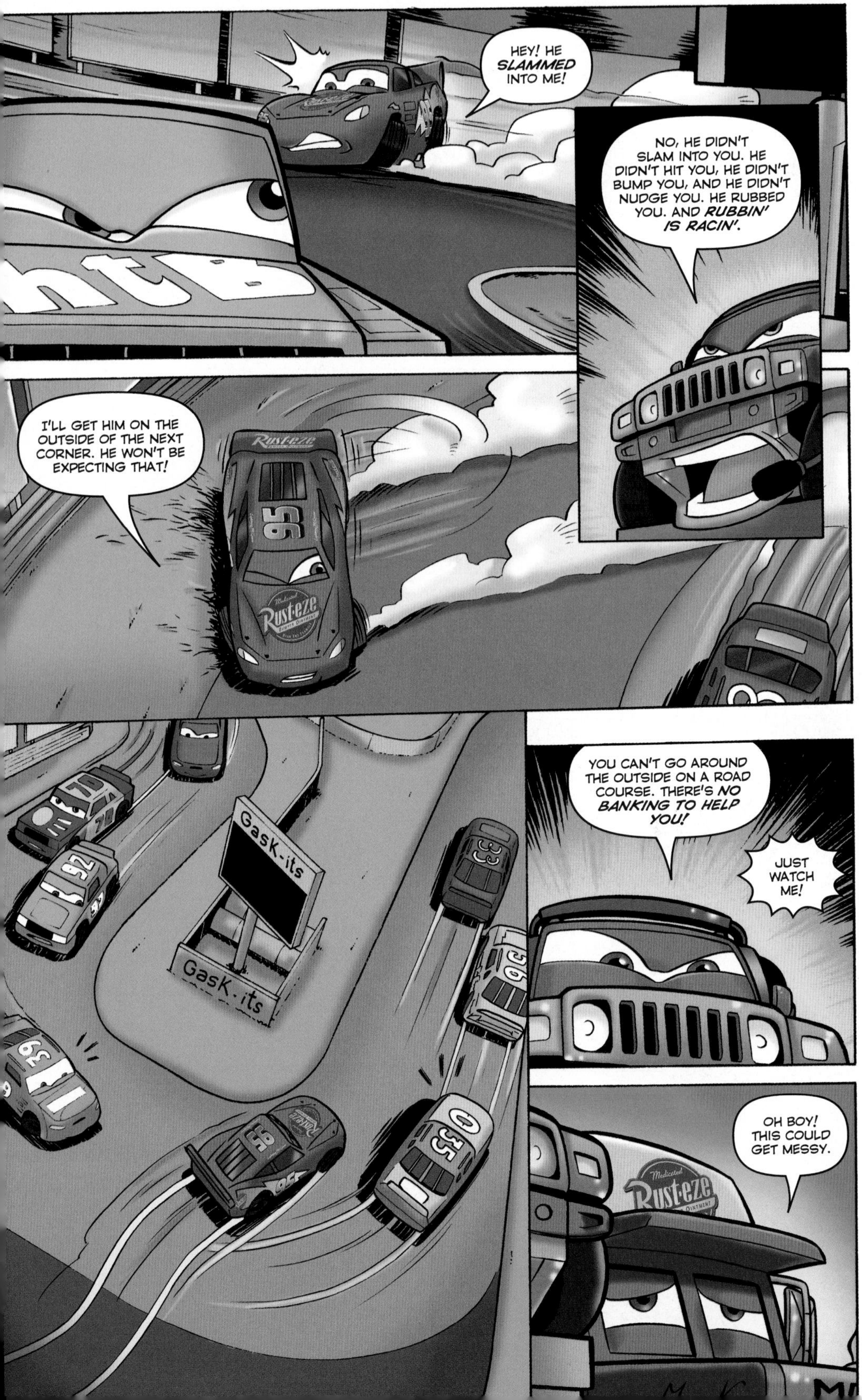

HEY! HE SLAMMED INTO ME!
NO, HE DIDN'T SLAM INTO YOU. HE DIDN'T HIT YOU, HE DIDN'T BUMP YOU, AND HE DIDN'T NUDGE YOU. HE RUBBED YOU. AND RUBBIN' IS RACIN'.
I'LL GET HIM ON THE OUTSIDE OF THE NEXT CORNER. HE WON'T BE EXPECTING THAT!
YOU CAN'T GO AROUND THE OUTSIDE ON A ROAD COURSE. THERE'S NO BANKING TO HELP YOU!
JUST WATCH ME!
OH BOY! THIS COULD GET MESSY.

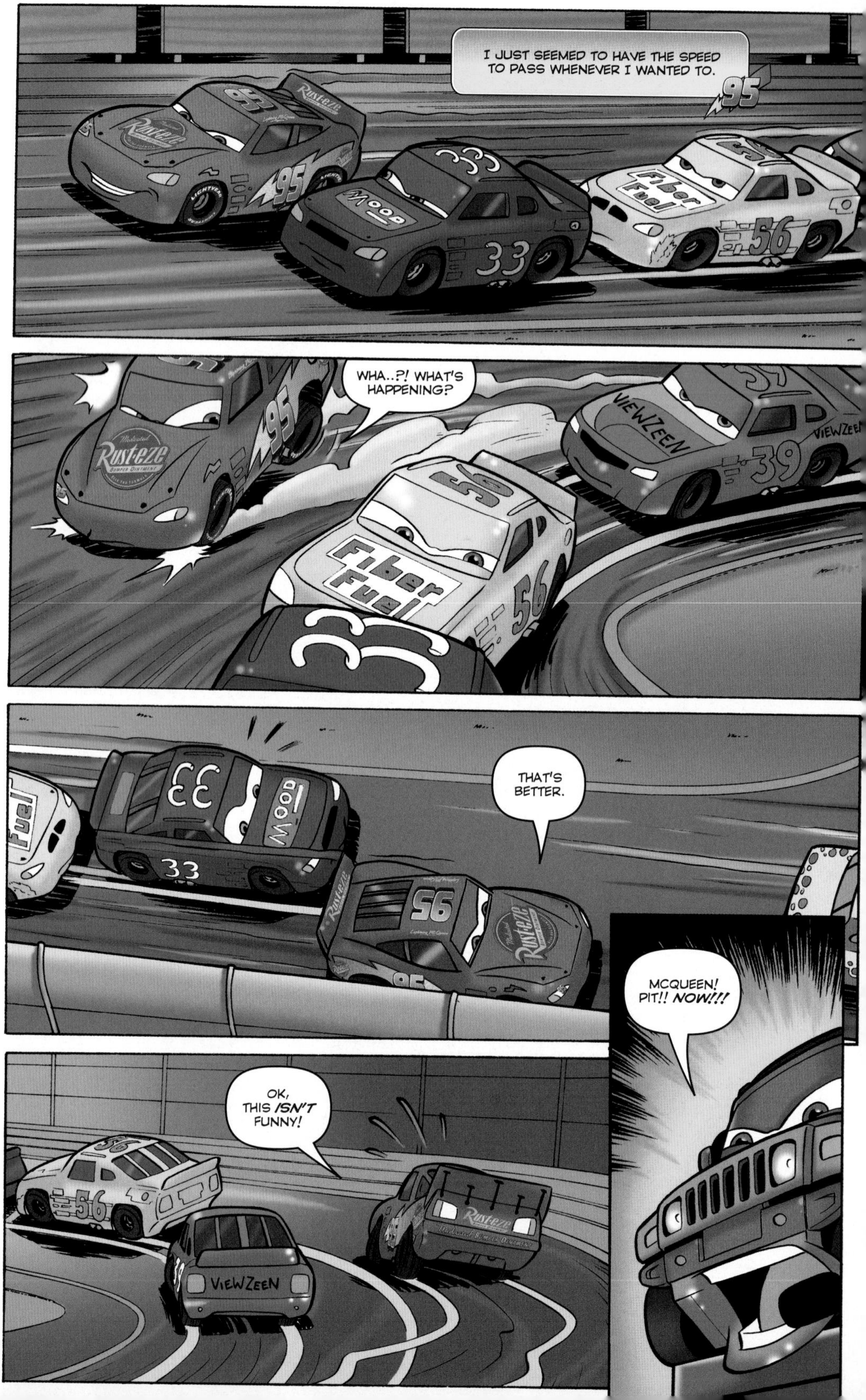
I JUST SEEMED TO HAVE THE SPEED TO PASS WHENEVER I WANTED TO.
WHA..?! WHAT'S HAPPENING?
THAT'S BETTER.
MCQUEEN! PIT!! NOW!!!
OK, THIS ISN'T FUNNY!

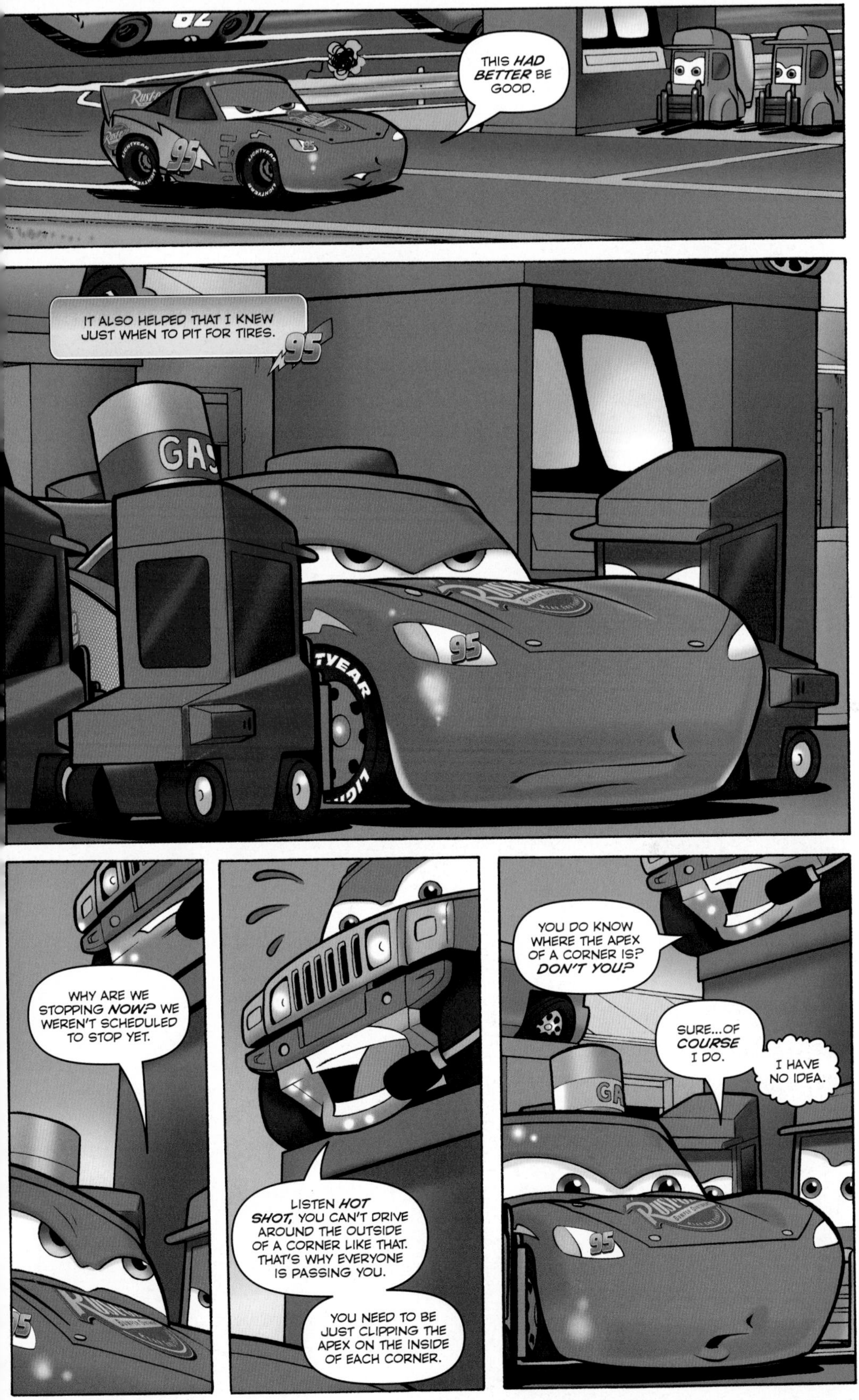
THIS HAD BETTER BE GOOD.
IT ALSO HELPED THAT I KNEW JUST WHEN TO PIT FOR TIRES.
WHY ARE WE STOPPING NOW? WE WEREN'T SCHEDULED TO STOP YET.
LISTEN HOT SHOT, YOU CAN'T DRIVE AROUND THE OUTSIDE OF A CORNER LIKE THAT. THAT'S WHY EVERYONE IS PASSING YOU.
YOU NEED TO BE JUST CLIPPING THE APEX ON THE INSIDE OF EACH CORNER.
YOU DO KNOW WHERE THE APEX OF A CORNER IS? DON'T YOU?
SURE...OF COURSE I DO.
I HAVE NO IDEA.

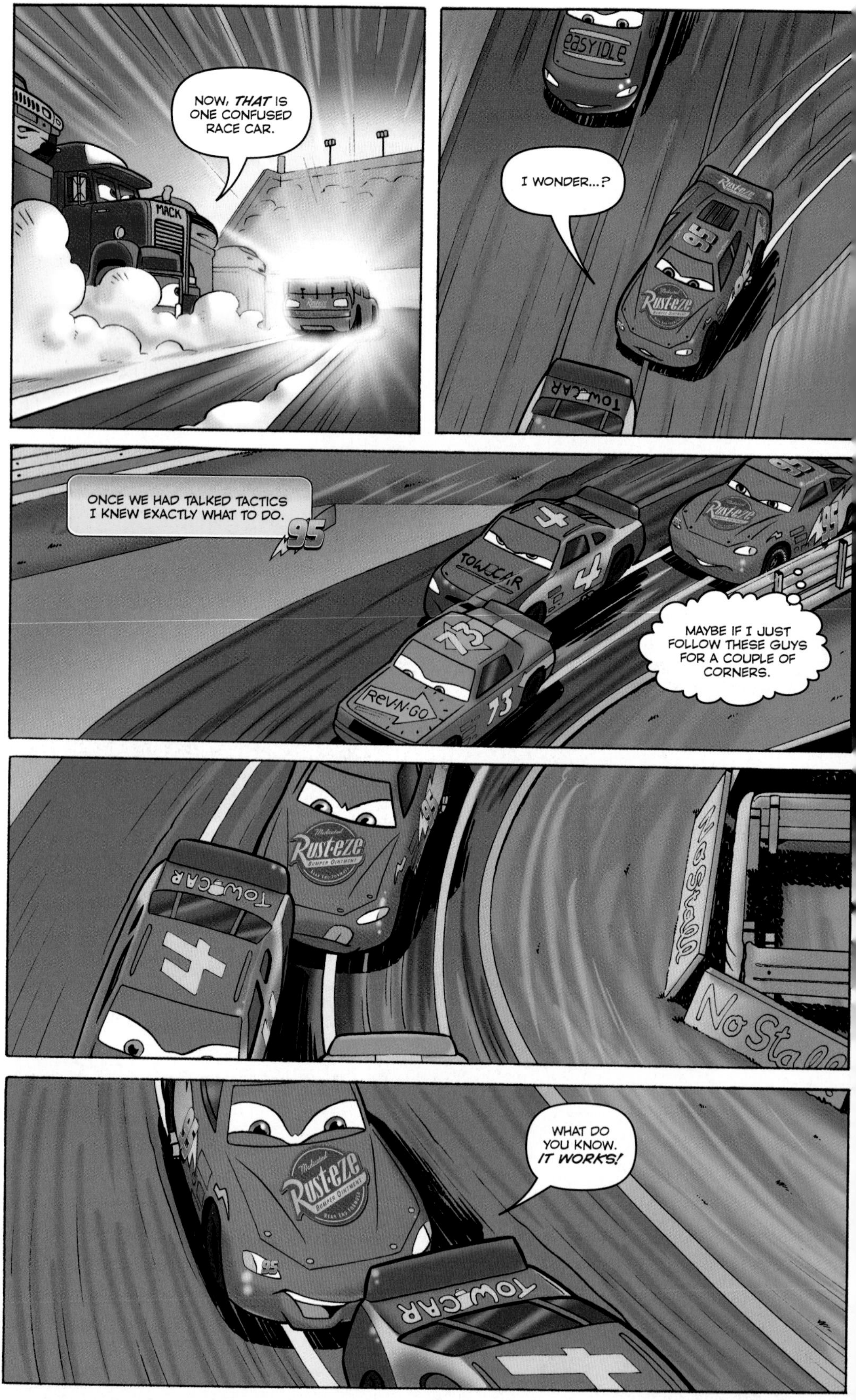
NOW, *THAT* IS ONE CONFUSED RACE CAR.
MACK
EASYIDLE
I WONDER...?
Rust-eze
95
TOW CAR
ONCE WE HAD TALKED TACTICS I KNEW EXACTLY WHAT TO DO.
95
TOW CAR
4
73
REV-N-GO
MAYBE IF I JUST FOLLOW THESE GUYS FOR A COUPLE OF CORNERS.
Rust-eze
BUMPER OINTMENT
No Stall
WHAT DO YOU KNOW. *IT WORKS!*

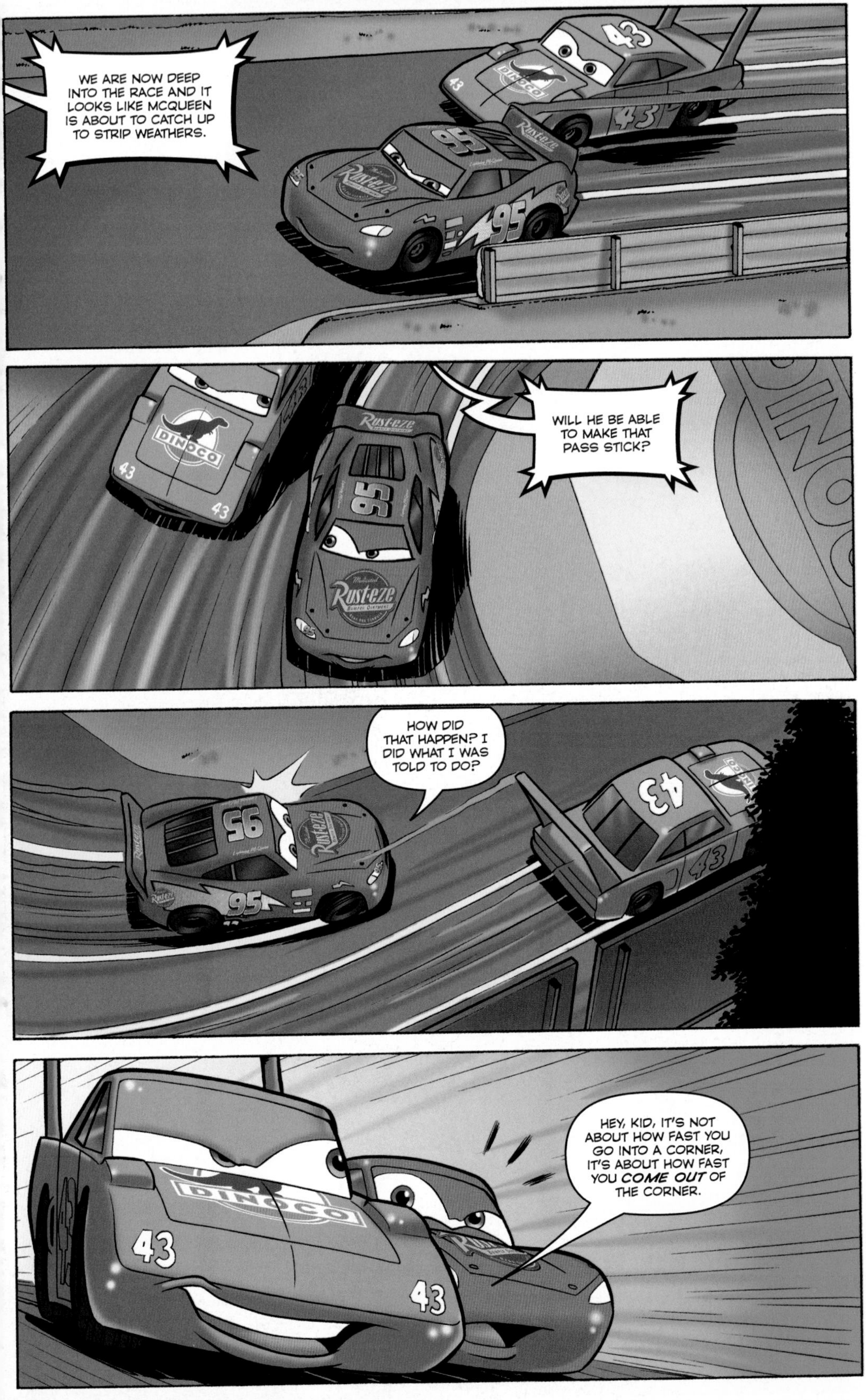
WE ARE NOW DEEP INTO THE RACE AND IT LOOKS LIKE MCQUEEN IS ABOUT TO CATCH UP TO STRIP WEATHERS.
WILL HE BE ABLE TO MAKE THAT PASS STICK?
HOW DID THAT HAPPEN? I DID WHAT I WAS TOLD TO DO?
HEY, KID, IT'S NOT ABOUT HOW FAST YOU GO INTO A CORNER, IT'S ABOUT HOW FAST YOU *COME OUT* OF THE CORNER.

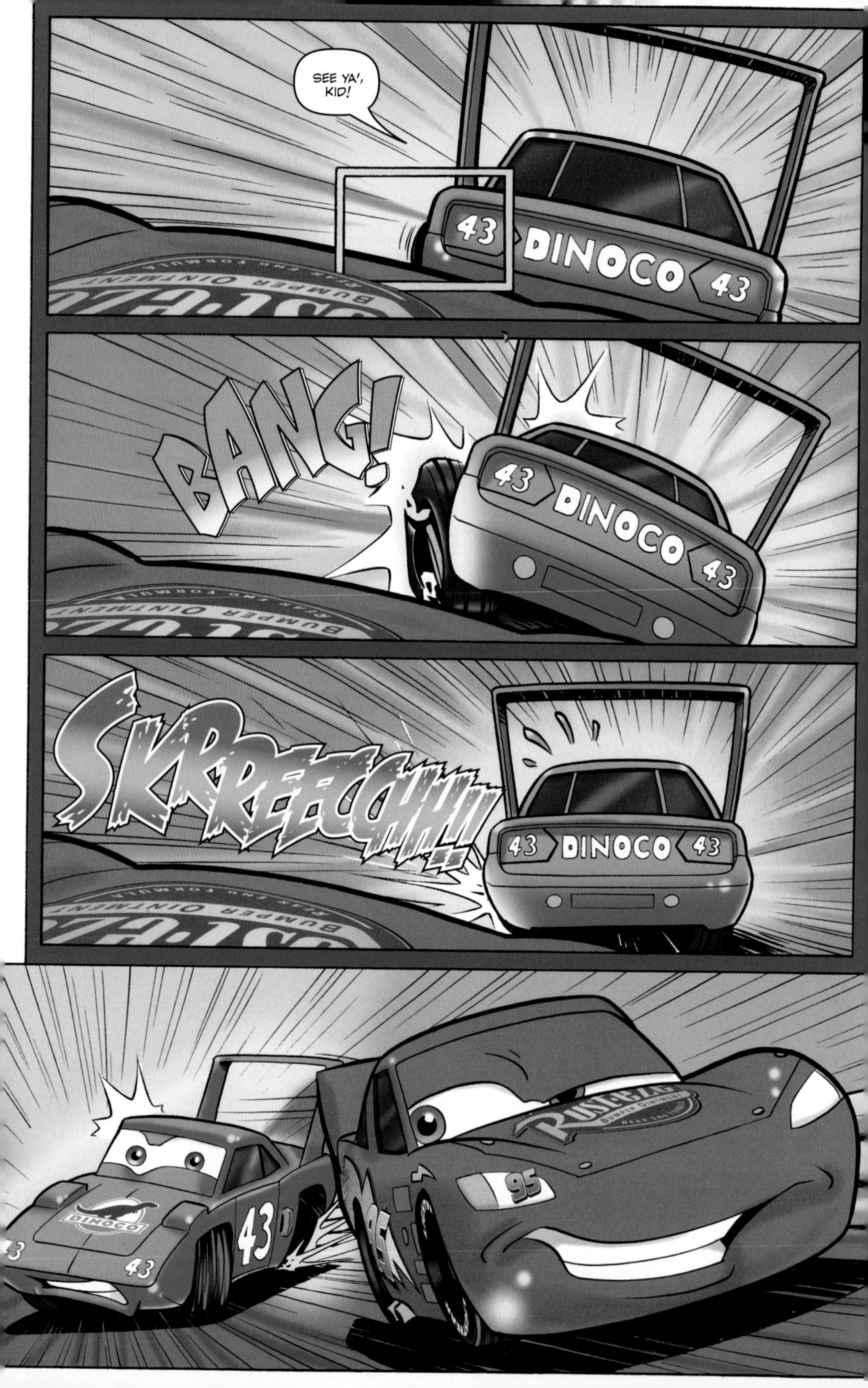
SEE YA', KID!
BANG!
SKREECHH!!

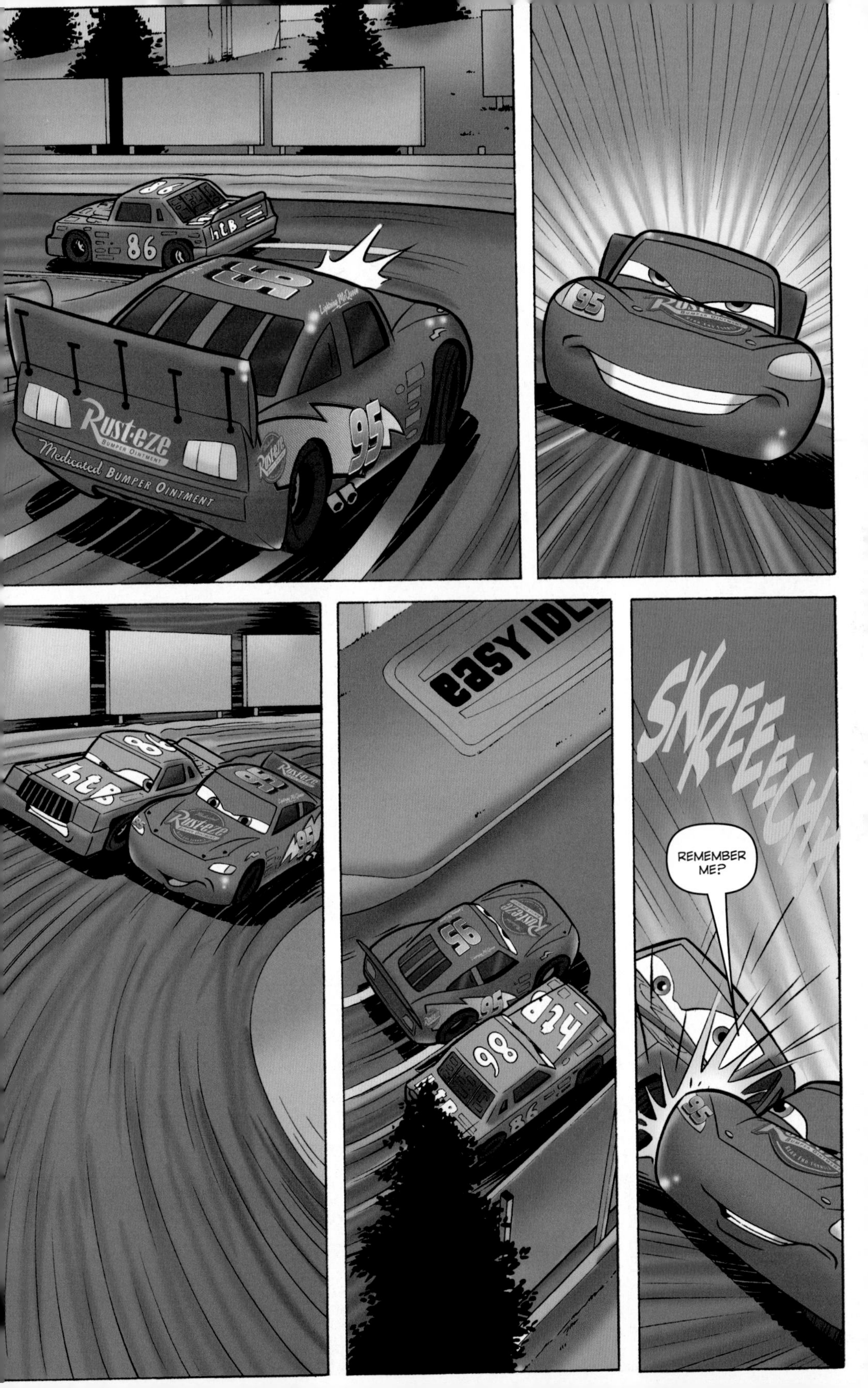
Rust-eze
BUMPER OINTMENT
Medicated BUMPER OINTMENT
REMEMBER ME?

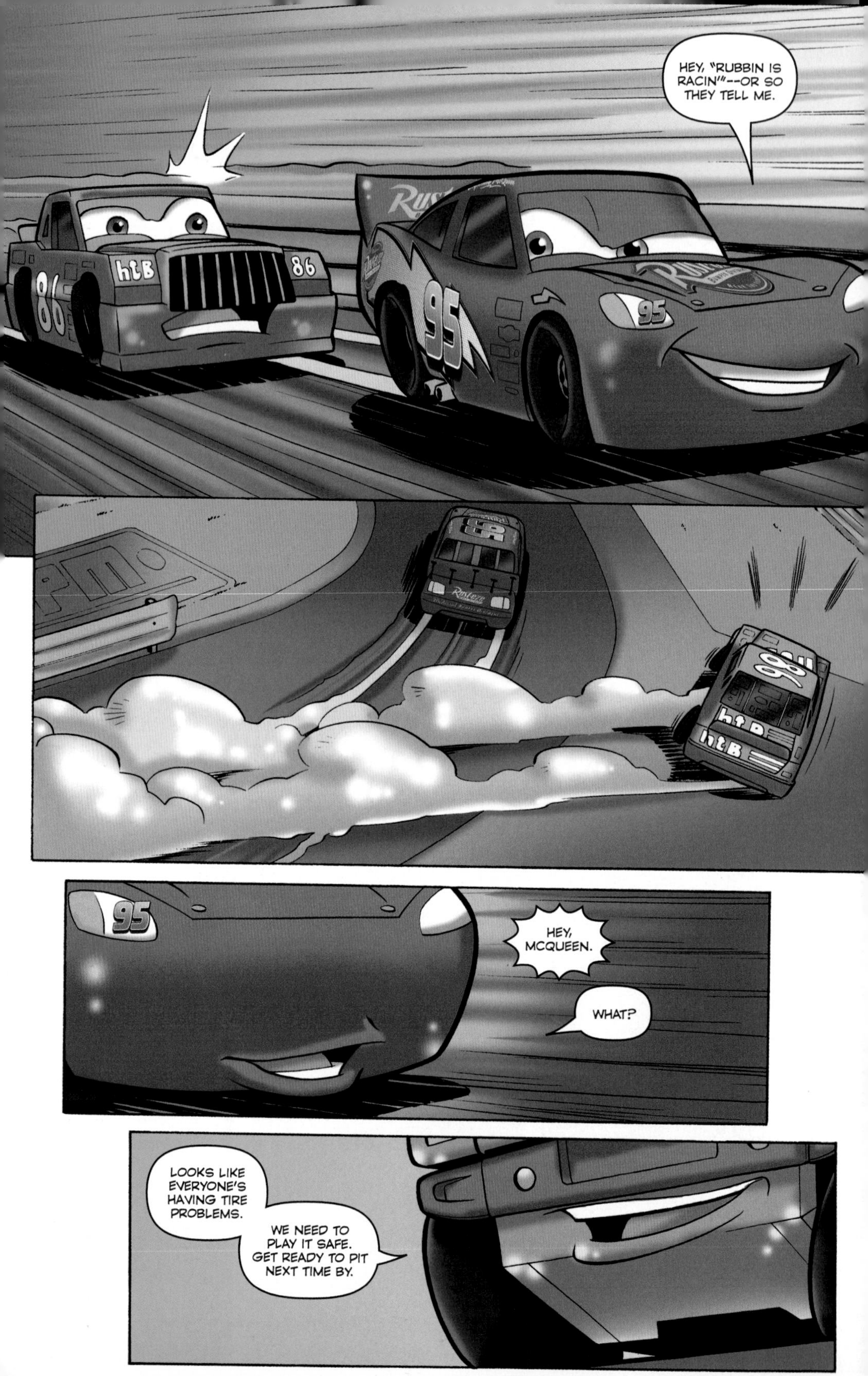
HEY, "RUBBIN IS RACIN'"--OR SO THEY TELL ME.
htB
86
95
HEY, MCQUEEN.
WHAT?
LOOKS LIKE EVERYONE'S HAVING TIRE PROBLEMS.
WE NEED TO PLAY IT SAFE. GET READY TO PIT NEXT TIME BY.

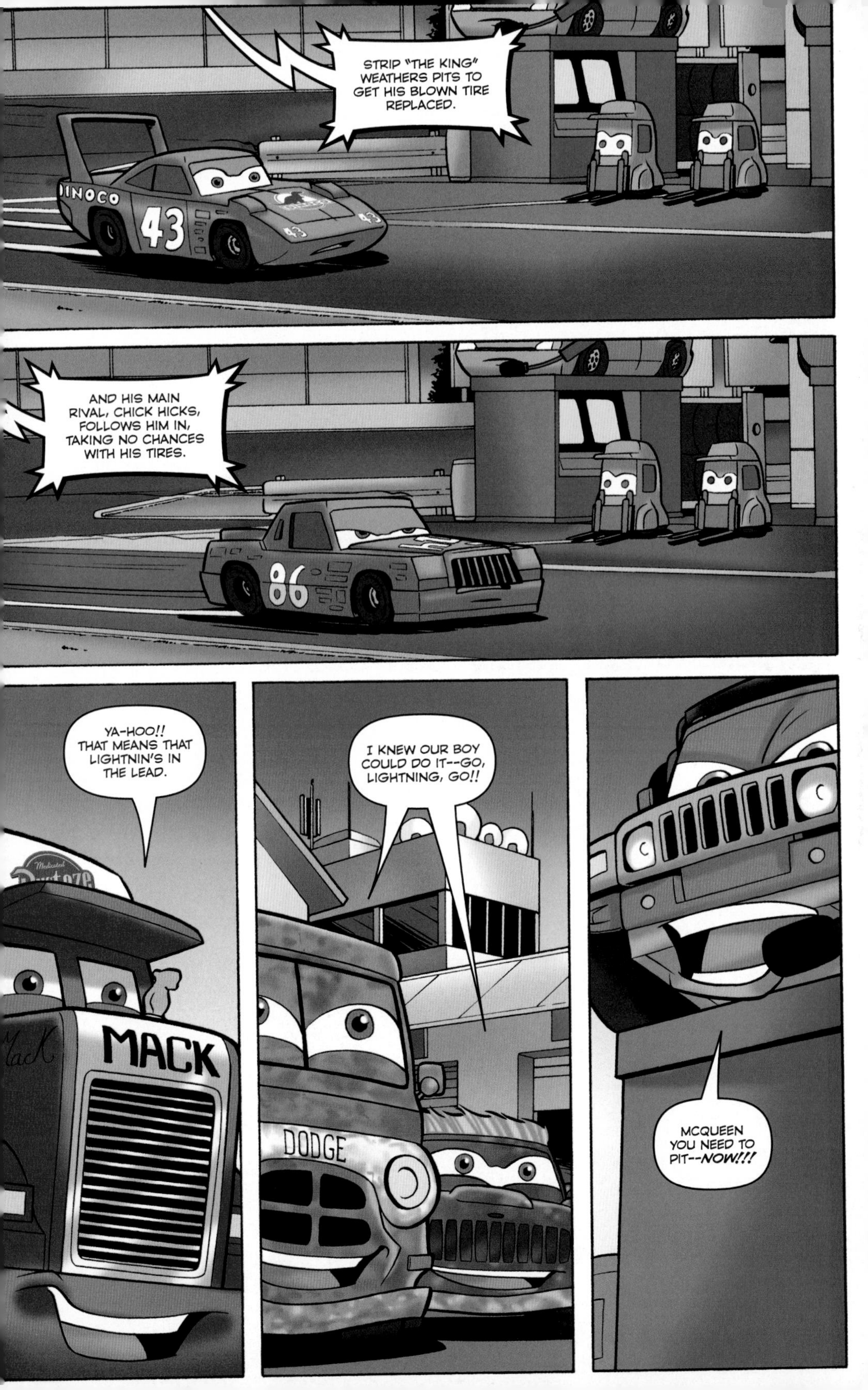
STRIP "THE KING" WEATHERS PITS TO GET HIS BLOWN TIRE REPLACED.
DINOCO
43
AND HIS MAIN RIVAL, CHICK HICKS, FOLLOWS HIM IN, TAKING NO CHANCES WITH HIS TIRES.
86
YA-HOO!! THAT MEANS THAT LIGHTNIN'S IN THE LEAD.
MACK
I KNEW OUR BOY COULD DO IT--GO, LIGHTNING, GO!!
DODGE
MCQUEEN YOU NEED TO PIT--*NOW!!!*

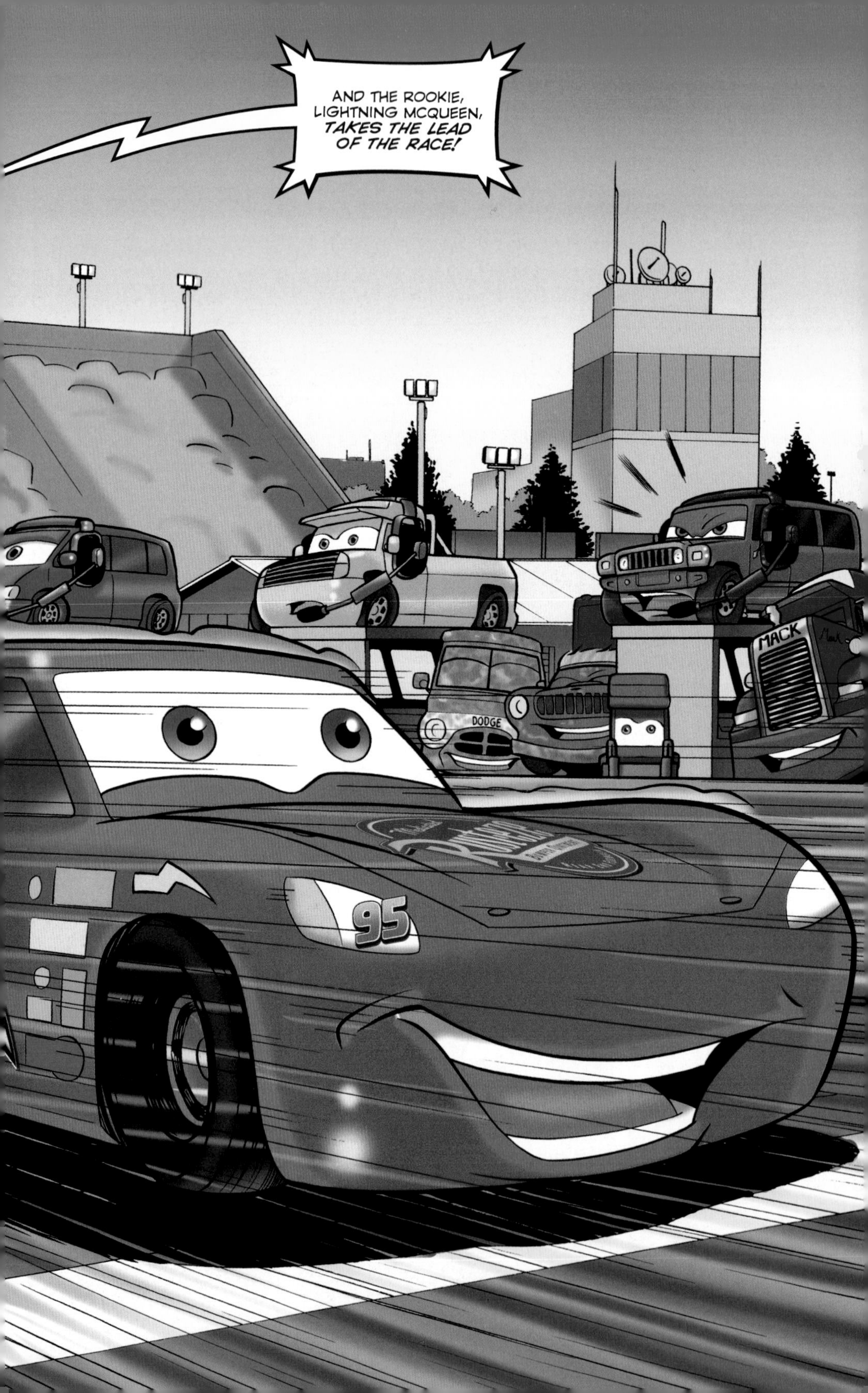
AND THE ROOKIE, LIGHTNING MCQUEEN, TAKES THE LEAD OF THE RACE!
DODGE
MACK
95

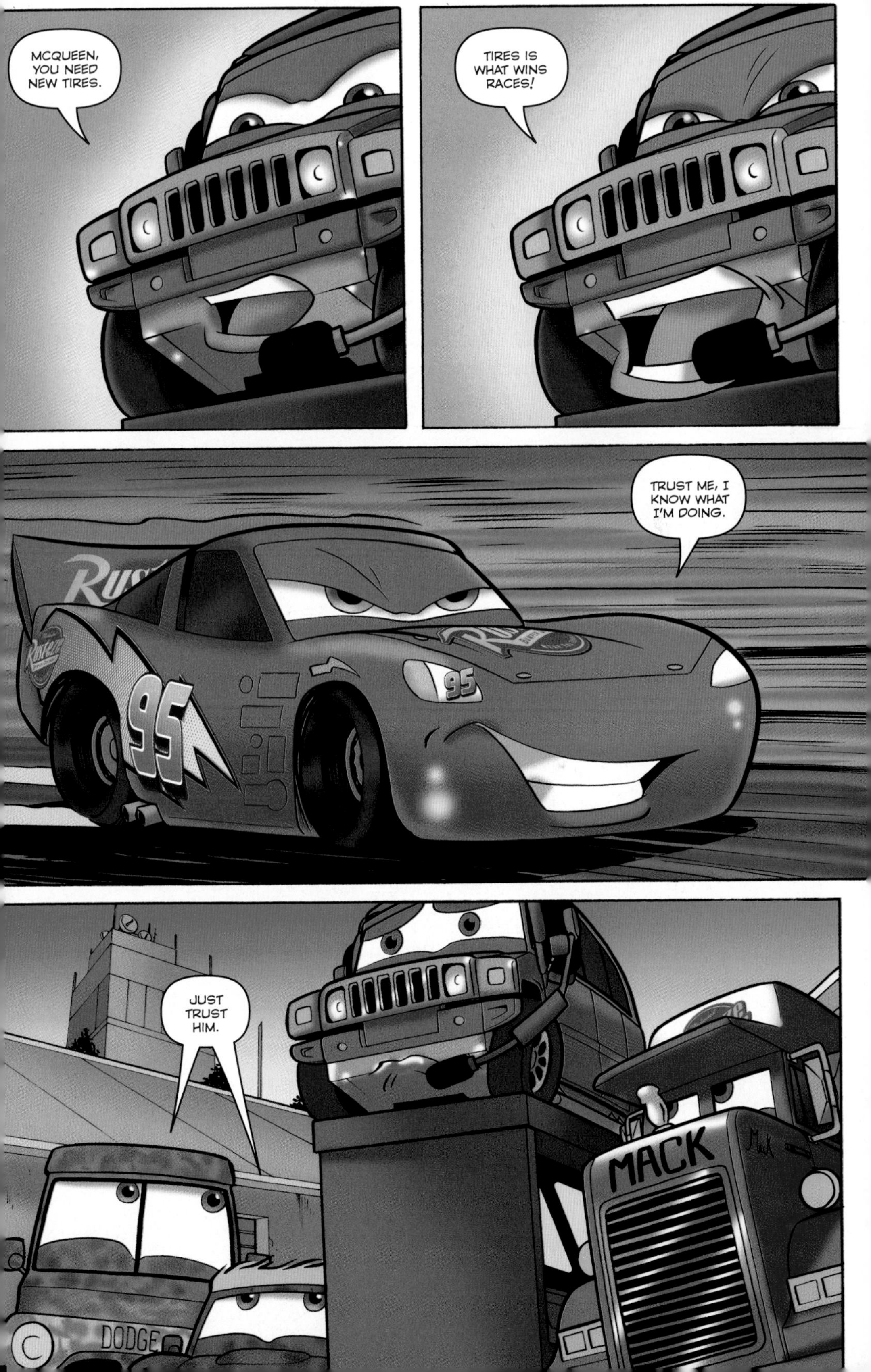
MCQUEEN, YOU NEED NEW TIRES.
TIRES IS WHAT WINS RACES!
RUST
95
TRUST ME, I KNOW WHAT I'M DOING.
JUST TRUST HIM.
MACK
DODGE

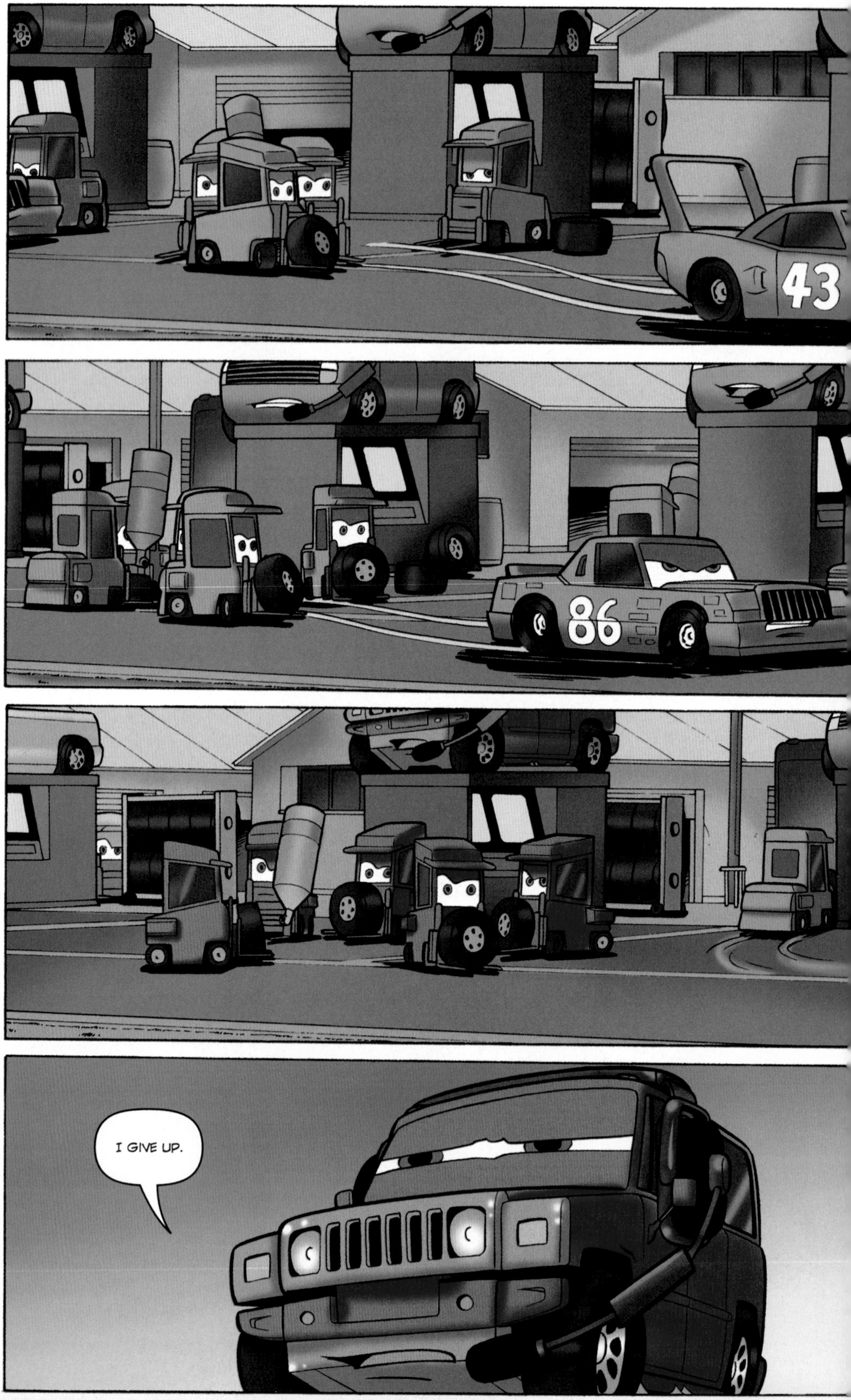
43
86
I GIVE UP.

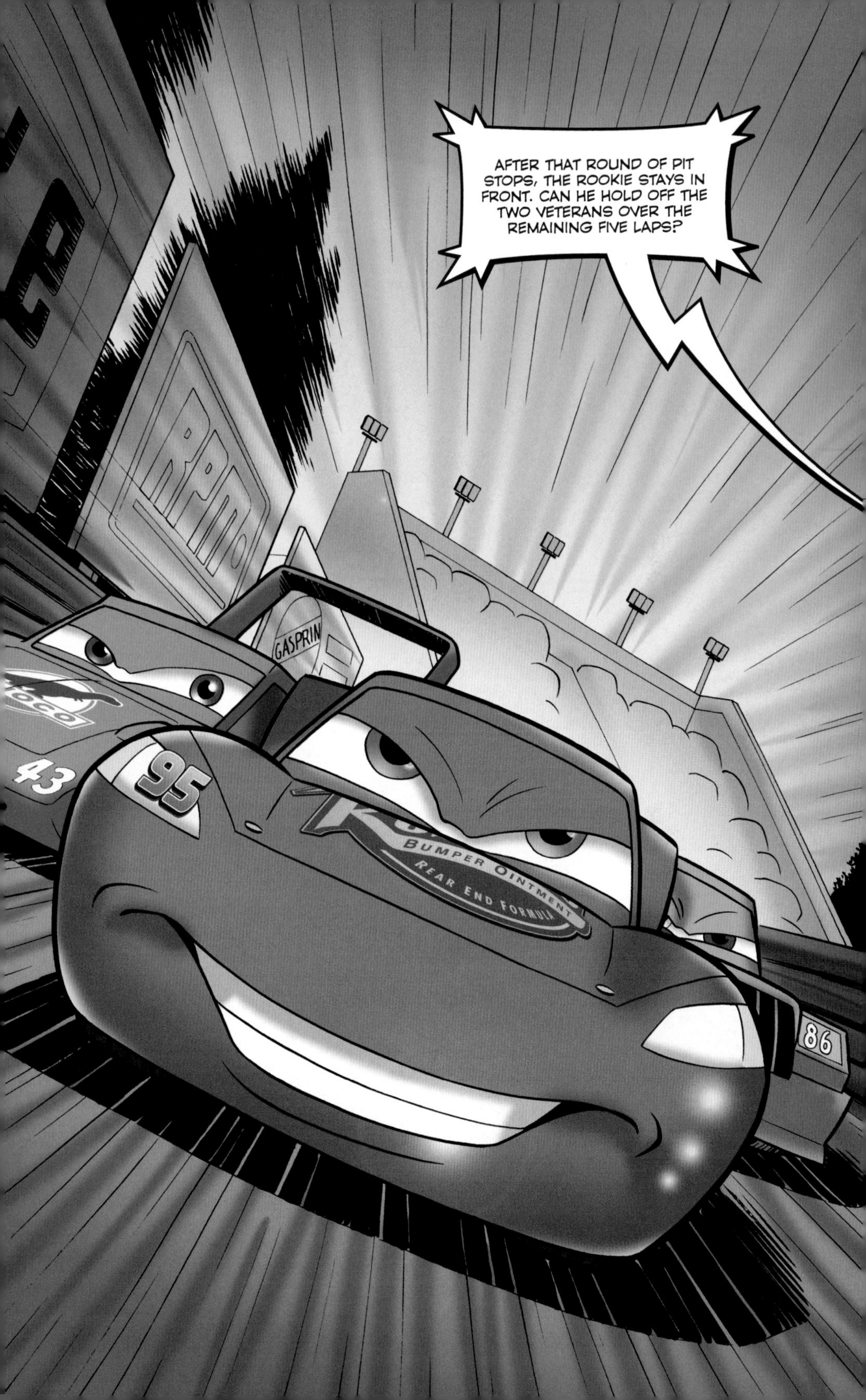
AFTER THAT ROUND OF PIT STOPS, THE ROOKIE STAYS IN FRONT. CAN HE HOLD OFF THE TWO VETERANS OVER THE REMAINING FIVE LAPS?
95
BUMPER OINTMENT
REAR END FORMULA
43
86
GASPRIN

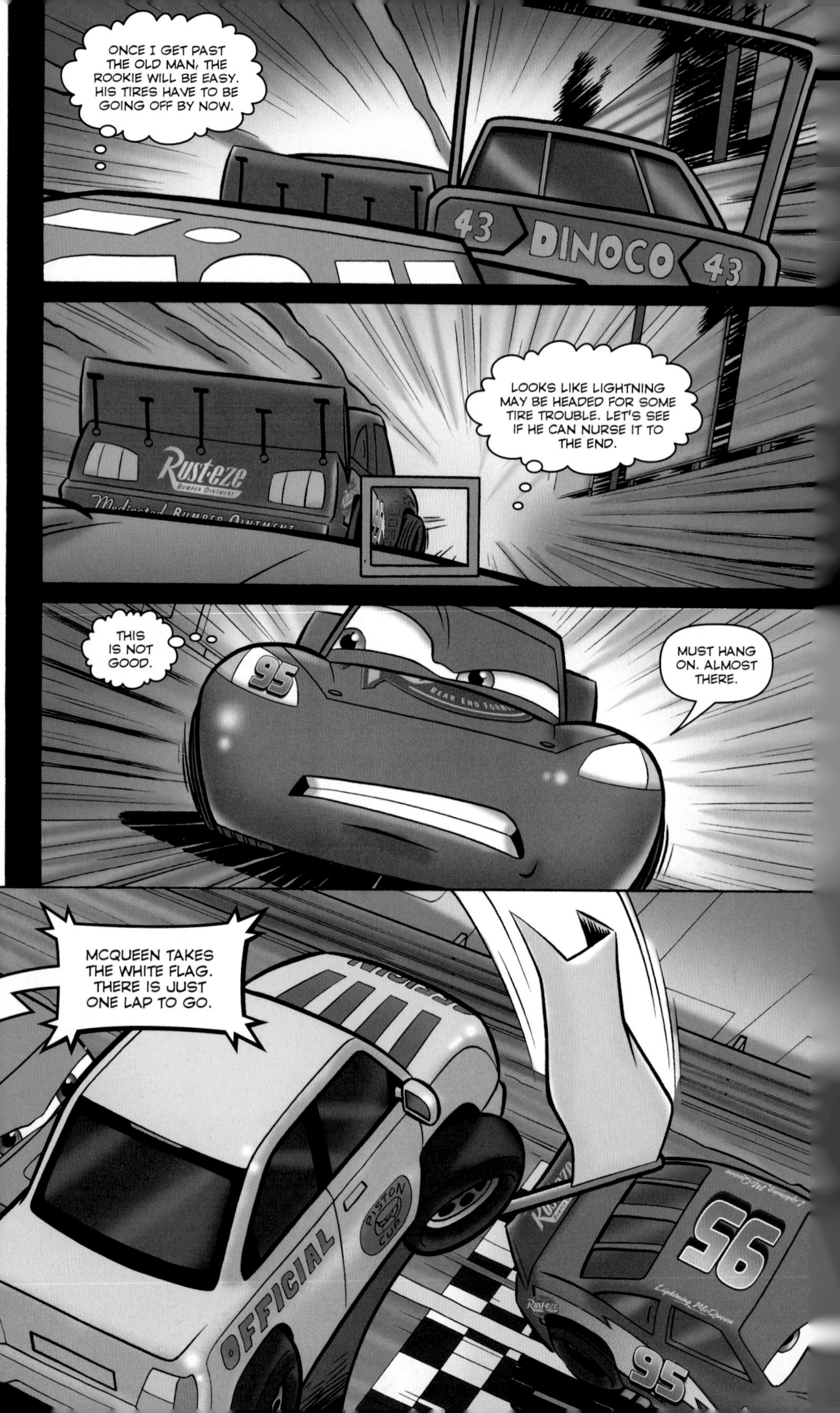
ONCE I GET PAST THE OLD MAN, THE ROOKIE WILL BE EASY. HIS TIRES HAVE TO BE GOING OFF BY NOW.
43
DINOCO
43
Rust-eze
BUMPER OINTMENT
Medicated BUMPER OINTMENT
LOOKS LIKE LIGHTNING MAY BE HEADED FOR SOME TIRE TROUBLE. LET'S SEE IF HE CAN NURSE IT TO THE END.
THIS IS NOT GOOD.
95
MUST HANG ON. ALMOST THERE.
MCQUEEN TAKES THE WHITE FLAG. THERE IS JUST ONE LAP TO GO.
OFFICIAL
PISTON CUP
95
Lightning McQueen
95

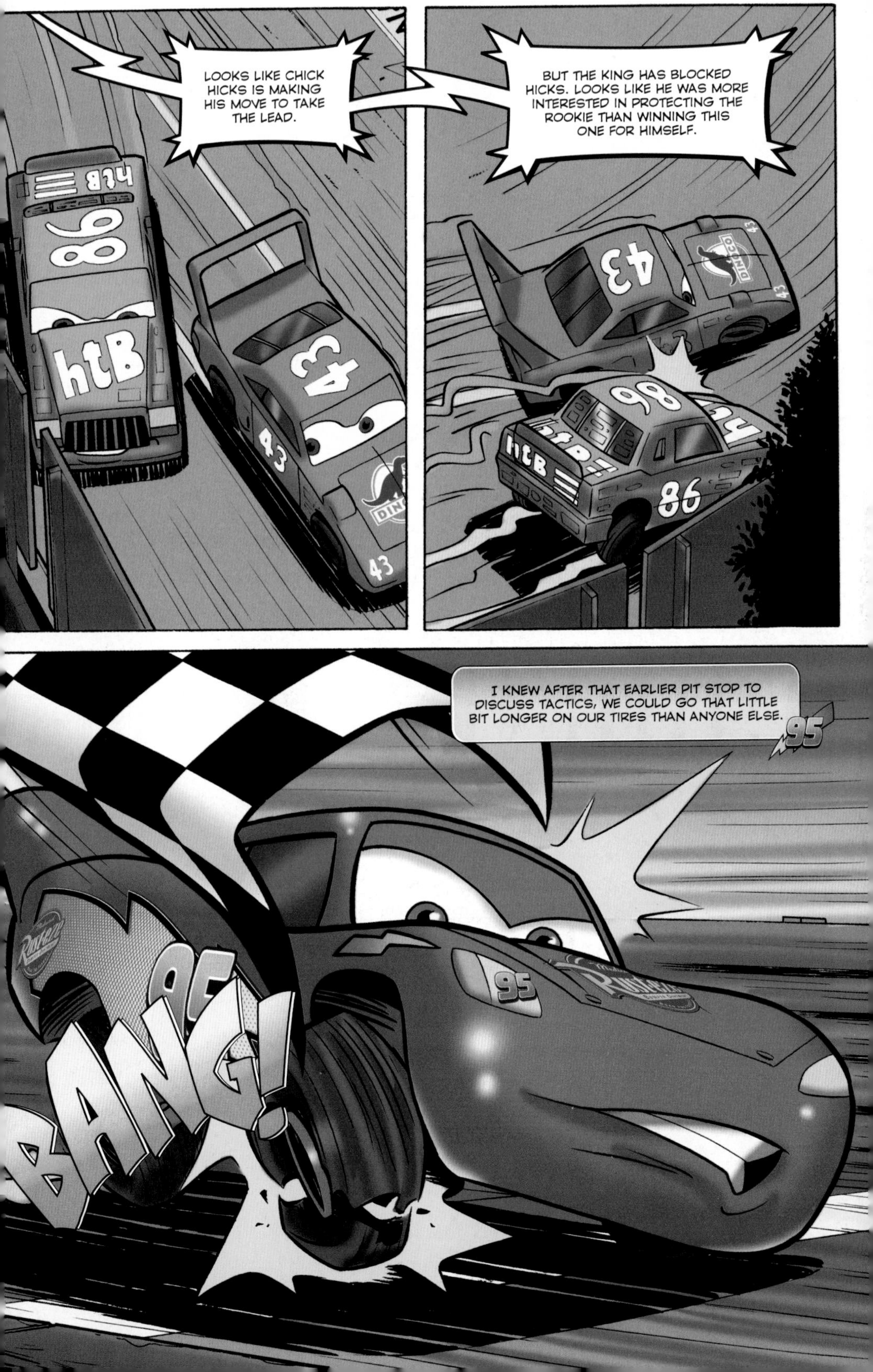
LOOKS LIKE CHICK HICKS IS MAKING HIS MOVE TO TAKE THE LEAD.
BUT THE KING HAS BLOCKED HICKS. LOOKS LIKE HE WAS MORE INTERESTED IN PROTECTING THE ROOKIE THAN WINNING THIS ONE FOR HIMSELF.
I KNEW AFTER THAT EARLIER PIT STOP TO DISCUSS TACTICS, WE COULD GO THAT LITTLE BIT LONGER ON OUR TIRES THAN ANYONE ELSE.
BANG!

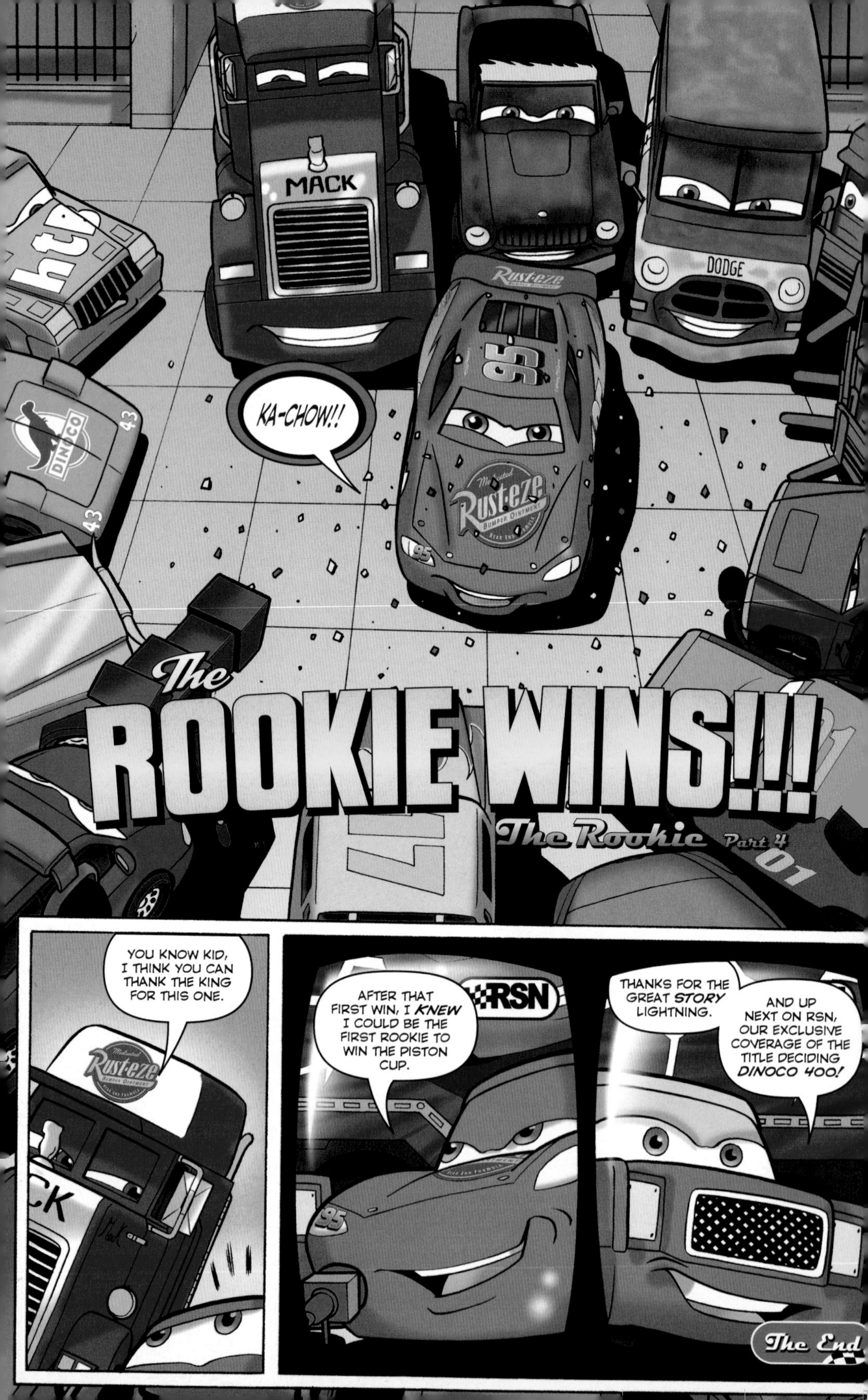
KA-CHOW!!
The ROOKIE WINS!!!
The Rookie Part 4
YOU KNOW KID, I THINK YOU CAN THANK THE KING FOR THIS ONE.
AFTER THAT FIRST WIN, I KNEW I COULD BE THE FIRST ROOKIE TO WIN THE PISTON CUP.
THANKS FOR THE GREAT STORY LIGHTNING.
AND UP NEXT ON RSN, OUR EXCLUSIVE COVERAGE OF THE TITLE DECIDING DINOCO 400!
The End

DISNEY • PIXAR

THE WORLD OF Cars

Cover Gallery

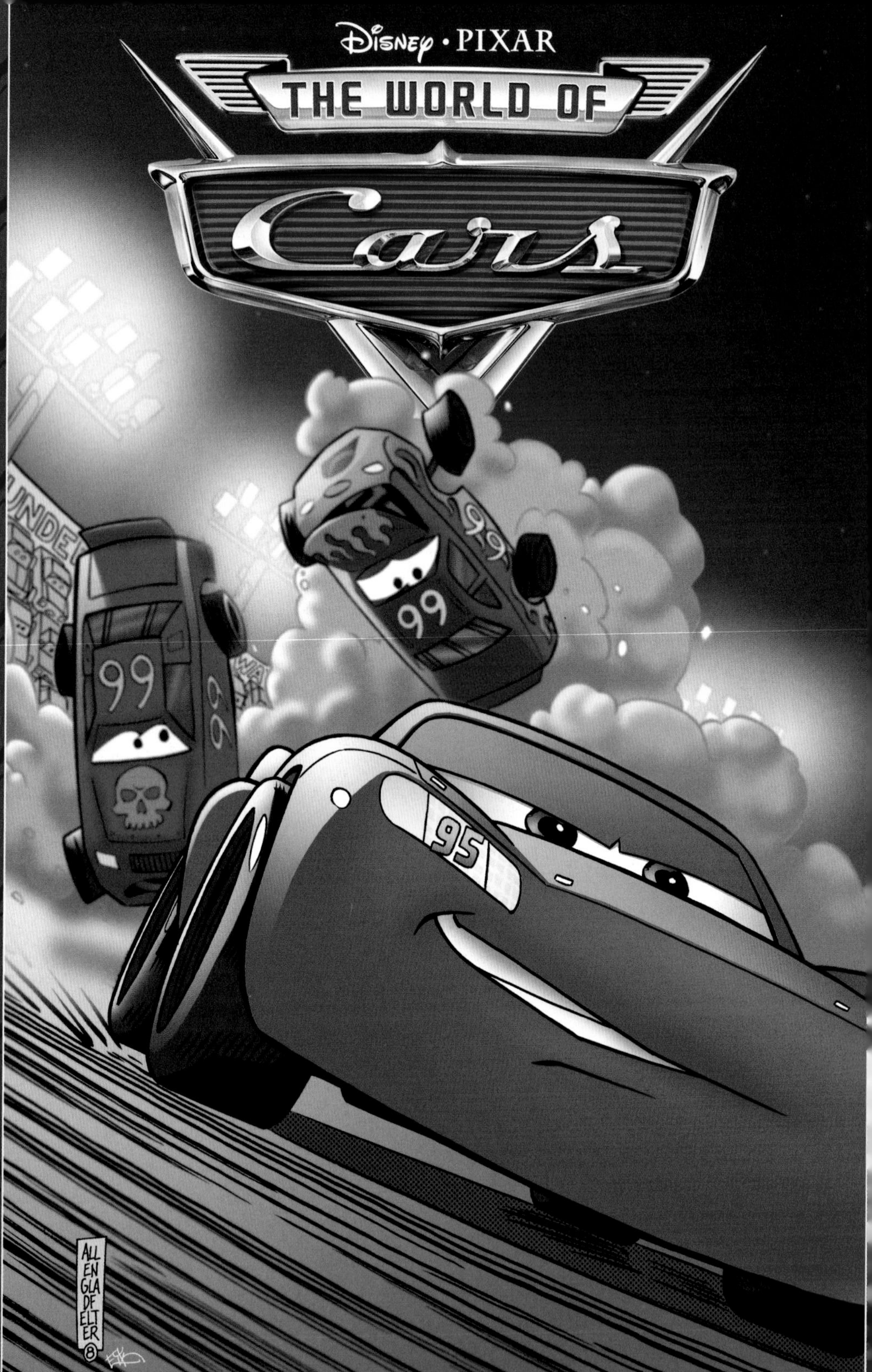

Disney • PIXAR
THE WORLD OF
Cars
99
99
99
95
ALLEN GLADFELTER

COVER 1A
ALLEN GLADFELTER

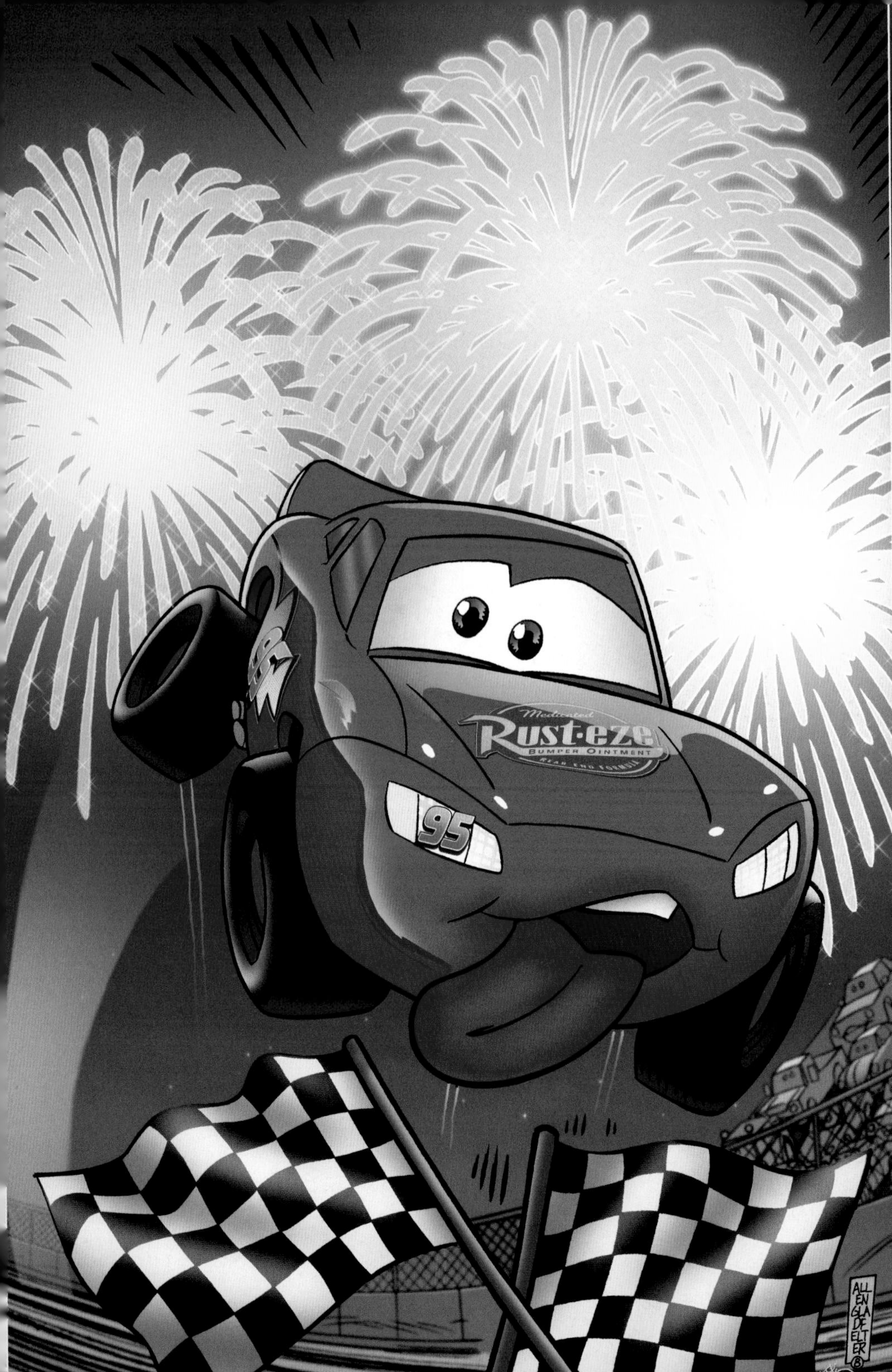
Medicated
Rust-eze
BUMPER OINTMENT
REAR END FORMULA
95
95
ALLEN GLADFELTER

COVER 1B
ALLEN GLADFELTER

Disney • PIXAR

THE WORLD OF

Cars

COVER 1C
PHOTO COVER

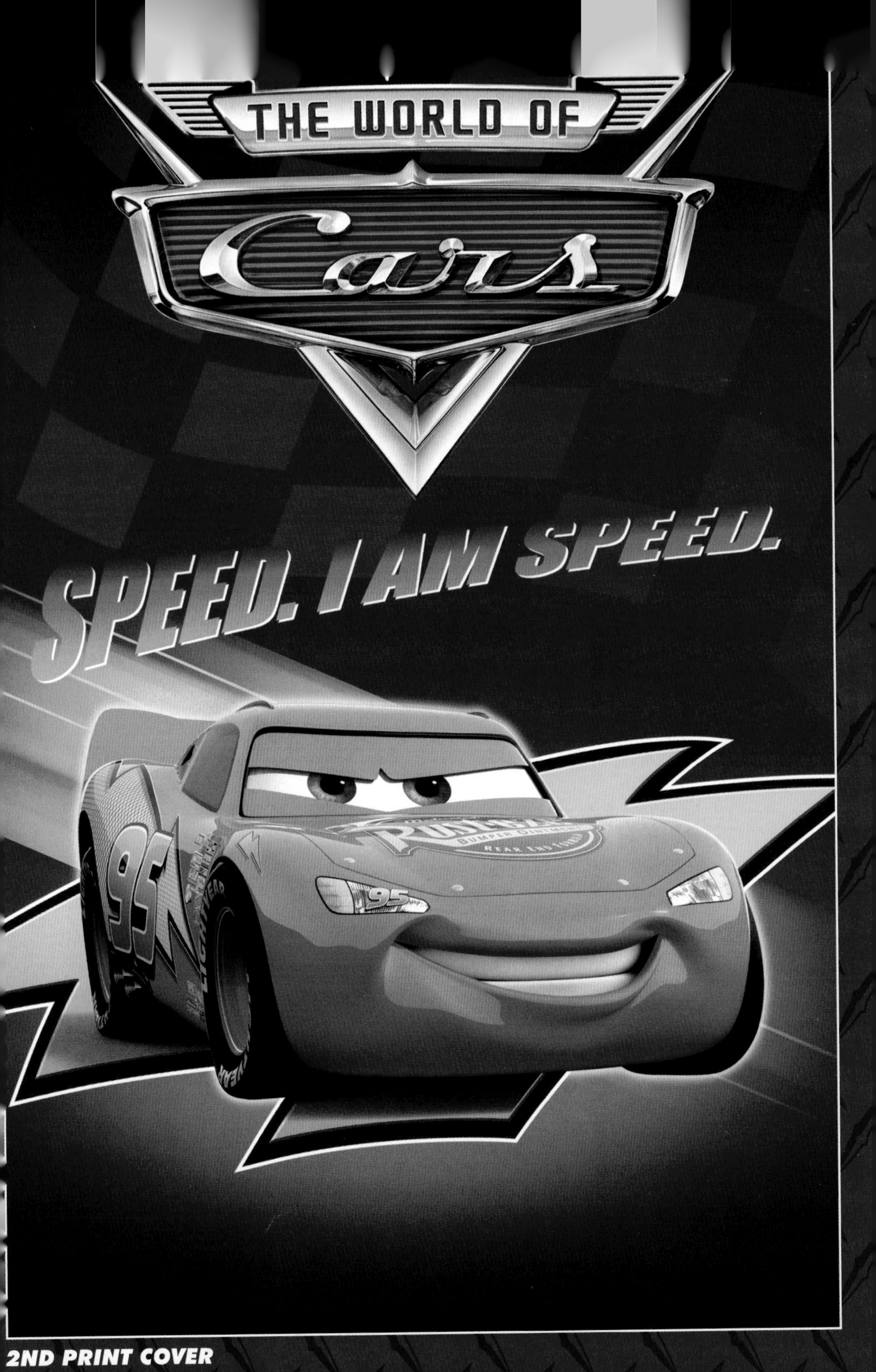
THE WORLD OF
Cars
SPEED. I AM SPEED.
95
BUMPER OINTMENT
REAR END FORMULA

2ND PRINT COVER
PHOTO COVER

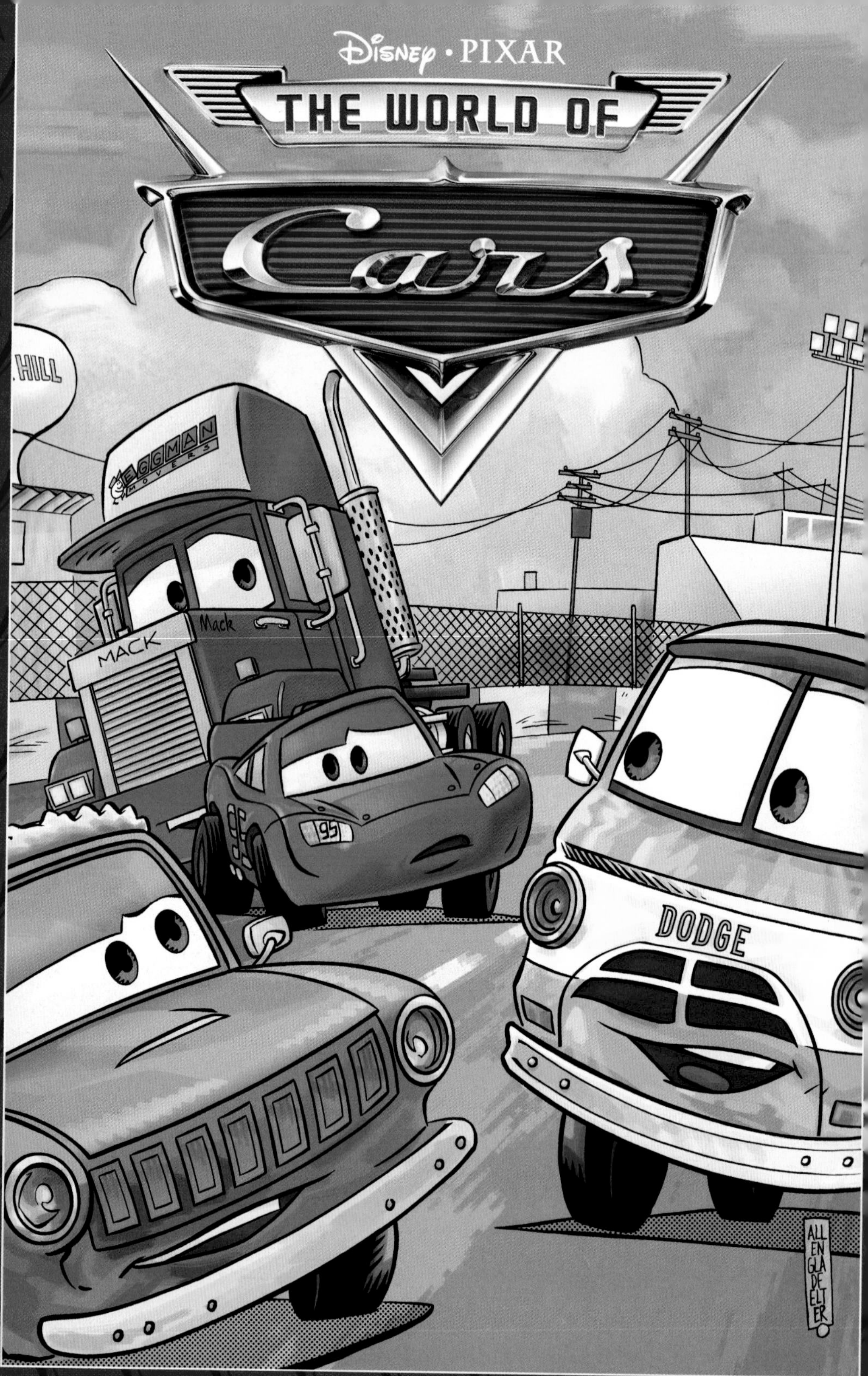
Disney • PIXAR
THE WORLD OF
Cars
HILL
EGGMAN
MOVERS
Mack
MACK
95
DODGE
ALLEN GLADFELTER

COVER 2A
ALLEN GLADFELTER

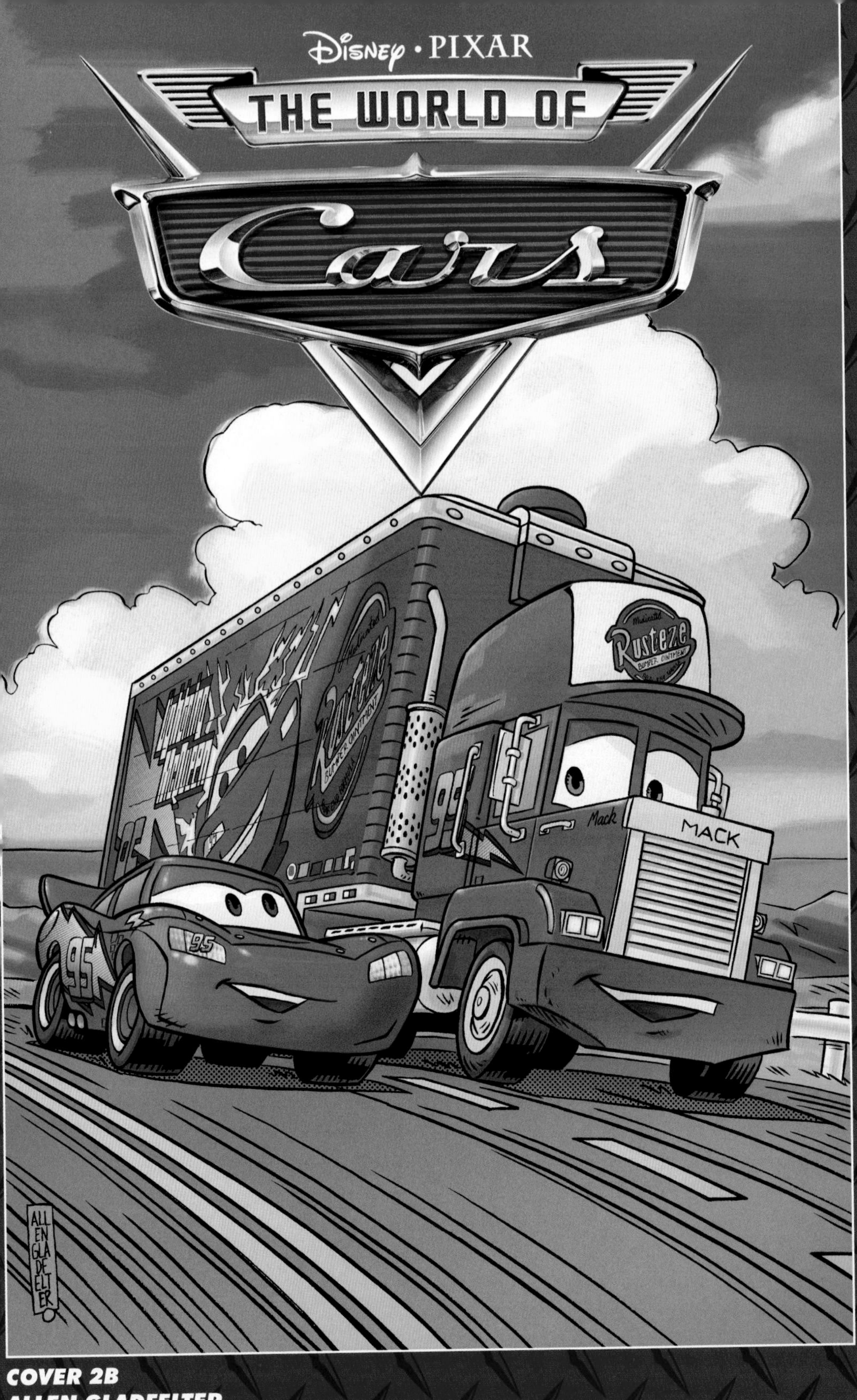
Disney • PIXAR
THE WORLD OF
Cars
Rusteze
BUMPER OINTMENT
Mack
MACK
95

COVER 2B
ALLEN GLADFELTER

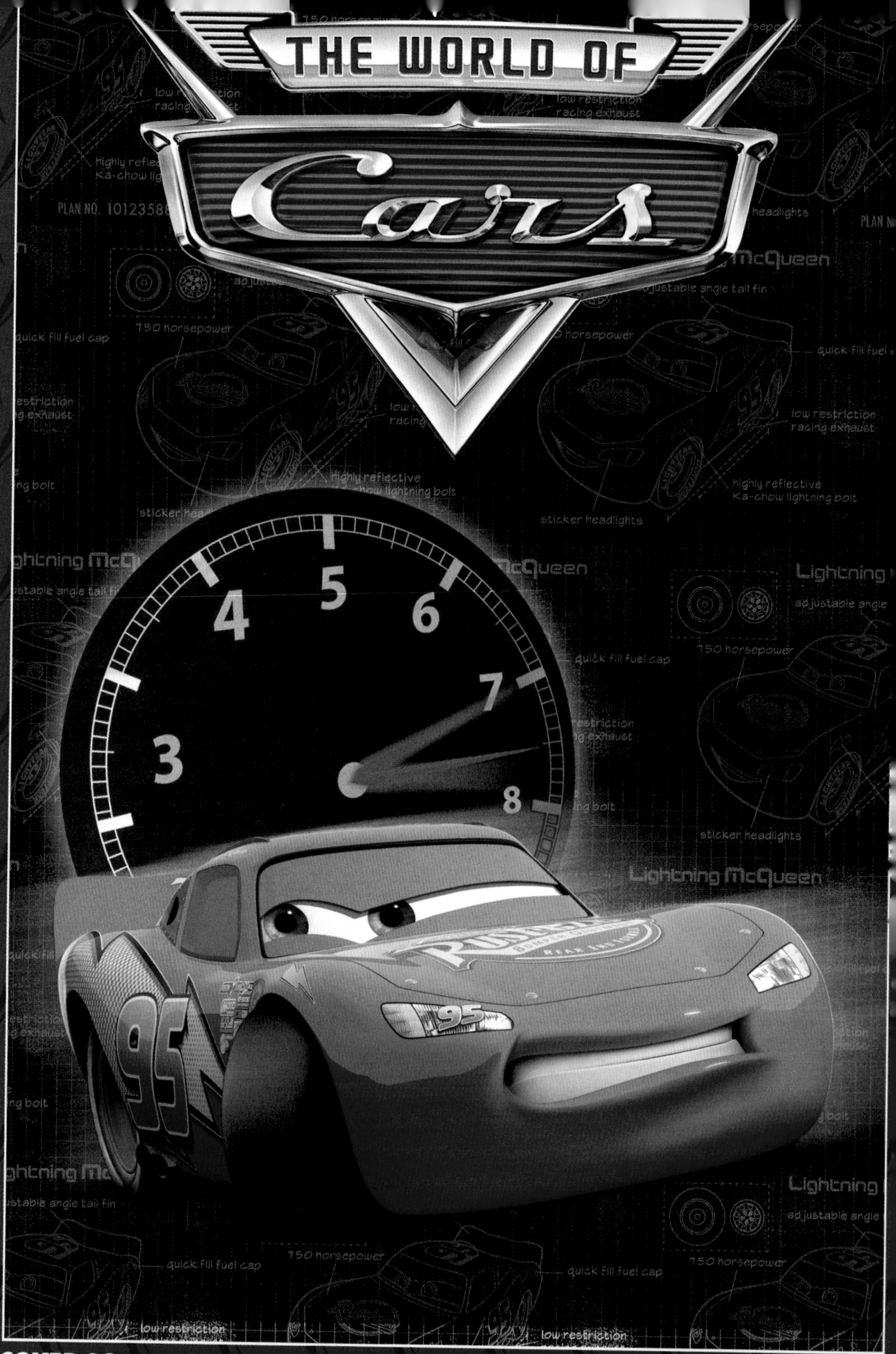
THE WORLD OF
Cars

COVER 2C
PHOTO COVER

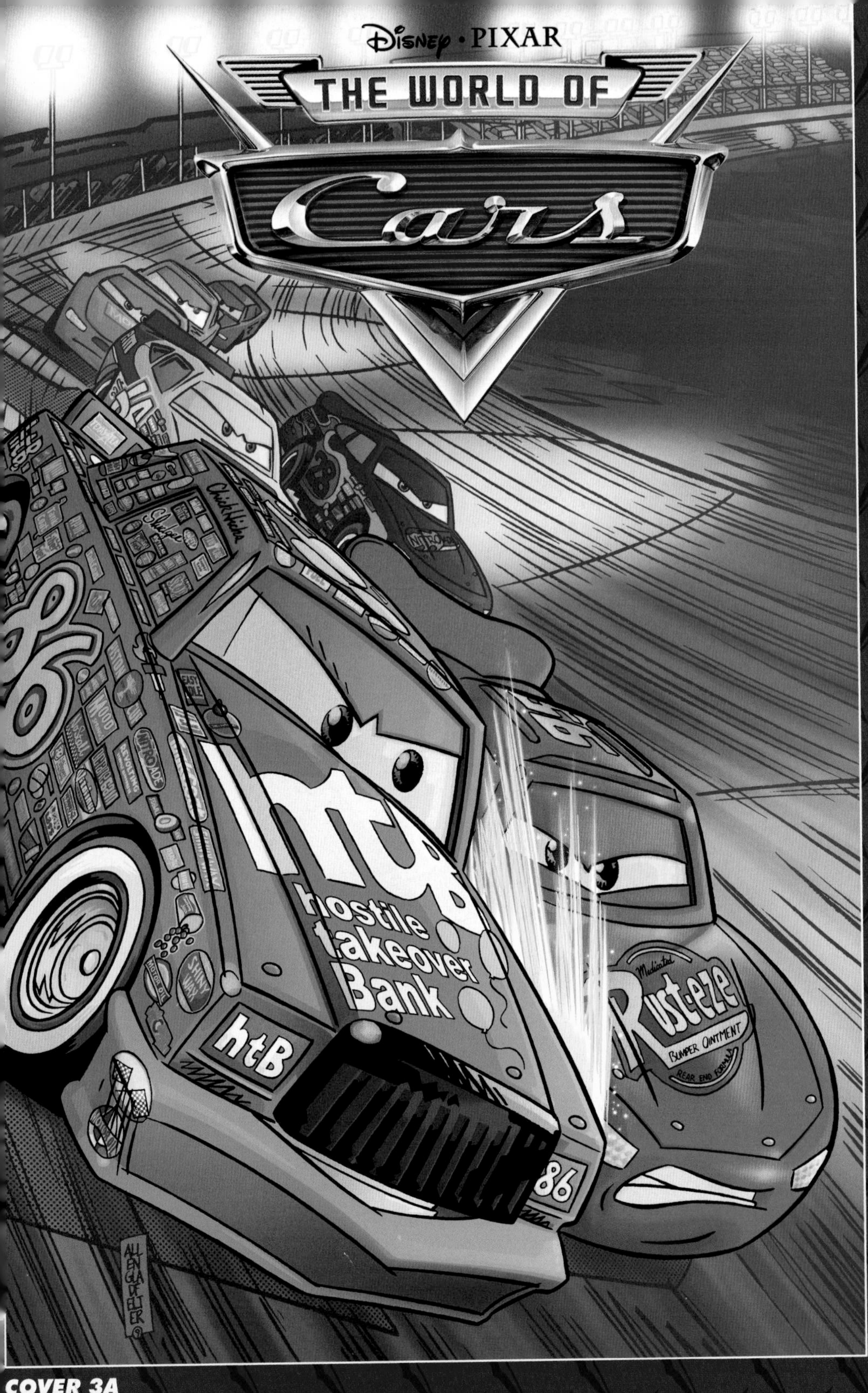
Disney • PIXAR
THE WORLD OF
Cars
Chick Hicks
htB
hostile takeover Bank
htB
86
Rust-eze
Medicated
BUMPER OINTMENT
REAR END FORMULA
NITROADE
SHINY WAX
ALLEN GLADFELTER

COVER 3A
ALLEN GLADFELTER

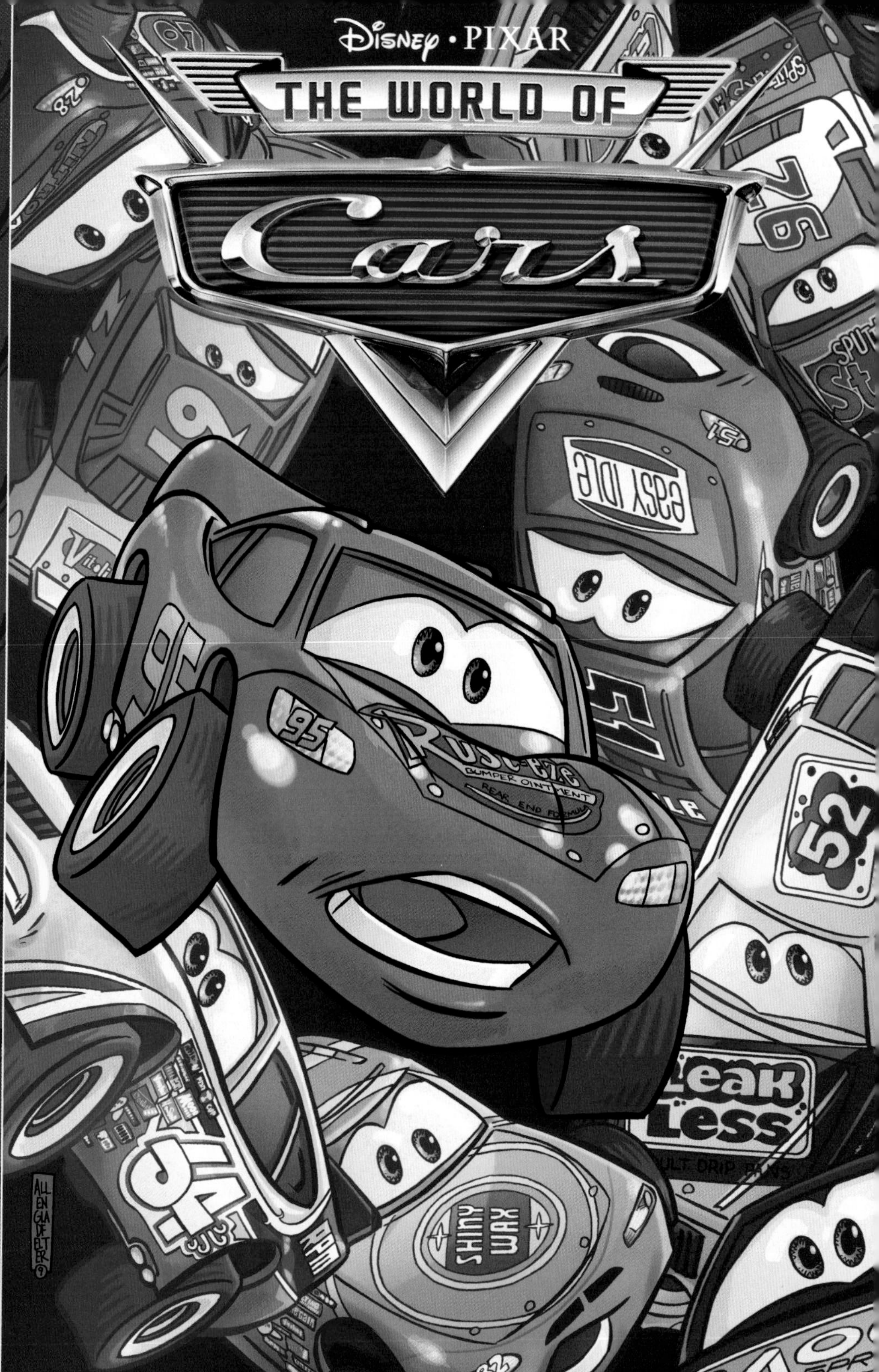
Disney • PIXAR
THE WORLD OF
Cars
easy idle
Rust-eze
BUMPER OINTMENT
REAR END FORMULA
Leak Less
Shiny Wax

COVER 3B
ALLEN GLADFELTER

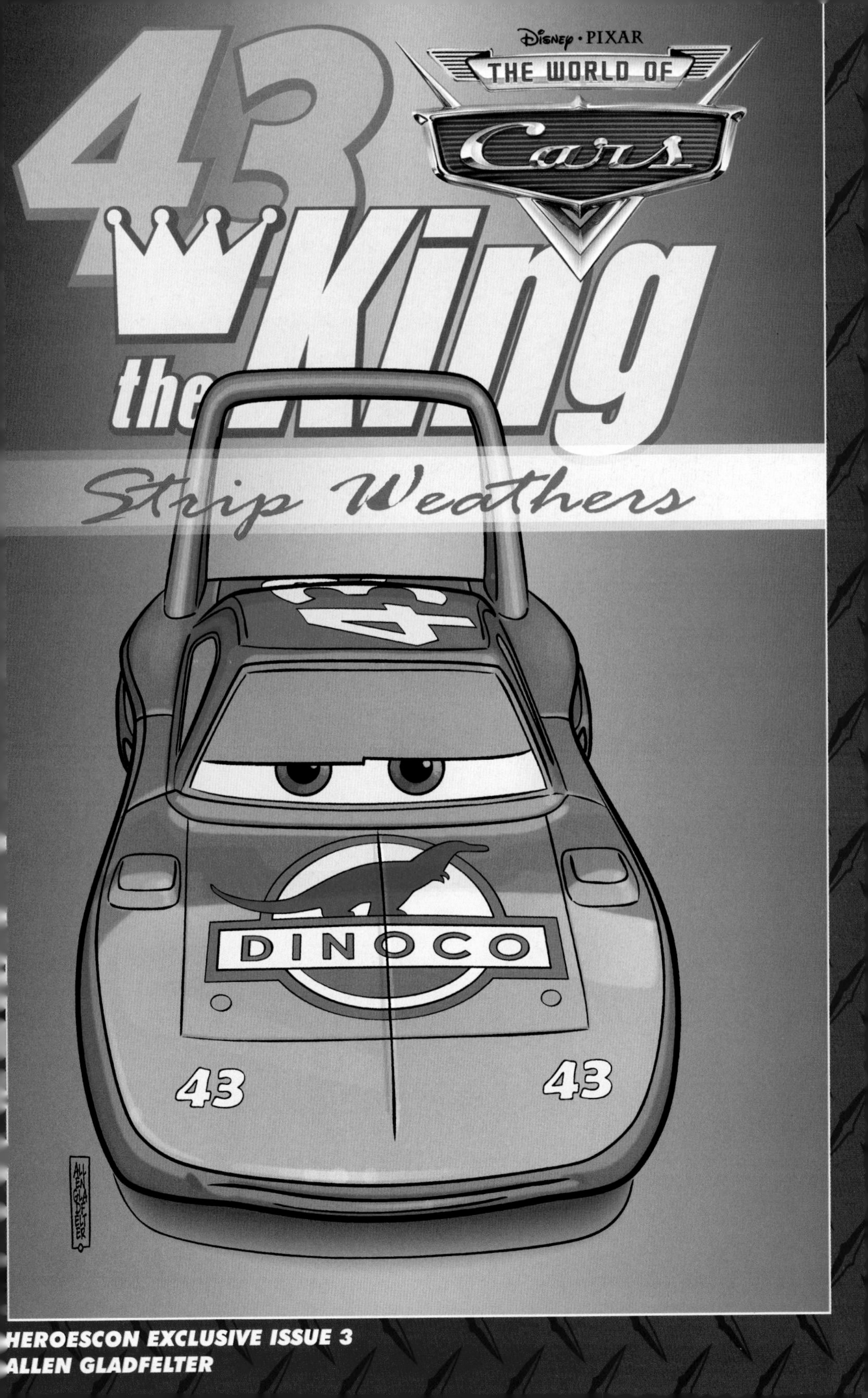
Disney • PIXAR
THE WORLD OF
Cars
43
the King
Strip Weathers
43
DINOCO
43
43

HEROESCON EXCLUSIVE ISSUE 3
ALLEN GLADFELTER

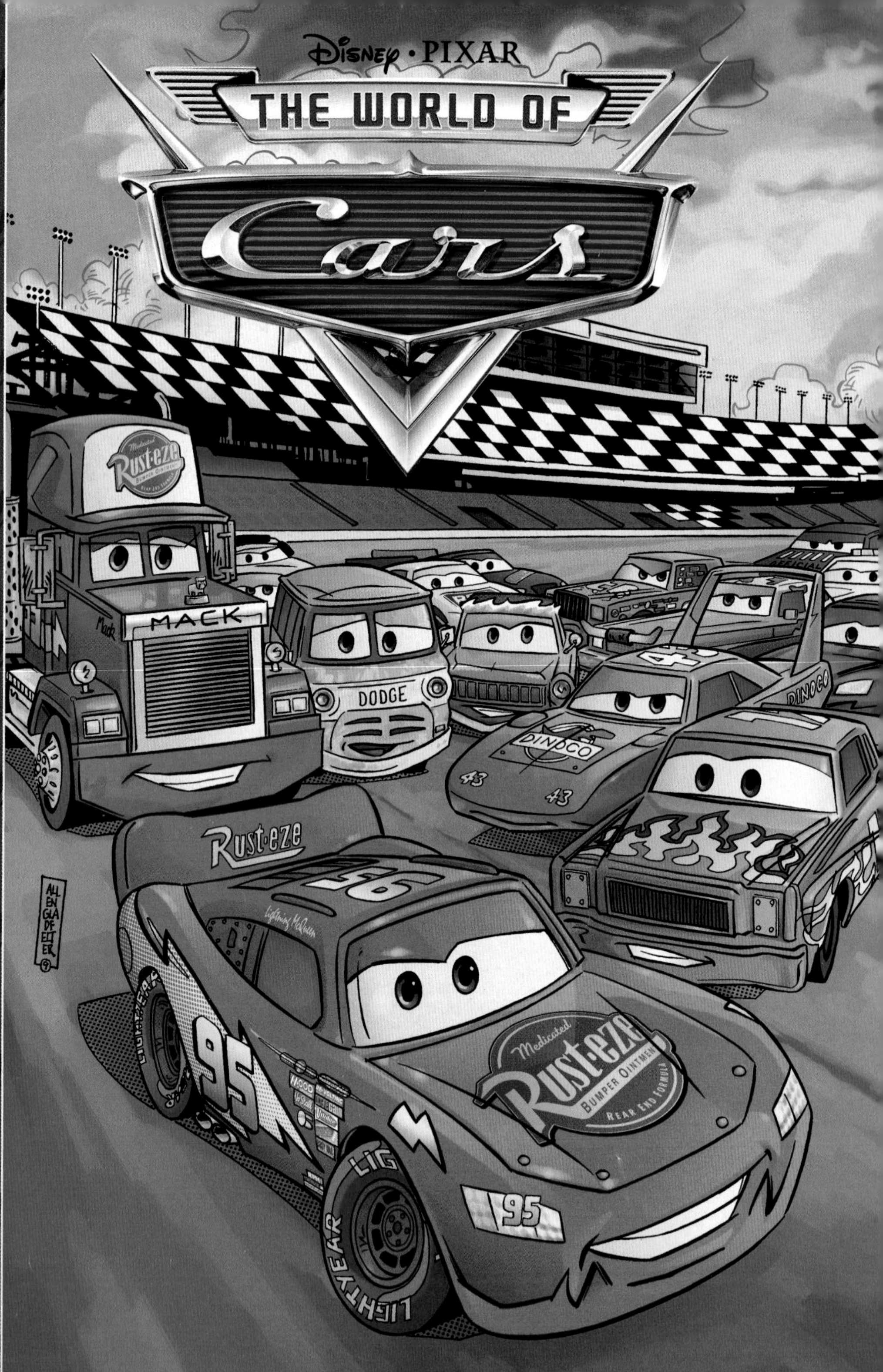
DISNEY • PIXAR
THE WORLD OF
Cars
MACK
DODGE
DINOCO
Rust-eze
95
LIGHTYEAR

COVER 4A
ALLEN GLADFELTER

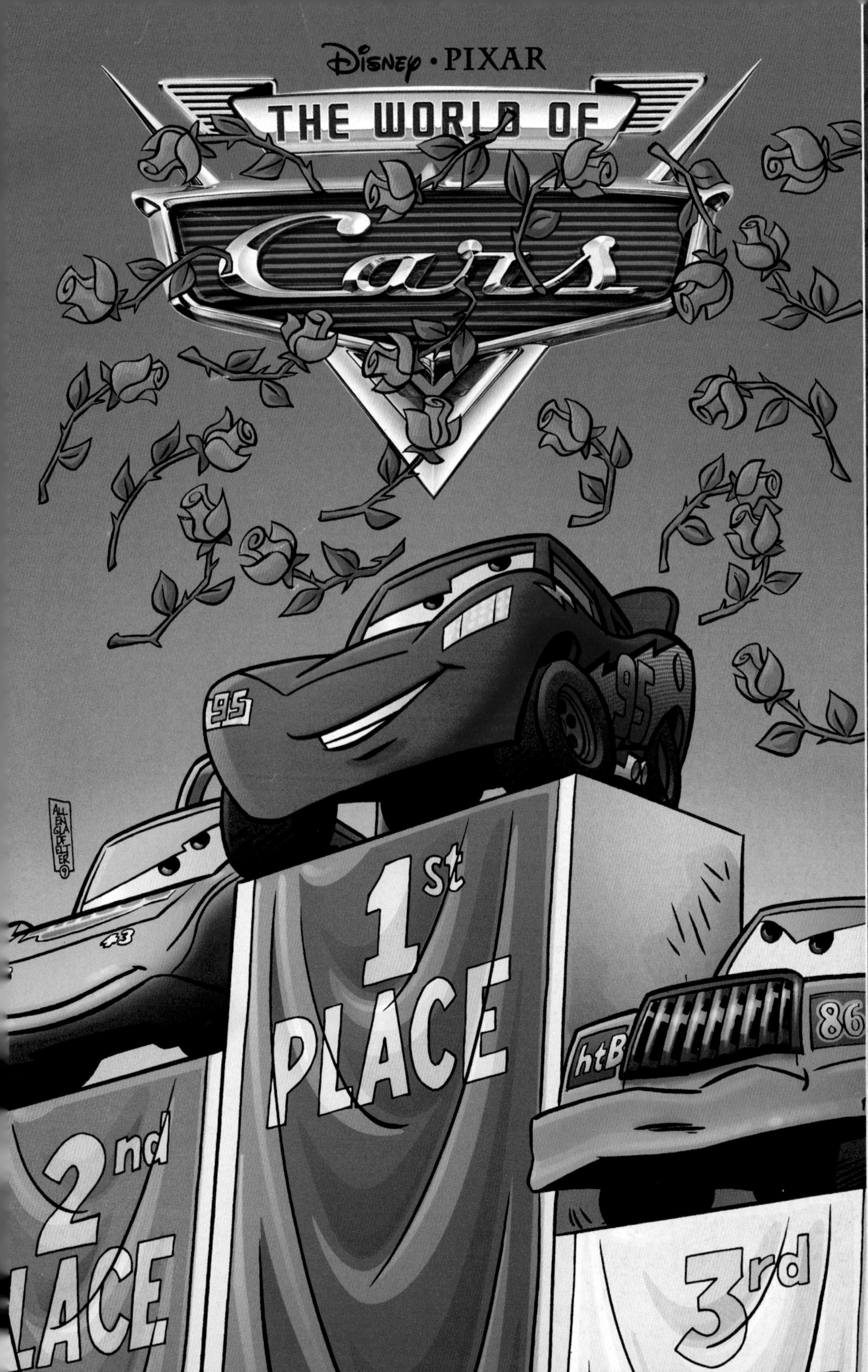
DISNEY • PIXAR
THE WORLD OF
Cars
95
95
43
1st PLACE
2nd
LACE
htB
86
3rd

COVER 4B
ALLEN GLADFELTER

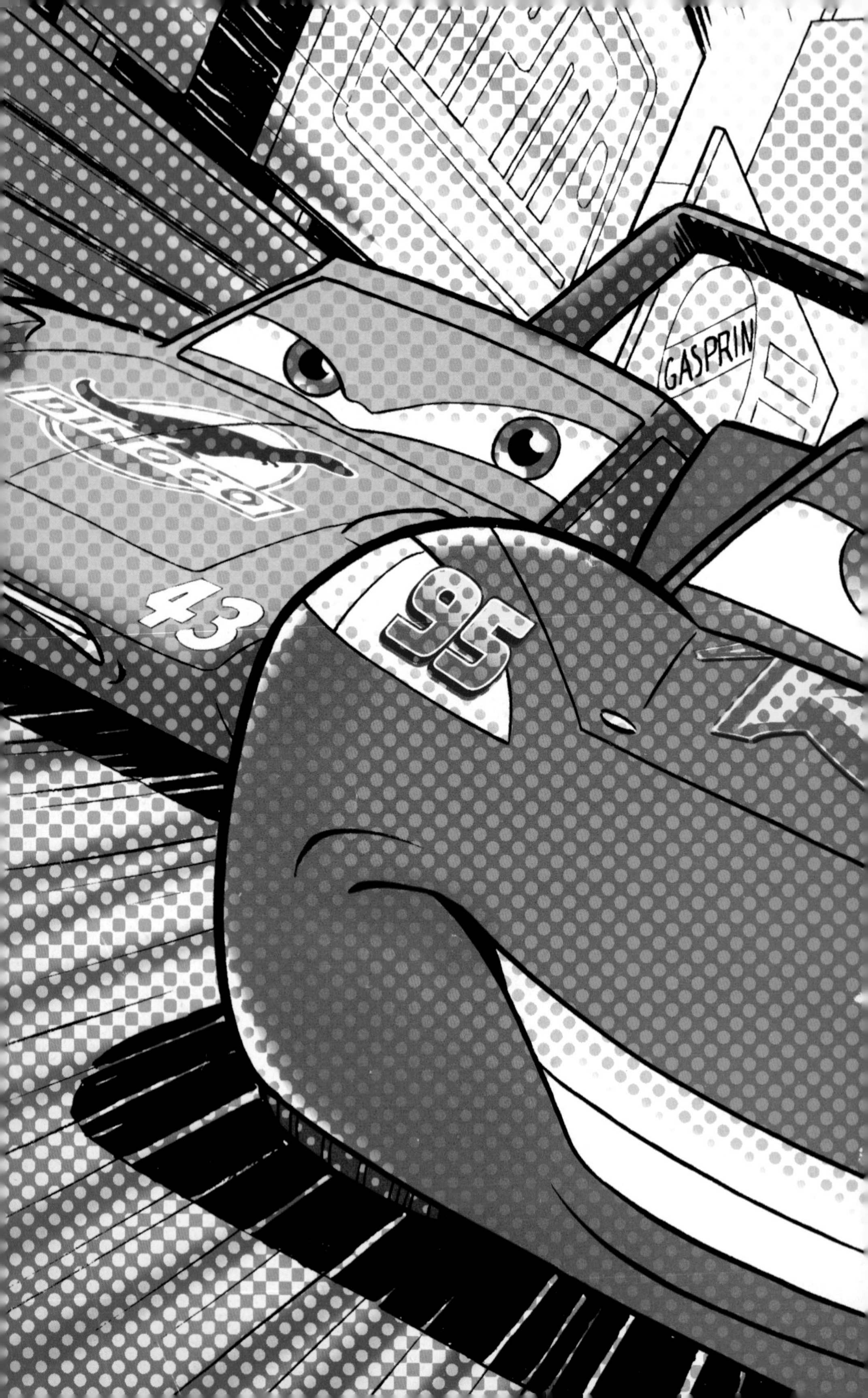
GASPRIN
DINOCO
43
95